MW00364160

WHEN REASON SLEEPS

TOM SEHLER

WHEN REASON SLEEPS

VIKING
Mystery
Suspense

V I K I N G

VIKING
Published by the Penguin Group
Viking Penguin, a division of Penguin Books USA Inc.,
375 Hudson Street, New York, New York 10014, U.S.A.
Penguin Books Ltd, 27 Wrights Lane,
London W8 5TZ, England
Penguin Books Australia Ltd, Ringwood,
Victoria, Australia
Penguin Books Canada Ltd, 2801 John Street,
Markham, Ontario, Canada L3R 1B4
Penguin Books (N.Z.) Ltd, 182–190 Wairau Road,
Auckland 10, New Zealand

Penguin Books Ltd, Registered Offices:
Harmondsworth, Middlesex, England

First published in 1991 by Viking Penguin,
a division of Penguin Books USA Inc.

1 3 5 7 9 10 8 6 4 2

PUBLISHER'S NOTE
This is a work of fiction. Names, characters, places, and in-
cidents either are the product of the author's imagination or
are used fictitiously, and any resemblance to actual persons,
living or dead, events, or locales is entirely coincidental.

LIBRARY OF CONGRESS CATALOGING IN PUBLICATION DATA

Sehler, Tom.
When reason sleeps / Tom Sehler.
p. cm.
ISBN 0–670–83938–8
I. Title.
PS3552.U7325W47   1991
813'.54—dc20   90–50757

Printed in the United States of America
Set in Times Roman

TO

ROGER AND JACK

*I would like to thank
Lieutenant Jerry Hoover of
the Boulder, Colorado, Police Department
for generously sharing his time
and his wide knowledge of
cults and ritual crimes.*

WHEN REASON SLEEPS

WHEN REASON SLEEPS

They were five, three girls, two boys. They picked their way along the rim of cliffs that overlooked the dark Pacific. Behind them, tiny lights marked the streets and homes of Mission Beach. In the farther distance, Pacific Beach formed a glistening crescent against the black of the sea. Ahead, halfway out Point Loma, the glow of the Fleet Combat Training Center gleamed against a sea haze that threatened to thicken into fog. But the rough spine of the Point kept the harsh lights from glaring in their eyes and cast darker shadows around their groping feet.

Despite the chill, all were dressed for the shore. The girls' two-piece bathing suits showed lithe, nubile figures beneath light beach jackets. The boys wore swimming suits, too, and against the mist one had on a brightly colored Ocean Pacific pullover with the hood up. The other clutched a large dark beach towel around his shoulders.

The boy with the towel went first. Familiar with the sandy trail, he led them past the end of a closed access road and through thorny brush and shrubs. Now and then he waited for the rest to catch up; once he gestured to the girls to stop their nervous whispering and laughter, and they paused to listen for sounds in the night: the beach patrol making rounds, a local property owner coming to investigate their noise. But the only sounds came from a channel buoy on the other side of the Point—a one-second horn and ten seconds of silence—and a steady thud of waves as the high spring tide came in against the rocks and gravelly patches of beach a hundred feet below.

Dropping into dimness, the leader passed another sign warning of unstable cliffs. He guided the other boy down a twisting path between stinging weeds and sharp rocks to a small ledge thrust out over the pounding surf. The second boy moved hesitantly, stepping with an insecurity that contrasted with the easy agility of the girls. His dragging pace, his general awkwardness in reach and stride, marked him as handicapped in some way. His fear of heights kept him as far back from the rim as the cliff allowed. One of the girls took him around the waist and smiled, placing his arm around her own warm, smooth flesh. The other two girls picked their way to the edge of the sandstone cliff and stared down at the streaks of dim white foam blossoming and fading around the rocks. Between them stood the boy with the dark towel. A light breeze from shore flapped it out and away from his body.

He, too, stared down. Then he stepped back into the small bowl of wind-scoured stone, grit, and tenacious weeds whose leaves and stems began to collect the mist into droplets. From a small pack slung over his shoulder, he took a bottle and poured a liquid into five handleless cups. He unfolded a pale cloth and laid it on the ground and walked around it to anchor each corner with a different object taken from the pack. Placing a cup at each corner and one in the middle, he beckoned the others and showed them where to sit around the white pentagram inked in the center of the cloth. Solemn now, the girls watched as the caped figure tilted a vial to dribble something on the point closest to the ocean. Then the boy in the bright beach jumper was placed there with his back to the cliff.

They lifted the cups. The youth with the towel still wrapped around his shoulders said something and the girls answered in unison. Their voices made a stagey wail slightly louder than the surf. The boy in the jumper didn't know the words but he moved *his lips trying to mimic what they were saying. Gradually the softly chanted words increased in tempo. The four began to sway rhythmically until the words and motion became a sinuous continuity, both hypnotic and portentous. At the chant's climax, the four stood, arms and faces raised to the foggy night sky. They held a long, tense salute to the still-seated boy who watched with dull attention. Then the four drained the cups and threw them over the cliff; the girls swept down on the seated figure and caressed him, kissing him and drawing arms and hair along his cheeks and shoulders and thighs as they hoisted him to his feet and, still swaying, began to chant again as the other boy raised a sputtering candle. The handicapped youth began to squirm. He tried to pull away from the soft hands of the girls. Gnawing at a fist hard enough to draw blood, he felt himself grow erect, eyes both frightened and fascinated as the girls' hands caressed his body, and he felt a wrenching throb clench his loins. The girls' lips brushed his cheeks and eyelashes as their voices rose in hypnotic repetition. Then the caped figure, his own voice a hoarse counter to the girls', stepped forward to stare into the boy's eyes. As the chant reached its climax, he shoved the boy's shoulders. In front of the girls' horrified eyes and suddenly silent, gaping mouths, the figure teetered and, too shocked to scream, toppled out and down into the blackness above the glimmer of surf.*

CHAPTER

Whistle-blowing is suspect behavior in any government agency. Forget all the crap you read about letters of commendation for honesty or awards for public-spiritedness. The whistle-blower is someone who can no longer be trusted by those who want to take advantage of someone else's trust. What made it worse for this whistle-blower was that I was a mere lieutenant-colonel, USMC, and the whistlee was a member of the U.S. House of Representatives. A senior member who served on the Armed Services Committee. Over the years in Washington, he'd traded for a roster of cronies and debtors that read like a lobbyist's "A" list. I suppose it was that cushion of contacts and connections that made the good congressman believe he could do whatever the hell he wanted to—up to and including actions that for a mere citizen would have been treason. Or maybe he just had a severe case of Potomac fever. It affects most congressmen and senators sooner or later: an atrophy of the sense of humility, a swelling of the glands of arrogance. As one of the saltier NCOs had muttered behind the back of the commandant of the Eighth and Eye Barracks, Your ass gets kissed long enough, pretty soon you want it kissed all the time. And everything in Washington, D.C., is designed to make each senator and congressman think his posterior deserves to be caressed by the world's puckered lips.

But nowhere among a congressman's long list of franks, privileges, retirement pay, and other perks was the right to peddle national secrets to a foreign government. At the time, a big part of my job was to catch those who were endangering national security, so I did my job.

I've been asked if I would do the same thing again. I've got to admit I had no idea the congressman would be able to pull me down with him—I thought I was protected by the evidence, by my orders, and by those who issued them. But there were those who were afraid I'd prove embarrassing not only to an august body of state but, more importantly, to the Navy Department, whose budget was scrutinized by cronies of the man who suddenly retired from office "for reasons of health."

An officer with more than twenty years in is vulnerable.

And an officer who makes waves is even more vulnerable.

An officer who splashes those waves on a congressman is most vulnerable of all.

Yet this officer wouldn't have done a damn thing different.

Still, I was glad Eleanor's death had come before she had to suffer additional pain—the sudden fading voices, the sliding glances of strangers who had heard about me, the false heartiness of a grinning hypocrite embarrassed to bump into me at an official function. The subtle distancing of those who had once called themselves friends. It would have hurt her as much as the cancer. She would not have found an answer to her statement that I did my duty. Ollie North had put his loyalty to the President above his sworn loyalty to the Constitution. I did what I pledged to do when I received my commission: uphold the Constitution against all enemies foreign and domestic. North became a hero; I was ordered to step down. All very politely and according to protocol. Even sugared by a graveyard promotion to colonel and, thanks to a few remaining friends, the opportunity of a job on the West Coast with the

Osiris Foundation—if we found ourselves mutually compatible after the six-month probationary period.

Therefore I have sailed the seas and come . . . not to a holy city or to Byzantium, but simply to my home of record, San Diego. Accumulated leave and travel time before reporting in to Osiris: forty-three days. Of which only five had been used and now the remaining time stretched ahead like a desert watered by self-pity. I'd written both Karen and Becky, telling my daughters only that I'd been placed on the inactive list and that I was looking at a job in Southern California. I'd get in touch with them as soon as things settled down. Karen, newly married and, with her husband, just starting her career as a lawyer in Sacramento, had tracked me down and surprised me with a telephone call last night. And, God, it was good to hear her voice; I didn't have to force any excitement and pleasure into mine, but I did gloss over the reasons for my unexpected retirement. Becky was taking her junior year abroad at Bordeaux and I didn't know if my letter'd even arrived there yet. Karen said she thought her sister was on one of those lengthy vacations European universities seem to have a lot of.

Was I planning on staying in San Diego? Karen asked. It looked like it; I had a job offer with a group whose national headquarters were in San Diego, so that worked out fine. What kind of job? Oh, defense contracts, providing services to military commands—the kind of thing retired officers do when they're still too young to quit working. But what about all your friends? What about the house in Fairfax? I'd had to sell that house to afford the new one in Coronado. She and Chuck would have to come down as soon as they had time; I was sure they and Becky would enjoy the new place. As for friends, she knew how it was in the Corps: the world was a network of duty stations where the same faces showed up sooner or later. As a matter of fact, I'd already been in touch with a couple of old friends.

That wasn't quite true. All but a few of the "friends" in Washington greeted my absence with a sigh of relief. And my arrival in San Diego hadn't generated any kind of ceremony.

But, I reassured her and maybe myself, I had run across an old high school buddy, Tom Jenkins, and a retired friend of my father's, Admiral Combs. In fact, the admiral had asked me to drop by his home.

"Dad," her voice was hesitant. "I don't know exactly what happened back there . . . I read a little about it in *Newsweek.* But I want you to know I love you. And I'm very, very proud of you."

"That means a lot to me, Karen." And it did.

Admiral Dalton Combs (USN-Ret.) gripped my fingers with a hand that was still strong despite the years that had shrunk the flesh on his face and put a slight curve in a ramrod-stiff back. "We're damned glad to have you home, Jack." He closed the heavy door and guided me into a spacious living room that held few mementos of navy life. It was, he said, Jenny's doing. Since his wife had to look after the home for months and years while he was at sea, she got to choose the decor. The only military memento was a large portrait over the dark fireplace that showed the admiral in dress blues standing against an angry red background. "Retirement gift," Jenny explained. "When old shipmates drop by, they ought to see their gift." She, too, had grown thinner with age. An already small woman, she now seemed sparrowlike in both fragility and the quick pecking of her hands. "We're having our evening martini. I hope you'll join us."

"Sun's below the yardarm," said the admiral, pouring.

I sipped carefully at the unfamiliar drink and answered questions about my mother's health and welfare. It was generous of the admiral to invite me to his home—and perhaps even a bit brave, too, considering. But then my father's old friend had won a reputation for courage in two wars—make that one war and one "police action." I saw, and was grateful, that neither he nor Jenny was about to let what happened change their opinion of me.

"Well, hell, call it fortunes of war and let it go, Jack." That had been the advice from one of my own friends, just after; but I couldn't help remembering that he still held his commission. He had also held his tongue. But I realize now that it would have done no one any good if he or anyone else had spoken up. A command decision had been made and no one was looking back. That was the way I should take it, too. The admiral was right.

"So now you're going to work for the . . . what do they call it, Jack?" Jenny offered another pass with the martini pitcher but I shook my head.

"Osiris Corporation."

The admiral's cheeks fell in slightly as he sucked on his cigar. Its glow etched lines in a face that had clenched against tropic sun and ice-laden winds. His hair, still cropped in a crew cut, was as thick and white as Jenny's. Even though the man was a decade or so younger than my father, I thought of them as the same age—perhaps because the admiral, as my father's executive officer on the *Saratoga* and then later at NAS Jacksonville, had shared an adult world while I was still in short pants. "Why that name?"

"I don't think it has a meaning, sir—the usual security technique." Or because Osiris was king of the underworld. And as far as the Marine Corps was concerned I was paid off, dead, and buried.

Another puff of smoke, carefully directed toward the ceiling away from Jenny and me. "So if you take your punishment honorably, that's part of the payoff, eh? Well, the work will be in your line, anyway." The gray cloud rose against the patterned stucco. I had a feeling the admiral's words meant more than they said. Jenny, too, seemed to wait in silence for more. The whole spacious home, in fact, was poised and quiet despite the increased heavy traffic half a block away that had been created when the San Diego Bay Bridge was finally completed. It was still new to me; I hadn't spent any time in Coronado for several decades. I'd seen the bridge on brief trips through North Island or Camp Pendleton. But until moving back last week, I hadn't realized its effect on what had been quiet corners of a sleepy town. In a way I was glad Eleanor hadn't lived to see those changes. Yet her death was still a big hole in my life, and it was most poignantly felt in those blank times when there was no familiar voice to talk the changes over with. Or in moments like these, when I saw the admiral and his wife sharing the end of a long life together.

"Your youngest daughter has finished college now?" The gin had brought a spot of color into Jenny's cheeks. There was a slight deliberation in the lacing of fingers that had once been long and straight, but were now bent with arthritis.

"My elder has." As I brought them up to date on Karen and Rebecca, Jenny nodded. She was far more interested in news of my family than in my fortunes of war.

"I keep forgetting you're younger than our Margaret. Still, it's hard to think of you being almost a grandparent."

"Don't rush him, Jenny—he and the girls will get there soon enough."

She smiled somewhat sadly and started to say something, then thought better of it. The admiral spoke quickly. "This Osiris Corporation, it's a civilian outfit?"

"Entirely. That's its reason for existence."

"But it does contract work for the services."

"For the Navy Department, but not officially. The idea is to provide avenues and opportunities that military intelligence is restricted from taking."

"Um. Wasn't my area of operations. We appreciated good information, though." Another puff of smoke. "How's it funded?"

"Subcontracts. Like a defense supplier or a university research contract."

"No line-item budget, then."

That was the idea. "No, sir."

He scraped a ragged fringe off his cigar into a large ceramic ashtray. "You know the CIA's hired a number of ex-military men who left the service for a variety of reasons. In fact, I hear it's part of the target profile."

"I'm not interested in them, Admiral." And I doubted that they would be interested in a whistle-blower.

"I see."

"I'm sorry we didn't get a chance to tell you how badly we felt about Eleanor, Jack." Jenny's soft voice broke the silence as she steered the conversation back to family.

"Yes," the admiral added. "We were very sorry to learn of that. From what the skipper told us, she must have been a wonderful girl."

That's what the admiral still called my father: "the skipper."

I know my father wouldn't have said much to him or anyone else about his family life, but it was kind of the admiral to pretend differently. "Thank you," I said. I could have added that the girls and I still missed her deeply, that we probably always would. But people who had lived as long as the admiral and Jenny knew the meaning of loss. It would be an insult to imply that they didn't. "How are Margaret and her family?"

Jenny's face tightened slightly and the admiral wagged his head once. "We don't see too much of them."

"Have they moved from La Jolla, then?"

A shrug from the admiral. "No. They just don't have much time for us old folks."

Jenny looked up from swirling the olive in her drink. "Why don't you ask him, Dalton."

The words rang like a tiny bell in the quiet room, urgent and tense and timid. And they confirmed a growing feeling: that there had been another reason for the admiral's invitation. In the silence, the man heaved a long sigh through his nose. But he said nothing.

"Ask me what, Jenny?"

"Please, Dalton."

"She wants . . ." The rigid man couldn't find the words.

"She's your granddaughter, too." She watched the admiral

mash the cigar end between his teeth. Then she turned to me. "We want to ask your help, Jack. All of our friends our age . . . Well, we're so out of touch with things. We thought perhaps you might know what to do."

"I'll sure help if I can. What do you need?"

The admiral jabbed his cigar into the large ashtray. "We didn't invite you over on false pretenses, Jack. We wanted to see you—to welcome you back. This"—his hand waved vaguely, the stone in the heavy Naval Academy ring glinting— "this came up . . . we got a call this morning. And I swear to God, we don't know what to do about it."

"It's Dorcas. Our granddaughter. Margaret's worried she might be in some kind of trouble." Before I could ask what kind of trouble, she added, "Margaret wouldn't tell me much else . . . She—Margaret—she's not well, Jack. Henry doesn't admit that anything's wrong with her, but . . ."

"But their marriage has been lousy for years, Jenny. You know that. I don't know why Margaret married him in the first place, and I don't see why she stays with him."

They had brought the issue up and now circled around it, the admiral embarrassed to have to ask for help, his wife hesitant for some reason of her own. "Did Margaret say what kind of trouble?"

"Only that they don't know where she is."

"They're afraid she's run off," snorted the admiral. "Quit her job, left her house—run off."

Jenny added quickly, "They called the police—sheriff— whoever, but those people are no help. Dorcas is over twenty-one and Margaret has no evidence that she didn't leave willingly. No evidence of anything . . . bad . . . happening."

The admiral picked up his cigar to stare angrily at the crumpled and still smoldering tip. Then he tossed it back. "Theirs isn't a happy family, Jack. Never has been. But Margaret's got too damned much pride to call it quits. And she's a grown woman—it's not our place to butt in where we're not asked." He cleared his throat. The anger gave way to a worry that pinched his white eyebrows together. "And Dorcas's life hasn't been a happy one, from what.I've seen. I don't know what the cause is; hell, I've been on sea duty most of the girl's life. But I remember her as a bright, laughing little thing. Just a beautiful little sprite who was into everything—just like Margaret used to be."

"How long has she been gone?"

"It's been over a week, now, I think."

"Margaret waited until today to tell you?"

The fragile woman looked even smaller. "She called to know if we'd heard from her. When I said no, she told me about it." Jenny studied her knotted fingers. "We—Margaret and I—were never as close as we should have been, Jack. There were so many things . . . time passed so quickly, and then she was grown and gone . . ."

"They've called her friends? Places where she might visit?"

"Henry did," said the admiral. "No one's heard anything from her."

"I'm not sure what you want me to do."

Jenny leaned to place her fingers with their swollen joints on my arm. "Can you talk to her? To Margaret? Dalton's told me something about the kind of work you've been doing. Maybe you can think of some way to help find out where Dorcas is, Jack. I know Margaret's worried about her. We are, too. But we don't know what else to do. We don't know who else to ask."

"Why don't you give me her address and number? I'll call and make an appointment to see her."

CHAPTER

The voice on the other end of the telephone had a tautness that tried to mask tension but only served to increase it. It reminded me of the voices reporting on one of those nightmare operations that had gone wrong: things were out of control and people were hurting, and no one could help now. But this voice wasn't an operations officer; it was Henry Wilcox, Margaret's husband and Dorcas's father. I hadn't talked with the man for over a decade and remembered him only slightly, and with no particular warmth.

"The admiral suggested you come over?" A stress on the first two words suggested sarcasm and an awareness of Admiral Combs's feelings toward his son-in-law.

"He thought I might be able to help. Is Margaret there? May I talk to her?"

As I spoke, I gazed through the window of a living room whose angles and echoing emptiness still smelled of fresh paint. Outside, sprouting from cramped and newly sodded backyards, small docks anchored a forest of masts and rigging. Beyond the marina, San Diego Bay spread gleaming and flat in the sun.

"She's not awake yet."

Even though it was a weekday morning, some sailing club was having a regatta. Distant bright spinnakers ballooned in silent explosion as the crews rounded a buoy into the downwind leg of the course. I watched one of the tiny blossoms tangle and collapse and jerk angrily from the thrust of a jib pole. Despite what I felt like telling Wilcox, I'd promised the admiral and Jenny I would do what I could. "It'll take me an hour to get there. That's enough time for her to be up and about, right?"

Another long pause told me that Henry was definitely unhappy at the idea of some agent of his father-in-law nosing into his life. But finally he said grudgingly, "I guess it can't hurt. God knows I've done every damn thing I could." And he gave me directions to his home.

The drive to La Jolla took longer than an hour; traffic north on the San Diego Freeway was snarled for no apparent reason, and the Mission Freeway dumped additional cars into the lanes like someone cramming marbles down a slot. There used to be a rush hour, I remembered, but now that hour had turned into gridlock. The rest of the day was the rush. Still, beneath all the changes and swollen growth that covered what used to be dry and empty hills north of San Diego, I could see remnants of the old. Even this stretch of the freeway had a familiar feel, one that recalled the restless high school years and my beat-up Triumph motorcycle that had terrified my mother. Then, speed and motion were the popular narcotics; it was enough to be going somewhere—anywhere—down those warm and sun-filled lanes of empty concrete, the wind popping my shirt and stinging tears from my eyes. Sometimes Tommy Jenkins would ride behind, his boot stuffed into the exhaust trumpet to muffle the rap of the engine when we passed a highway patrolman. It didn't seem that long ago, and I regretted having to call Tommy and ask for a rain check on today's lunch. But the man had understood—"Hey, Jack, somebody needs your help, go to it"—and we would be getting together soon.

The twin bands of busy freeway swept past the flat, man-made islets of Mission Bay. Marinas and parking lots were both crowded. The green parks glimpsed through billows of pink and white oleander were dotted with strollers and joggers. Above the frayed tufts of palm trees, bright kites shaped like swallows or airfoils or long, snaking dragons hovered and dived in the wind. West, over the Pacific, a line of haze marked the fog that followed the chill waters of the Japanese current offshore. North toward the rise of Soledad Mountain and La Jolla, the sun glinted on thousands of whitewashed houses half hidden by trees. This California green was different from the urgent, moist green of the Virginia countryside. The freeway, despite its familiar blue information signs and green exit markings, lacked the tunnel effect of tall trees crowding the interstate to screen colonial brick homes and shopping centers from the constant traffic around Fairfax. Here, the highway lifted away from the bright irrigation of park and lawn and arced between brown, dead-looking manzanita that covered hillsides too steep and sandy for development. Above, cresting the ridge against the sky, the fringe of dull green started again: the exclamations of Lombardies, the showy burst of date palms, the dark, well-watered hedges of oleander protecting homes perched over the canyon's rim. My two memories of landscape—one sharp with recent severing, the other beginning to stir under a blanket of years—churned up echoes and juxtaposed emotions and brought that unreal feeling of not actually being where I was.

I hadn't felt that way in years, not since childhood. Then, uprooted by my father's transfer from one duty station to another, I often had a sense of disconnectedness that cushioned me from the surrounding world until, gradually, I could center myself in the new landscape. It was strange to feel that again after so long, and I found myself recalling an associated game from that same childhood time: searching the days and deeds for favorable and unfavorable omens, for hints of whether this new place would be welcoming or hostile. Strange, I didn't remember feeling it in Viet Nam. Maybe it was the intense map study. Maybe it was my unblinking focus on treeline and ridge and avenues of approach. And though I'd never felt at home in Viet Nam either, by God I knew exactly where I was when I was there.

The La Jolla exit swung me onto the twin lanes of Ardath Road. This, too, was new. The asphalt swerved to pulse traffic between clusters of shops separated by dry and brushy canyon walls. Finally the road tangled with the more familiar streets of downtown La Jolla where crowded, stop-and-go traffic glittered in the mid-morning heat like crumpled aluminum foil. I kept glancing at the directions Henry had given over the telephone. If I needed a reminder that talking with Henry wasn't something I was all that eager to do, it was the fact that I did have to keep studying the road names and turns. Jobs I was eager for needed only a single glance and I had the directions memorized.

But my father's friend had asked for help, and it was Jack Steele to the rescue. Not quite sure what he was supposed to do or how he was supposed to do it, but admitting more than a little relief at shifting his attention from his own sour memories to someone else's problem. Maybe that's one of the wellsprings of benevolence, the discovery that another's worries can dwarf our own.

The final turn was beyond the La Jolla Cove with its facing high-rise apartments and dignified hotels. A winding lane tilted steeply up from the blue of ocean and into an older, half-remembered residential district. Set back from the street, the homes were protected by curving brick walls or thick shrubbery that masked houses and insured privacy despite tiny lots. The Wilcox house was like a lot of the homes I thought of as typically Californian: shouldered down among a rich variety of trees and bushes, it offered only the garage door and a sliver of wall for greeting. Then the house opened to the secluded patio area with its pool and sliding glass doors surrounding. Henry, an unsmiling man almost my height, gripped my fingers once and dropped them. The gesture said he wasn't one to forget his manners despite an apparently unwelcome intrusion.

"So the admiral thinks you can help us somehow?" He led me through the entry and living room and an open patio door. A small swimming pool filled a yard surrounded by oleander. "Margaret's out here."

The man's creased face with its heavy ears and long, graying hair seemed even more weary and houndlike than I remembered. Our last meeting had been more convivial; that was the time Henry welcomed any friend of Margaret's, especially those who might have an interest in putting money into an exciting new project of beach-front condominiums. When Eleanor and I hadn't warmed to the idea, the camaraderie chilled.

"Jack?" Margaret, wearing sunglasses, shielded her eyes from the glare as she looked up. "My God, you haven't changed at all in—what is it, ten years now?"

"About that, Margaret. How are you?"

She didn't look well. The flesh peeking beneath the sunglasses was a puffy and unhealthy gray. Her lips had shriveled into a tight wrinkle that pinched the corners of her mouth. On the glass breakfast table shaded by a bright umbrella stood a pitcher half-filled with cheery red liquid. "I mixed up a batch of Bloody Marys for you, Jack. I remembered how much you and Eleanor used to like them."

That wasn't true, but I accepted a glass anyway. Margaret apparently needed some kind of excuse for mixing a drink. Henry shook his head. "I'm having coffee. Can't you remember that?"

Ignoring Henry, she settled me onto one of the wrought-iron patio chairs and drank deeply. "I talked with Daddy last night. He said you were coming over. I hope you can help us, Jack."

"When did you last see Dorcas?"

She listened to the faint clink of ice cubes in her drink as she counted back. "It's been almost a month now."

"She's been missing that long?"

"No," said Henry. "That's the last time we saw her, which is what you asked. We also talked to her on the telephone a couple weeks ago."

"She called you?"

"Yes."

"How soon after that did you know she was missing?"

Henry shrugged. "We're still not certain that she is. That's why the police are no damned help—they say there's no proof of any crime being committed."

"But obviously you're worried about her."

"We hadn't heard a thing from her since she called," said Margaret. "So Henry went up there to see if she was all right. She was gone. No word to us or to anyone. Just gone."

"Up where?"

"Near Julian." Henry sipped at his coffee and leaned back in the iron chair. His animosity gradually ebbed as he talked about his daughter. "It's a small town about fifty miles east, in the San Bernardinos. Dorcas likes the mountains."

"She lives up there?"

"Yes. She has a job in a gift shop—wanted to be on her own, she said. Away from us, anyway." The man stared into his cup and then looked up. "Some people complain about their kids moving back in with them after college. Dorcas came home for a few months and couldn't wait to get away again. So she took this two-bit job up there because she said she liked mountains."

Henry made it sound like a social disease. "Have you talked to her employer?"

"Of course. A Mrs. Gannet. That's how we found out Dori was gone—we called the shop to talk to her. Mrs. Gannet said Dorcas was gone. That she simply stopped coming to work. She went by her cabin a time or two, but nobody answered the door. She has no idea where Dori is. So I drove all the way up there and saw just what Mrs. Gannet did—nothing."

"Friends? Boyfriends?"

Henry shrugged again and looked at Margaret. She shook her head. "I'm not sure . . . She doesn't really tell us much anymore. She wants her freedom, she says. You know how young people are . . ." She looked across the blue water of the kidney-shaped pool. "You have daughters, don't you, Jack? You know how they can be."

I had daughters, yes, but thank God both of them were considerate enough to let their old man know what was going on. Which was more Eleanor's influence than mine. "Dorcas never mentioned any friends at all?"

Margaret seemed to be drifting away in her thoughts. From somewhere beyond the thick barrier of shrubbery came the steady scrape of a gardener raking leaves under bushes surrounding the neighbor's pool. Finally, she shook her head. "Only her friends from high school. She calls a few of them when she comes home for visits. There are three or four friends she keeps in touch with, mostly just gossiping on the phone."

"You talked to them?"

"I did," said Henry. "They didn't know anything. Not that they'd tell me, anyway."

"What's that mean?"

He shrugged. "Just the secrets the young keep from the old." He snorted into his coffee cup. "Making up for those the parents keep from the children, I suppose."

"But you told them she might be missing?"

"They said they hadn't talked to her in weeks. I don't think they were lying. And I don't know why they'd have any reason to."

The man had shifted his gaze from his coffee cup to the pool. A stray breeze made quick traces across the surface of the blue water and Margaret, too, watched the busy shadows on the pool floor.

Hers was an aching pensiveness that called for gray, overcast skies and a steady drizzle, weather suitable for moroseness and reflection. But it was spring in Southern California and it wasn't raining. The sun was that beautiful, misty gold of the Pacific coastline, and this La Jolla home was a long way from a dreary moor. It was hard to reconcile a setting like this with the festering unhappiness that Margaret and Henry showed. We may not be able to make every place heaven, but we seem able to make any place hell.

"How about a private detective, Henry? I'm sure your family lawyer would be able to recommend a good one."

"Daddy suggested a private detective. Henry said no."

A stubborn look made his creases deepen. "I—we've—thought of that. But I don't want anyone I don't know meddling in my family affairs."

Nor anyone he did know; especially the admiral. Margaret waved the pitcher at my still-full glass and then refilled her own.

"When Daddy said you were coming by, I was so relieved. He said you've had a lot of experience in investigations. And because you have daughters of your own, I know you can understand how we feel."

"I have no experience in the civilian sector, Margaret—"

"Please, Jack. We don't know where she is! Or why she's gone. We don't know if she needs help or if she's just going through a phase. We need to at least know that she's alive and well. Oh, God, I need to know!"

"Margaret, that's enough!" Henry set his empty coffee cup down with a sharp rap. " 'Daddy' said you would help, Jack. And people usually do what 'Daddy' wants, by God! Now are you going to help or not?"

"Is it what you want, too, Henry?"

The man sucked a deep breath, then he nodded. "The admiral assures me you're a friend of the family. Certainly I accept his assurances. Just the same, I want this on a businesslike basis. I expect to pay a reasonable sum for your services. What sort of fees do you anticipate?"

"What you're suggesting is probably illegal in California, Henry. I'm not a licensed professional. Let's just call it a learning experience for both of us."

His pale blue eyes blinked at my refusal; then he cleared his throat. "That's very generous. However, I do insist on paying any and all of your expenses."

"That's fine. I'll let you know what they are. Now why don't you tell me everything about Dorcas since she came home from college—friends, any names she might have mentioned, all the places she's lived or worked."

The rest of the visit was spent completing what could be called a background questionnaire. In addition to names and addresses, I tried to find out as much as I could about her car and license number, bank accounts and credit cards, insurance policies and medical programs, church membership, any possible fingerprints taken for any reason, any arrest record, and, finally, a recent color photograph that showed a tall girl whose blond hair was swept back into a ponytail just visible at her left shoulder. She wore a loose turtleneck sweater that hinted at full breasts. A pair of frayed jeans outlined a nicely curved hip and long leg. She was smiling at the camera, though not widely. Large, round glasses gave her face a seriousness that emphasized the regularity and balance of features that were clean-cut but not overly pretty. Still, she had grown up a lot from the skinny twelve-year-old kid I remembered.

"She's an attractive girl."

Margaret, looking at the photograph, nodded. "We took this just after she came home from college . . ."

"She looks better when she wears her contacts," said Henry. "She insists on wearing those damned goggles instead. I don't know why."

"You're sure she didn't have a boyfriend?"

"Not that I know of."

If a girl like this didn't have some male panting after her, maybe the unisex revolution had gone too far. "Has she ever disappeared before?"

Henry glanced at his wife. After a long silence, he nodded reluctantly. "Two times. Once in high school and once in her third year of college."

"Tell me about it."

He did, in a halting fashion with occasional sidebars from Margaret. She smiled apologetically to take any blame for the disappearances on herself. Henry dismissed a lot of it with the phrase "You know how kids are about their parents bugging them all the time." In the first instance, she had disappeared for three weeks, returning home finally after calling from a runaway shelter in Los Angeles. The second time she had simply dropped out of college and started working as a waitress at a Lake Tahoe ski resort. "That one wasn't anger or whatever. She just said she was tired of books and people who lived only in books. Said she wanted a change of pace."

"How long was she missing that time?"

Henry sighed. "A month or more. We didn't even know she'd left school. They thought she'd returned home, and we thought she was happily attending classes. Then the dean's office called about her absences."

"She didn't get in touch with you."

"She didn't bother to. I suspect she was afraid I'd try to talk her into returning to school. Which I would have—there was no damned refund on tuition."

"But she did graduate?"

"A semester late. With a degree in philosophy, of all things. Then came home to live with us for a couple months, and then took that fool job up in Julian." He added, "We told her she could stay here and come and go as she pleased—I was hoping she'd settle down and start looking for real work. But she wanted to be entirely on her own. She wanted to think things over, she said."

"And she's been up there for a year?"

"About that."

It was possible that, after a year, she just wanted another change of scenery. Perhaps she had in mind a place that would cause her father more anger if he knew about it. "Her pattern seems to be to leave and then get in touch with you after her emotions settle down."

Margaret looked up from staring at the pool's surface. "I hope that's it, Jack. I hope that's all it is."

"Any reason why it shouldn't be?"

The woman's head quivered "no." "I just want to be sure, that's all."

I set down my half-full glass and stood. Henry gathered up papers and notes that he had brought from the house to answer some of my questions about Dorcas. "I'll do what I can."

"Don't forget what I said about your expenses."

"I'll keep a record, Henry."

He followed me to the door, manners back in place. "Fine. Frankly, I expect she's not in trouble or we'd have heard, but you saw how Margaret's on the edge . . ." He held the door open and for the first time smiled. "And someday maybe I can hear your side of that mess you got into in Washington."

CHAPTER

There were things I should do in San Diego before driving up to Julian. Instead of winding back to the freeway, I guided the car through the early-afternoon traffic on La Jolla Drive. Here the changes were less noticeable than in other areas of town. Modest homes were still modest, and homes that had been imposing when I was in high school were still imposing. Nevertheless, change was not totally absent. Old palm trees towered a bit taller, spacious grounds had been cut into smaller lots to allow other mansions to shoulder in, and the modest homes were now owned by doctors and lawyers rather than shopkeepers.

Mission Beach still had that same transient and temporary quality of seasonal rentals, but totally new and confusing was the Mission Bay area. Signs directed me and the other tourists to Sea World; strings of fast-food restaurants and strip malls mushroomed on the fringes of the sprawling man-made bay. A tangle of traffic circles threw me off course toward Point Loma, and I found myself on Sunset Cliffs Boulevard and climbing the Point into neighborhoods which had breathed affluence and contentment for half a century. The rental cottages and seasonal beach homes that had once squatted in shabby ease had been refurbished with manicured landscaping, paint, and quaintness to become year-round residences.

Below the cliffs, cadenced swells lifted brown, scabby patches of kelp before lunging at the rocky shore. It was a sight that pulled me to the curb for a moment to stare. Here and there, the waves peaked to spill trails of foam, and surfers scratched water to catch their faces. There were a lot more surfers, now; it was a sunny day and the waves looked good—four, maybe five feet, nothing great but consistent and not bad for this late in spring. We'd spent a lot of time off these cliffs—Tommy, Arthur, Scott. And me. Often, in those days, we had been the only four in the cold ocean. We'd push out into a fog so dense you couldn't see the cliffs, and from that gray mist, silent swells swept in as thicker gloom. Finally, a towering, dark wall like the coming of night sucked the kelp pods under with ominous little hisses. The wave of the day and a ride blind against the fog and blown spume and plunging surf. The only thing to do was hang on and trust luck and your own skill to keep the board crackling against the glassy face of the curling wave. A metaphor for life, maybe. Which, looking back to that long-gone foggy day and almost forgotten ride, suddenly seemed to have sped as quickly.

When we'd talked, Tommy told me about retiring from his stint in the air force and starting his second career as a restaurateur. It was either that or go into real estate, he'd said, and he liked being around food a hell of a lot more than being around salesmen. Scott was still an engineer in one of the high-tech aerospace industries that crowded south Los Angeles. Arthur, who'd had his troubles in high school, was an occasional rumor of drunkenness, violence, and waste. And now I'd come back, pushed out of the Corps and on the edge of my own second career. Yet despite the years and the knowledge that none of us were the same, those ghosts brought the past forward and gave a shape to a present that startled me with its familiarity.

Had those days been so different from the ones that faced

Dorcas Wilcox now? God knows, staring at the surfers and remembering, they didn't seem so long ago. To my daughters, my early life was from some ill-defined time labeled "before we were born." It had to be that way for Dorcas, too. Like the problems my daughters had faced, her problems were new to her and therefore new to the universe. And the parents who could have given her answers were parents she no longer trusted.

Dorcas—Dori, as she was sometimes called. But the girl in the photograph wasn't someone I'd known. The Dorcas I remembered was a thin girl with straight, pale hair and blue eyes— eyes that in the newest photograph were masked by lenses. In my memory they had been neither confident nor speculative, but pleadingly hopeful. A mix of hurt and trust. In fact, I'd contrasted Dorcas's solemnness with the bright, chatty eagerness of Karen and Becky, and wondered then at the difference. Now, try as I might, I couldn't dredge up anything more about her. Yet, after so much change for both of us, our paths crossed again.

Twisting through the one-way streets of downtown, I located a parking spot near the gray tower of the San Diego County courthouse. Long columns of windows, recessed between modest pilasters, rose to meet in arches thirty or so stories above the sidewalk. Above the uppermost windows, little awnings looked like startled eyebrows. It was another of those landmarks that hadn't changed. As a lieutenant in charge of interviewing military personnel held by civilian authorities, I'd made the Monday morning trips down from Camp Pendleton. The records office was where I remembered it, and a slow-moving clerk took my request and the fees required for the search. Then she handed me the receipt and said it would be a few minutes.

It was more than that, of course. But eventually my number was called and another clerk, this one younger but just as methodical, took my receipt and handed me printouts describing Dorcas's car and license, her driver's license number, a negative report on any county arrest record. It wasn't much, but it was a start. The county recorder listed no deeds, leases, or licenses in her name. The voter registrar told me Dorcas had voted only in the last Presidential election and not in any of the subsequent local ones. She listed her father's La Jolla address as her legal place of residence, and was registered—like her parents, I assumed—as a Republican. Nothing strange in that. Not that there weren't Democrats in La Jolla—there were; I'd heard about someone who met both of them. But Dorcas's penchant for rebellion apparently didn't extend to political spheres.

Finally I went upstairs to the sheriff's department and told a sheriff's officer what I wanted. He said they had Jane Doe descriptions for unidentified bodies found in the past four weeks.

"We don't have information on all the unidentifieds, sir." The black officer punched a code into a computer. "Just the ones located in our jurisdiction."

"She lives up near Julian."

"Uh-huh. That'd probably be us, then. She Hispanic?"

"No. Anglo."

"That cuts out some." He scrolled another file up the screen. "Get a lot of Hispanics. Mostly coming up from Mexico." He paused again. "How long you say she's been missing?"

"Two weeks or so."

"Here's one—blond, approximately twenty years old, five-seven. Found one week ago near Chula Vista." He read further. "Any tattoos?"

"None that I know of."

"This one has a rose tattoo on her left buttock. Other identifying marks or scars?"

"A birthmark on the back of her right thigh."

He shook his head again. "Not on this report. Don't mean much though. She missing any teeth?"

"No." I showed him the photograph and waited for his nod.

He only grunted. "This one had false front teeth. Top four teeth missing a long time."

I felt my shoulders sag with relief. The sheriff's officer scrolled again and then shrugged. "Nobody we got fits who you're looking for. Try the city morgue yet?"

Henry told me he had called them himself, but sometimes when you didn't want to discover something, you didn't probe deeply enough. I got a list of the regional police and hospital agencies and thanked the officer. Out in a car hot from sun and closed windows, I used a map to sketch an itinerary that took me in a large loop and used up the final hours of the day. By the time I drove up the Strand from Imperial Beach, the sun, an inch or so above the Pacific, was a red ball filtered by the distant sea haze. It gradually flattened and broke against the purple water.

It was a long afternoon's tour: offices, waiting rooms, service counters, punctuated by three visits to viewing rooms. The silent and chill cubicle was usually furnished with a few tubular chrome chairs and a dim reading lamp. Cozy morgue decor. A coroner's assistant would come into the room just before another man wheeled the loaded gurney into the small alcove beyond the viewing window. Then the alcove's harsh overhead light flared on and the covered figure was silently pushed up close to the glass. The morgue attendant folded back the sheet from the cadaver's head and neck and stood back. He kept his eyes on the coroner's assistant and avoided my face. In the glare of the strong lighting, the dead woman's features always seemed chiseled and any bruises or cuts were etched darkly against the bloodless skin. And, so far, the answer was the same: not Dorcas Wilcox.

Easing the car into the garage of my new house, I paused in the kitchen to pour myself a beer. Then I flipped on a couple of lights to chase the darkness from the rooms, the stereo to rid the silence with the mellow saxophone of Spike Robinson, and rummaged through the refrigerator for something to remove the hunger. The thing I really wanted to get rid of was the lingering vision of dead women blindly facing that harsh light. And the thoughts that had come with seeing the sprawling county's unnamed human detritus. The scraps of food and the beer helped, but the painting of Karen and Becky hanging behind the small dining table helped most of all. I could see the light strokes of Eleanor's invisible hand in the minute shades of pigment. The colors were arranged in the pattern her mind had created and brought her closer. I didn't remember Eleanor painting this work—it had been done as a surprise while I was on one of those unplanned and unheralded assignments that weren't supposed to be mentioned. But she had proudly hung it to greet me when I got back, and her pride was justified. It was a calming pleasure to imagine her alive and intently lost in stroking the rough paper with those little *whish-whish* noises of pastels, and radiating that warmth of someone in control of her work and thoroughly enjoying its discoveries.

I rinsed the dishes and added them to the breakfast stuff in the dishwasher. One of these days it would fill up enough to run, but until then I had plates and forks enough to last. The mail had come and was mostly the stuff of occupants' dreams: free prizes, quick and easy loans, introductory coupons for hundreds of discount dollars. A comic greeting card wished me good luck in my new home and was signed "In haste—letter coming—love, Karen and Chuck." She had mailed it before we talked on the telephone, and it brought back the worry I had about Becky—the suddenness of my retirement and move to Coronado. It would certainly surprise her, but I hoped it wouldn't be upsetting. Karen had tried to reassure me: Becky wouldn't be upset—she was too involved in her own life now, and that was good. Besides, Karen laughed, it would probably be more exciting to her than traumatic. Her younger sister always did like to move to a new duty station more than she did. And I reminded myself that Rebecca had been talking of staying in Europe until school started in the fall. Perhaps she'd want to spend some time here in the new house—there were worse places for a lovely girl to stay for a few summer months, and she'd have a chance to visit her sister. But it would be her decision; Eleanor and I had tried to instill independence in the girls. We'd wanted to counter the losses brought by constant moves and changes of school which could rob a child of security and leave her emotionally stunted and unsure. Now I saw in them the same self-confidence and fair-mindedness that had been their mother's. Perhaps Eleanor and I had done it right; perhaps the girls had been old enough when their mother died that they could cope with that shock. More likely, they had inherited enough of Eleanor's courage and blessed good humor to survive with as little hurt as possible. Still, I'd have to send Becky several photographs of the new house with its vacant boat slip just beyond the back door. And promise that she could help choose the boat that Eleanor and I had been saving for over so many years.

The admiral answered my call and had me hold while he asked Jenny to pick up an extension. I told them what I'd spent the afternoon doing.

"Those poor girls," said Jenny. "But thank God none of them were Dorcas!"

"What's your next step, Jack?"

"I'll head up to Julian tomorrow morning and start from there." My question wasn't easy, but it had to be asked. "Jenny, how would you characterize Dorcas's relationship with her parents?"

The line was silent for a long moment. "It's not a happy family, is it?" she said.

"Did Dorcas ever talk to you or the admiral about it?"

"Not for a long time. Not since she was in high school. By her senior year, she seemed . . . accepting. She wasn't happy, but she seemed to have reached some kind of understanding."

"Was that before or after she ran away the first time?"

"She ran away?"

"In her senior year. Margaret didn't tell you about it?"

"No! This is the first I've heard of it. I don't know why she didn't tell me."

The admiral's voice broke in. "I damned well do: Henry. He wouldn't want us to suspect he failed at being a father like he's failed at being a husband."

"Dalton, it's not all Henry's fault. Margaret isn't a very strong person herself."

"I grant that. But by God—"

"Dalton, please!"

I spoke into the angry silence. "I'll be in touch with you as soon as I know anything more, Admiral. Good night, Jenny."

My next call was to Tom Jenkins to tell him I might be out of town for a day or so and why.

"You're doing what?"

"That's the help Admiral Combs asked for. So I told him I'd do what I could."

"God, I haven't seen him in years. How's he doing?"

"Still a tough old buzzard." I told Tom about Jenny, too, and Margaret and Dorcas. Tom wasn't as close to them as I was; but in a town as small as Coronado, he'd known Margaret and there were a few summers when we'd done odd jobs and yard work for Mrs. Combs.

"Well, I hope you're better at playing detective than you were at the four-hundred-yard dash. But any time, man. Just give me a call, and I'm available."

The four-hundred-yard run. Tommy always would remember winning that regional track meet by half a step. I had almost forgotten, but Jenkins's reminder brought back the sting of that loss. Tommy had gone on to the state meet and placed third, which was probably a hell of a lot better than I could have done. At the time it seemed important, all the more because our rivalry was intense. Fortunately, it had been based on friendship rather than enmity, and I was glad to learn that Tommy still had his fundamental good nature: he didn't sound sore about another delay of our get-together.

There had been rivalry in surfing and skin-diving, as well—who could get the biggest wave, who brought in the biggest langosta. And thinking of that made my mind touch on other names and events and especially on the atmosphere, the way things used to look and feel. Some people said they remembered faces accurately; for me, faces were impressions surrounded by settings that were often more important. And anchored by moments. Now that I dredged it up, I could see Tommy at the edge of my vision, head thrown back in straining effort and elbow high with the lunge of his torso toward the tape. Then that white banner pulling away and taking with it all my dreams of glory as Tommy's chest crossed the line first.

Strange how the past keeps welling up into the present. Images, flavors, sounds—all bringing back trivial moments that persist in memory. And it seems the importance of those moments is less for what actually happened than for the meanings that continue into the present.

CHAPTER

The mountain town spread among pines and up and down hillsides. From the highway a grid of side streets led into the shadows of trees and past quiet houses. Aside from the motels and inns, most of the homes were small. The familiar clusters of gas station, restaurant, grocery store, and a dozen or so shops were strung along the highway. Graveled parking areas waited for the weekend influx of tourists. This far from the coast, the sun burned despite the altitude. A haze of pollen from the pines dusted the ground with yellow and gave a resiny tang to the air. The Golden Bear gift shop was on the edge of town, one of four adjoining stores linked by a boardwalk that tried to look rustic. Two horses were tied at one end, stamping and quivering their haunches against the bite of flies. In the hot silence of midday a distant car whined up the long hill toward town. Somewhere beyond the heavily treed ridge a small plane droned in the blue.

"Mrs. Gannet?"

The woman in a brightly flowered muumuu turned from arranging the greeting card selection. I introduced myself.

"I'm looking for Dorcas Wilcox. Her father tells me she works for you."

"She did. I don't know where she is now." The woman patted

at the knot of graying hair held at the back of her head by two long hairpins. It was a Spanish touch that matched her olive skin and dark eyes. "I haven't seen or heard from her in three, four weeks. I told her father that. As well as the deputy that came by asking the same thing." The knot of hair wagged once. "Poor girl."

"When did the deputy come by?"

"About a week ago. A few days after Dori's father did."

"Did she work for you long?"

"Over a year. Did a good job, too. Mr. Steele your name is? Well, Dori had a real nice way with the customers, Mr. Steele."

Maybe it was my cheerful personality or just the fact that I was asking questions, but Mrs. Gannet's tone carried a note of blame for losing a good clerk.

"And she left without saying where she was going?"

A curt nod.

"Did you see her leave?"

"No. All I know is she's somewhere else and not here."

"Can you tell me about any friends she had? People who might know where she went?"

"You some kind of detective? That what you are?"

"No. I'm just a friend of the family. Her grandfather asked me to help. I have two daughters, so I have a pretty good idea what her parents are going through."

She studied my face for a moment. "And if you find her, you're going to make her go back, that it?"

"No. She's over twenty-one. I can't make her go anywhere she doesn't want to go. What I'm trying to do is find out whether or not she needs help. If she doesn't, fine. If she does, somebody ought to know."

The woman scratched again in the bun of hair and seemed to ponder something. "She was trying to be on her own. She said the last thing she wanted was help from her parents."

"I can understand that. My daughters like their independence, too. But if they happen to get into more trouble than they can handle, I want to know about it. I'm sure you'd feel the same way."

The woman's lips pressed into a thin line. "I really don't know where she is. Dori's a nice person—the quiet kind, maybe, but she's got a good heart. And that's the ones usually get hurt. I just hope that poor girl's not in bigger trouble than she was when she left."

"What kind of trouble was she in when she left, Mrs. Gannet?"

The brown eyes blinked a time or two. "Pregnant."

I digested that snippet of news. "Did she tell her parents?"

"She doesn't want them to know. That's why she didn't want to see her parents when they came up a month or so ago."

"But she told you."

"Didn't have to—I know the signs. A man might not, but a woman who's had her own kids knows the signs."

"And you saw the signs."

"I did."

"Do you think she was afraid to tell her parents?"

The hostility was replaced by puzzlement as the woman shook her head. "No, I don't think that was it. I honestly don't. I mean it's not like getting pregnant's a big sin anymore. I mean there's all these movie stars knocking each other up and showing their bellies off in the newspapers, and all these high school classes for teenage mothers. So it's not that big a deal. That's what I told her." She sought her words. "But Dori didn't like to talk about herself a lot. Good with the customers—talk about the weather, whatever, but it was like pulling teeth to get her to talk about herself."

"Do you think she's gone to have an abortion?"

The woman's head shook again. "I asked her if that's what she was planning. Besides, she would have done that a while back—you know, after missing only a couple periods. What she said was the baby was a bond."

"A bond? With the father?"

"Didn't say that. Just that it was a bond. And a pledge to the future—exact words: 'a pledge to the future.' "

"Did she say who the father was?"

"No."

"Do you have any idea?"

A brief snort. "Some damned man, wouldn't you say?"

I sure couldn't say it wasn't. "Can you tell me about any of her friends?"

She mentioned a few names, people in the community whom Dorcas talked with or saw every day. "As far as any real close friends, men or women, I can't say, and she didn't talk about them. She could've been living with somebody, but I wouldn't know. I never went to her cabin until she started missing work."

"Mrs. Gannet, I'm not going to harass Dorcas. I'm not going to make her do anything she doesn't want to—I couldn't. But her family is very worried about her; they have no idea if she's safe, if she's happy, if she needs help." I added, "That's all I want to learn—that she's all right."

"If I knew where she is, I'd have told the sheriff. I don't know, so I can't tell you, either."

"Can you at least tell me how to get to her cabin?"

That she could do.

The cabin sat back from a graveled county road; a two-rut dirt track led to it between scattered ponderosas. A deep porch ran around two sides and a wooden swing seat dangled from rusty chains. Its windows were framed by pierced bargeboard touched up with red and blue painted flowers. That gave it a Swiss look and drew attention from the badly faded stain on the log siding. A window box showed a tiny smear of color from geraniums that were surrendering to drought. My heels clumped loudly on the varnished boards of the porch and I pulled open the creaking screen door to knock on the wooden one. As Henry had said, the place was empty—looked empty, sounded empty, felt empty. I didn't expect any answer to my knock and that's what I got.

After a second and louder try, I walked around the building, listening for noises and looking at the tightly closed and curtained windows. Behind the cabin the round silver ball of an LP gas tank seemed jarringly out of place against the pines and rock outcroppings. A small building served as a storage shed and pump house. On one side, a stone barbecue grill rose from a cleared patch of gritty dirt. A pair of sandy streaks and an oil patch showed where a car habitually parked. A rusted steel drum used as a trash barrel stood empty. Nothing looked disturbed; the dusty pine needles lay flat and unscuffed, and any footprints had been erased by wind.

I went back to the porch and slipped a plastic wallet calendar under the tongue of the locked doorknob. It was a trick I hadn't used in a long time, and I have to admit it didn't go as well as it did in training. But with a few choice words and a half-dozen tries, I finally popped the latch and opened the door to the musty smell of an airless room. A faint odor of gas came from the burning pilot light of the stove, and an electric shudder told me the refrigerator had kicked on. I spent a few minutes walking through the small rooms—the living/dining area had a portable television set. A bookcase was crammed mostly with paperbacks whose titles indicated interest in religions and mythologies, philosophy and ritual. The kitchen's open shelves were masked by gingham curtains that matched the yellow-and-white-checked cloth at the windows. In the bedroom a queen-sized platform bed took up almost all the space. A single bureau and a closet, also curtained off by gingham, made up the furniture. A tiny bathroom with a shower stall had been added off the bedroom. I started my detailed search there.

It wasn't too different from the old search-and-seizure training, except I didn't expect to find anything incriminating so I didn't have to worry about evidence bags and the chain of possession. What I did note as I finished with a survey of the refrigerator's contents was that Dorcas had apparently left willingly and planned only a short stay. The plastic containers of leftovers blossoming with hairy mold, the half-carton of sour milk, the open dish of butter, all indicated haste in leaving and possibly an intent to return soon. But her toothbrush was missing from the bathroom, as were the cleansing solutions for her contact lenses. No deodorant. An almost full box of sanitary napkins under the bathroom sink, which she wouldn't need if she was pregnant. No money or checkbook, no purse or wallet with necessary identification or keys. Some of her clothes filled the drawers and hung in the closet. But there was no suitcase or clothes bag, and a tangle of empty hangers was shoved to one end of the bar. A plastic napkin holder on a kitchen shelf held a few bills—telephone, electricity, and a gasoline company credit report. The telephone company's record of charges listed a total of five toll calls to two different numbers; the area code that wasn't La Jolla was 303, and that listed three calls. The gasoline bill had a series of fill-ups from a few stations in La Jolla and Brown's Full Service in Julian. The last entry was almost a month ago. I pocketed the slips and gave the cabin one last check. The trash can under the sink held smelly food scraps and some torn papers. Using a plastic Baggie for a glove, I lifted out a ripped sheet of paper and fitted it together on the sideboard of the sink. Through the blurs of dripped grease and splattered food, I could make out half of a letter written in now-smeared ballpoint pen: ". . . so if you do, it will blow your mind, Dori. I mean that. Shirley was all twisted up about it at first, you know what a sweat bead she can be, but she's really into it now and says it's really changed her life. Anyway I hope you can, you won't regret it, I promise. Always the same, Dwayne."

I slipped the letter into another plastic Baggie and took one last look around. Before I locked the door, I dumped a coffee can of water on the reedy geraniums—maybe that would hold them until the next rain, if it ever rained again in Southern California. At the end of the drive, I checked the mailbox. It

WHEN REASON SLEEPS • 39

held a handful of mail addressed to occupant. I left it there and
headed back up the graveled county road to Julian.

Brown's Self-Service sat surrounded by a sun-baked and oil-
stained concrete pad. A girl in cutoff jeans and a T-shirt advertising Foster's Lager Beer stood behind the cash register.

"Dori Wilcox? She's missing?"

"She may just be on a trip somewhere. But her family's
worried."

"You know, I haven't seen her in a while . . . She gets her
gas here maybe every other week, so I haven't noticed like I
would if she came in all the time."

"Can you remember when she was in last?"

The girl frowned and then shook her head. "I really can't.
She could have come by when I was off. You know, in the
evening or something."

"Could you look through your credit card receipts, say starting about two weeks ago?"

"That's a lot of receipts!"

"It could be very important." I practiced my friendly smile.
"You might have the only information that can tell me where
she is." Finally the girl nodded. "Thanks. I have to go by the
post office—maybe they know something about her. I'll be back
in a while."

For a dollar fee, the post office provides a person's change
of address if they've filed a c.o.a. card; for a few minutes' time,
the route carrier can often provide information about anyone
going on vacation or stopping their mail for a short while, or
even a new name that might get deliveries at an old address. I
didn't have to pay my dollar because, as I suspected, Dorcas
hadn't filed a change of address. But the postal clerk told me
where the carrier for that route would probably be eating lunch.
I found the woman's car, a "Caution—Frequent Stops" sign
taped in the four-wheel drive's back window. It was parked in
the shade of a county roadside park overlooking the coast range
and the haze-filled valleys below.

Lunch was a tuna fish sandwich. I smelled it on the hot breeze that lifted up the steep, rocky flank of the mountain. A deeply tanned arm spotted with turquoise jewelry waved at the occasional fly which smelled the same aroma. "Wilcox?" The name didn't register, but she was sorry to hear the girl was missing.

"She lives in a dark brown log cabin about a mile and a half down Country Road V."

Most reasonably honest citizens, I'd learned over years of investigative work, were eager to provide information if it didn't cost them anything. In fact, one of the challenges of interviewing witnesses was to be able to winnow fact from helpful invention—something the FBI agents often overlooked in compiling dossiers on suspects and which had contributed to ill will between that agency and my own. The mail carrier wanted to help but it wasn't until I described the cabin that she recognized the name. "Oh—the Potts place! Sure—Wilcox—moved in maybe a year ago, right?"

I nodded. "Did anyone else ever get their mail delivered there?"

The woman shook her head, curly dark hair spilling over the collar of her plaid shirt. As a contract carrier, she wore civilian clothes instead of a uniform. "Not that I remember. Just the one name." She explained, "I remember addresses better than names. Folks are always moving in and out of these cabins, especially in summer."

"Did she say anything about going away for a while?"

The woman shook her head again. Silver and turquoise Navaho earrings glinted in the sun. "I didn't see much of her—just the mailbox."

"And she didn't get much mail?"

"Books—she's the book one." The woman finished her sandwich and swigged at a thermos. "She was always getting these padded book mailers. Couple weeks ago she got a big one that didn't fit in the mailbox so I had to drive in and leave it on the porch."

"Remember where it came from?"

"Lord, no! It came from out of state, I think . . . I remember that. From an ashram or something. Had a little Buddha picture with flames all around it. But that's all I remember."

The girl at Brown's Full Service was waiting for me. "I found it!" She held up a dimly legible card with Dori Wilcox's signature and automobile license number for identification. Unleaded, eleven dollars and thirteen cents' worth, and the date was the sixth of the month. A little over a week ago. My guess was she filled the tank before driving wherever she was headed. And I guessed, too, that she might have used the credit card since then.

"Good work, miss! This may help a great deal."

The girl tried not to look too proud. "Well, all I did was look through the receipts."

"Does Dorcas have any particular friends in town? A boyfriend, maybe?"

"No, I don't think so. She pretty much stays by herself. I mean she's friendly and all, but I never see her with anybody, and she doesn't date any of the boys around here. A place this small, there's only a couple bars to go to and you see everybody there."

"Do you know what kind of car she drives?"

"Sure—a white Mustang convertible. A classic, you know? I told her if she ever wanted to sell it, I'd be interested. It's boss!"

I stopped at the post office once more, mailing a check to the gasoline company to cover Dorcas's bill. I also asked them to please note the new address for future correspondence.

CHAPTER

5

The California Bureau of Vital Statistics in Sacramento will, for a two-dollar fee per inquiry, provide information on marriage and divorce records as well as birth and death records. It was a long shot, but I took it, more to rest my conscience than with the expectation of finding anything. I'd telephoned both the admiral and Margaret when I got home from Julian to tell them my conclusions about Dorcas planning for a short trip. I didn't tell either one of them about her pregnancy. She wanted to keep that private and I respected her wishes. It's what I would have offered Dorcas if I'd found her, as well as what, by implication, I'd promised Mrs. Gannet. But that promise added urgency to the search. If the girl was in trouble, her pregnancy made it worse.

I spent the rest of the afternoon with my lap-top and the telephone. The first was to draft standard inquiries to various state bureaus. The latter was to call the highway patrol offices in neighboring states in case a white Mustang had been in an accident. Neither Arizona nor Nevada reported a Mustang with Dori's California plates, and that left Baja California as a possibility. But how to get that information was a puzzle which local federal agencies didn't solve. A call to Washington finally reached a woman in the State Department. She made it plain they were not inclined to endanger international relations with cavalier searches for missing Americans in Mexico. Most definitely, no one in the State Department would initiate any inquiries about an American citizen without bona fide evidence of peril. And if said citizen had violated any laws of the host nation, no action would be taken anyway. What she meant was State's interests were a hell of a lot more important than those of mere citizens and taxpayers. And by no means coincided. I felt the familiar stir of anger. The Washington establishment— major and minor—demanded, in the name of the flag, loyalty, sacrifice, and cash. But their real purpose was self-service. Not all patriots are scoundrels, but by God it seems all Washington scoundrels make loud use of patriotism. It's no wonder the word has come to feel bulgy and false on the tongue.

But anger wouldn't help. I reminded myself that without more evidence Mexico was just another possibility, and cursing the servants of the people wouldn't help. But even the next item, a call to the telephone company, was only a little more helpful. The directory had told me that area 303 was for northern Colorado; a recording told me the number had been disconnected. Sensitive to the company security, the operator would not tell me who the subscriber was or even which town the prefix referred to. Finally I called the reference desk at the San Diego State University library. They had a collection of telephone books, including several for Colorado. One listed the prefix as serving Kremmling and vicinity. A reverse directory would have told me who rented the number, but I no longer had easy access to that little jewel—it was reserved for government agencies.

Still, I did find out that Dorcas had made three calls to Kremmling, Colorado, in the month before she disappeared. A look at the map gave me the county that Kremmling was in—Grand—and more telephone calls let me know that no one by the name of Dorcas Wilcox and no white Mustang with California plates had come to the official attention of the county hospital or the sheriff's department. A clerk in the sheriff's office took the missing girl's name and solemnly promised to call if something should turn up. In my mind's eye, I could see the notice possibly making it as far as a crowded and little-read bulletin board.

I recorded the names and numbers I'd telephoned in a small notebook. The record was less for Henry's cost sheet than out of the habit of keeping track of all names and addresses relating to an investigation. In fact, I felt myself slipping easily into that old, familiar frame of mind which I called On the Hunt.

The next calls were to the names Henry provided as Dorcas's old high school buddies. One had married and still lived in La Jolla. The other numbers had prefixes that meant San Diego and the southern half of LA County. I tried the nearby one first. A recorded message played assorted roars and growls and then said Hi and told me it was feeding time at the zoo, would I leave a name and number or call back later, thanks. I left my name and number, saying it was very important. I didn't have the slightest temptation to bark good-bye. The La Jolla call was answered on the second ring by a woman with a heavy Spanish accent who said, "Just a moment, please." Then a young woman's voice said yes, it was Kimberly Overstreet Goddard, and, yes, Henry Wilcox had talked to her about Dorcas.

"But I really don't know where she might have gone. I mean, we really haven't talked all that much in the last couple years, and especially since my marriage and all."

"Do you know if she has a boyfriend or someone she's been dating lately?"

"No."

"How about anyone called Dwayne?"

A short silence. "Not that I recall. I mean she might, but like I say, we really didn't have all that much to talk about anymore. I mean she's interested in doing her own thing, and I've been more and more involved with my married friends and with the wives of my husband's associates—there's a very active social program for attorneys' wives here in La Jolla. So Dori and I've just sort of drifted apart."

"Do you know of anyone in Colorado she might have gone to see?"

"Colorado? No. But a lot of people from California go there. I mean, it's sort of an in place to go. All those mountains and open spaces, you know. In fact, my husband's been thinking of taking a position there—he's an attorney—but I don't know, the economy isn't all that great, I hear."

I let the woman talk through the possibilities of moving to Denver in the hope she might mention something pertinent. But the hope was false. All I ended up with was a hot ear and the repeated fact that her husband was an attorney.

The Santa Ana number didn't answer, nor did Riverside. To give my ear a rest, I changed into running clothes and headed across the highway for the long, surf-hazed beach on the ocean side of the Strand. By the time I trotted back, waving a hand to Mrs. Meisner, a next-door neighbor who was busily poking petunias into her tiny patch of new lawn, I had justified my thirst for a beer and worked up an appetite for that slab of swordfish waiting for the grill. I was halfway through an early dinner when the telephone rang and a female voice said, "This is Stacey Briggs. I'm returning your call."

Rinsing the rest of the fish out of my mouth, I told her who I was. "I understand Mr. Wilcox spoke with you earlier."

"Yes. And I don't know what more I can tell you—Dori called me sometime last month and that was the last time we talked."

"Did she mention any boyfriend? Or say anything about her health?"

"No. Is she sick?"

"That's one of the things I'm trying to find out. Did she say anything about making a trip?"

"No. We just talked about this and that. Nothing special, really."

"Do you know of any friends she might have in Colorado?"

". . . No. Do you think that's where she went?"

"It's possible. Do you know anybody named Dwayne?"

This time the pause was longer, and suddenly I wished I could see her eyes. "Dwayne who?"

"I don't have a last name yet. But apparently he was a good friend of Dorcas's."

"Call her Dori—she doesn't like 'Dorcas.' " A pause. "Dori has her own friends, now. I don't know all the people she sees."

"What about a Shirley?"

"No."

"Kimberly Overstreet or Margot Hoyer?"

"Oh, sure. We all ran around together in high school. But I haven't seen much of them in the last couple years. We talk on the phone now and then, but that's about it." She added, "Kimberly's married, and Margot's living up in Santa Ana, working as a paralegal. Her brother Jason's with one of their dad's banks out in Riverside. You might give them a call—I know Dori talked with them, too."

I thanked Miss Briggs and sat back to finish my dinner and to let the stray thoughts and impressions form into words. Then I dialed Henry and asked a few more questions.

One of the things I asked of Henry was Dorcas's high school yearbook. On my way north through early-evening traffic, I stopped in La Jolla long enough to look through the glossy pages.

"You think there might be something in this?" Henry, glass in one hand, handed me the yearbook with the other. Its richly padded cover had an engraving of palm trees and ocean cliffs. Rows of tinted portraits smiled back with clear-eyed faith in the future, and alphabetized names in the margins. Margaret, Henry said, had gone to bed early; the only lights on in the rambling home were the living room's soft lamps and the cooler flicker of the television room. Apparently, Henry spent his evenings there alone. The whole house was filled with a quiet gloom. It might have been despair over their daughter, but the mood seemed more routine than that. It was a kind of surrender to ennui, as if Henry and Margaret had created a refuge where no further effort was needed and nothing called for change. I could understand a young girl's unwillingness to live in that atmosphere. Or to bring her child into it.

My finger traced the names in the margins beside the rows of photographs. "It's just a hunch—that's about all I have to go on so far."

Henry swigged at his glass, ice cubes clinking. Finally he asked, "You don't think she might be dead, do you?"

I looked up from the glare of the shiny pages and tried to read his expression. "Do you think she might be?"

He shook his head. "I think she's just run off again. But Margaret's worried about it. And . . . and you read about things in the papers . . ." He drank deeply. "I want to know what you think about it."

That kind of question wasn't something you lied about. "I don't think she is. But it's a possibility."

He watched me bend over the pages of the yearbook. "Margaret told me you called earlier and what you said about Dori taking a short trip. I can't even let myself think she might be dead."

"Well, let's not, then. It's worrisome that she didn't return as soon as she apparently planned to. But there's a lot to find out before we can be sure of anything."

"Right, right." He cleared his throat. "But if you do find out bad news, tell me—not Margaret. She—ah—she has a hard time handling things like that, Steele."

"Will do." I found another Dwayne and jotted that name under the first one.

"What's that you're doing?"

"Dorcas had a letter in her trash from someone named Dwayne. It's possible he's another high school friend. I want to try out the names, anyway."

"Dwayne?"

"Do you recognize it?"

He shook his head. "I didn't know many of her high school friends. College, either, for that matter."

When I finally closed the yearbook, I had five Dwaynes and four Shirleys, which, I supposed, wasn't bad from a graduating class of several hundred. Henry walked me to the door, fresh drink in hand.

"You're going up to LA now? This late?"

I glanced at my watch. "I'll get there about eight or nine, depending on traffic."

"I—ah—do appreciate what you're doing, Steele. Margaret does, too." He added, "You'll be certain to let me know the minute you find out anything, right?"

I told him I would.

"Thanks. And good luck." The closing door made a slightly hollow sound in the street's silence.

CHAPTER

I paced myself through the traffic lights back to the San Diego Freeway, then headed north. Long rows of anonymous cars sped bumper-to-bumper twenty miles an hour above the speed limit. The familiar interchanges to Camp Pendleton and the El Toro air base dredged up a lot of echoes and even some hurt. But I pushed that away and concentrated on reaching LA in one piece. A river of cars in six oncoming lanes began to glitter with headlights. The evening's smog and dust settled in to shadow the streets below the elevated freeway, and neon signs glowed dimly against the thick mix of twilight and carbon monoxide. Marking main avenues, rows of tall royal palms lifted out of the haze in bushy-headed silhouette, emphasizing beauty in the delicate and deepening purple shades of poisonous gases. I made my descent down the ramp into a wide thoroughfare lined on each side by the smooth trunks. A couple of eye-watering blocks later, I turned onto one of those empty residential streets that make up so much of greater Los Angeles. Silent and seemingly vacant houses with blank picture windows faced each other across small lawns trimmed with flowering shrubs. Margot Hoyer's address was a corner fourplex in what was called California Mission design. Beneath a miniature bell-tower, the stucco entry arch led to a tiny patio whose only sound was the brittle splash of a neglected fountain.

She knew even less about Dorcas than Stacey Briggs did. "We chat on the phone now and then. Once in a great while we happen to be in La Jolla together, and we might have lunch. But as for knowing her plans . . ." The woman shook shoulder-length, crimped hair that flared like the sides of a brown tent around her face.

"Do any of these names sound familiar to you?" I showed her the list of Dwaynes and Shirleys.

Slowly, she read down the column. "Dwayne Hoover—he was in our high school class. Dwayne Vengley was, too." She looked up at me. "Shirley Ellman. Are all these from our class?"

"Yes. Do you know if Dorcas is still in touch with any of them?"

"In touch?"

"Writing. Talking to. Seeing."

The hair shook again.

"Have you talked to any of these people lately?"

"No—of course not. Why should I?"

"They're old classmates. Like Dorcas."

"Dori and Kimberly, Stacey and me—we were sort of a club." A small laugh, half scorn, half affection. "We called ourselves the Four Femmes." She handed the list back to me. "None of these were in our group."

"Did Dorcas mention any boyfriend at all?"

"Not to me."

There wasn't much more I could think to ask, and it was obvious Margot Hoyer would be happy to see me go. It was less obvious that she was avoiding something, but that feeling was there. I left my telephone number for her to call if she happened to remember anything at all that might help. The woman smiled widely and assured me she would.

Her brother's apartment was half of a ranch-style duplex that he shared with two other young men. When I called from a nearby telephone hood, Jason Hoyer—surprise clear in his voice—said he wasn't sure what he could say that would help any, but I was welcome to come by.

"I went out with her a few times—nothing heavy. Just movies and things. She's a nice girl and all, but we didn't have that much in common. She and my sister were big buddies. They had this clique, the Four Femmes, and I wasn't going with anybody at the time, so I sort of asked her out once in a while."

"You weren't in her senior class, though?"

"No. I graduated a year ahead. They were all a nice bunch of girls. Fun people, you know?"

Jason Hoyer was still slender with youth and exercise. But his heavy shoulders and hips promised bulk. There was some resemblance to his sister, especially around the eyes and the thrust of his jaw. He was tanned in a way that clerking in a bank would not provide, and I noted that, as the man reached for the list of names, his arm was brown far up under the cuff of his pin-striped shirt.

"The only one I know is Dwayne Vengley. He was in Margot's class."

"Did your sister or Dorcas have much to do with him?"

"Margot didn't, thank God."

"Why 'thank God'?"

"Aw, the guy was a real asshole—pardon my French. Always acting like he had some big secret nobody else was in on. Trying to make himself look important all the time. Crap."

"Did Dorcas see a lot of him?"

He shrugged. "Not while I was in school." Leaning back in the kitchen chair, he glanced through the open doorway to the living room where his two suitemates watched a television set mounted in the center of an almost empty bookcase. "I guess she might have her senior year—they were in the spring musical together. Dori was in the chorus and Dwayne was the cowboy—what's his name—the one who sings 'Oh, What a Beautiful Morning.' "

"Dorcas was in the school play?"

"Yeah. Kind of surprised me. She didn't usually do that kind of stuff. But she said it was her senior year and she felt she ought to try it. She'd surprise you like that now and then."

"And that's when she dated Vengley?"

"I guess. I was at the university so I didn't see much of the Four except when I came home. I remember on spring break, when the Gates thing happened, Margot was royally pissed at Dori and the others for even being there."

"The Gates thing?"

Jason looked slightly embarrassed as if he'd mentioned something better left unsaid. Then he shrugged. "Yeah. It was in all the newspapers. David Gates. He, Dori, Dwayne, Kimberly, and Stacey. They went on a picnic out on Point Loma and David got lost or something and died falling over a cliff. It was really a bad scene—the Gates kid was a kind of feeb, but he was all right, you know? That's the only time I ever felt close to sorry for Dwayne; he was really cut up about it. Crying, everything. They all were. Thank God Margot didn't go on that one." He shrugged again. "Nobody liked Dwayne. Dwayne the Pain we called him. I don't know why Dori was hanging around with him."

The rest of the questions dealt with any recent information Jason had about Dorcas, but there wasn't much. "She telephoned maybe six, eight weeks ago, just to talk. I was kind of surprised to hear from her, but she's like that: you don't hear anything for six months or a year and then she calls. Said she tried Margot but she was out, so she called me instead."

"Did she seem at all worried or upset?"

He thought about that. "No, I don't think so. It's hard to tell with her; she's pretty intense, you know? But she really holds herself in." He rubbed an earlobe in thought. "Kind of unhealthy, if you think about it. Maybe that's why she was getting into crystals."

"Crystals?"

"Healing power and visions. She met somebody up in Julian

who claimed crystals could cure cancer or something. She's always been into that kind of stuff. Even in high school."

"Despite a bachelor's degree in philosophy?"

"Because of it, I'd say. She claims philosophy raises more questions than it answers. I mean she's always reading. Weird stuff." He added, "What's she always saying . . . ? 'There's more to the mind than Reason or Freud.' Whatever the hell that means."

"What kind of weird stuff does she read?"

"Oh, Nietzsche, Bokanovski or whoever. I can't remember all the names. If it isn't business or economics, it just doesn't stick with me, you know?"

"Did you go to Occidental, too?"

"No. USC. I'm applying to the business school now, my MBA. They like you to have some work experience after graduation before applying."

"Did you see much of her after she went to Occidental?"

He shook his head. "Only on vacations now and then. Or when she'd drop by the house to see Margot."

"Do you know if Dwayne Vengley went to Occidental?"

The thought was new to him. "No. I sure don't."

Tom Jenkins's voice was the only message on my telephone answerer. "For a retired old fart, you sure don't sit on the front porch much. Give me a call if you get in before midnight." The number he cited was different from the one I had on my memo pad. Road-weary, I glanced at my watch—eleven forty-five—and opened a beer before punching the numbers into the telephone. The answer was a female voice whose briskness surprised me.

"The Lagoon."

"I'm trying to reach Tom Jenkins, please."

"Yessir. Who can I say is calling?"

I told her and a few seconds later Tom's rusty voice greeted me with an invitation to lunch tomorrow.

"Make it around noon, okay?" Tommy coughed away from the mouthpiece and then his voice came back. "I don't get out of bed until ten anymore."

That was fine with me. The next day I slept until my own alarm went off late in the morning. Then I made a few telephone calls before running along the beach to let the sweat and salty mist clear away the loginess. By the time I returned, I had an answer to one of the calls and an afternoon appointment with Dwayne Vengley's father. A quick shower and just time to meet Tom across from the Hotel del Coronado in a patio restaurant tucked behind a row of tourist shops.

Tom gripped my hand and looked me up and down. "By God, I'd hate to race against you now—a little gray hair, a few more lines and pounds, but by God—"

A waitress hovered beside me to take my drink order. Without asking, she brought Tom a bottle of mineral water. He, too, had put on weight. The runner's frame had filled out and a fold of flesh under his chin showed where the man struggled against even more pounds. But he still moved with suppleness and he made a point to tell me that he played handball two or three times a week.

"Did you ever learn to pick them off the back wall? You always were a sucker for that shot."

"Uh-oh." Tommy leaned back. "Somebody's looking for trouble. Dime a point?"

"I hate to take your money."

"Plus two bits for every ace."

I shook my head sadly. "But if you're going to throw it away anyhow . . ."

"Ha! Winner buys the drinks—just so you won't feel bad."

The ritual was more than twenty years old. It and the laughter that went with it carried us both back in time.

"By God, Jack, it doesn't seem that long ago, does it?"

"It doesn't. And it's damn good to see you again. Here's to."

We tipped glasses and drank. Then he filled me in on his marriage—second one and childless—and kids from the first marriage, the son working in a San Francisco investment firm, the daughter teaching high school in Descanso. The waitress slid a plate onto the table, warning, "The plates are very hot, sir."

"Good service."

"Yeah, well, it helps if you own the place."

I looked around at the airy patio shaded by a bamboo lattice overhead and given a cozy air from the uprights and the bougainvillea that climbed them. "Good business?"

"Christ, with any location at all, you can't help but make money around here." Tom laughed again, the grin making his face even more familiar. "And then lose it all."

In high school, Tom had been one of the restless ones. He led weeklong trips into Mexico and talked about the chance to see Tahiti before it got too touristy. "But, hell, after twenty in the air force and flying all over the goddamned world, I couldn't find any better place than right here." He swished a bubbly mouthful of water. "I went up to LA a couple times. Thought I might start a restaurant up there. Hell, all I saw was cars on four sides and no place to park. They got more people, even, than we do. And every damned one of them lives on the freeway." He took another long drink and nodded toward my beer. "Drink up. You look too damned healthy, and I'm envious. You're still running, right?"

We talked about that and other things, calling up names I hadn't heard in decades. Tommy was impressive in how much he knew about them; I was ashamed of my ignorance. My life had gone at a different angle from the rest of the class, and the few times I'd come through Coronado had been on business rather than pleasure. The thought crossed my mind that perhaps Dorcas, too, was moving away from the lives of her classmates. If so, it wouldn't be too long before she was as distant from them as I was from mine, and I suspected she would feel the same surprise at how fast it happened.

"So you've retired from the marines." Tom pushed a crust of bread across the remains of paella on his plate and glanced into the empty clay pot that sat between us. It was the house specialty, he'd said. I could understand why people were standing in line for a table even this long after the noon hour. "Remember Sonny McCrimmon? Went to the Academy? He sent me a news clipping with your name in it. About a year ago, maybe."

I remembered both Sonny and the news item. The *Washington Post* and *New York Times* had run stories. Their reporters had managed to find out about the shadowy role I'd played in the downfall of a U.S. representative. Although I told them nothing that wasn't already published or admitted publicly, both stories made me into something of a giant killer: lone officer courageously battles bureaucrats and self-interested politicians for the good of the nation. So much so, in fact, that I had received a telephone call from Admiral Burgnon himself. But it wasn't congratulations. Instead, he made it quite clear that Oliver North be damned—the navy and marines did not tolerate grandstanding in their officer corps.

"What I guess, Jack, is maybe you didn't volunteer to retire." There was a shrewdness in Tom's glance that said he, too, had learned a few things since high school.

"Let's just say I was eligible to stand down. Highly eligible."

"And there was no way you couldn't step on toes, right?"

"You got it." I tried to bury the sour taste in my mug of beer.

"Let me understand this, now: The bastard's a traitor. You find him out. You end up getting canned. That right?"

I nodded. The congressman had squawked loudly about vindicating himself in court, but the trial was never called. Too many national secrets would have been aired by the defense. After a suitable time, the man had resigned from his office and taken his fat and tax-sheltered pension with him. And I was an expendable embarrassment. It took the Pentagon a while, but the commandant of the Marine Corps, who took his orders from Burgnon, finally offered me a retirement package I couldn't refuse. My quiet but emphatic exit smoothed a lot of ruffled congressional feathers and reestablished a badly eroded power structure.

But Tom didn't need to know all that. And, as I told the admiral, I wouldn't have done a thing differently—I couldn't have. People had come up to me in empty corners of the Pentagon and out-of-the-way spots around Washington to say how much they admired my sense of duty and what a lousy screwing I was getting. That was true, but as I had told Karen and Becky when they were children, the only reward to expect for doing right was the knowledge that you did the right thing. Now I spent a lot of time reminding myself of that. One of the damned problems of being free with advice is that sometimes you have to take it.

Jenkins read my silence as an unwillingness to open wounds, and he was right. "Okay—so we change the subject. So what you got in mind for rest and recreation? Fishing? Traveling around?"

"Well, I have been thinking of buying a sailboat—but God knows taking care of a boat's a full-time job."

"Yeah. Like being married. Except a wife, at least she scrubs her own bottom." He leaned forward, habitually aware of listening ears at neighboring tables. "Listen, I know a couple guys in the boat business over at Shelter Island—there's always boats for sale, and they can get you a good deal."

I told him that sounded fine but I was still thinking it over. "I want to see how my daughters feel about the idea. Becky, especially. Hell, it's their inheritance I'm spending."

"Spend it on yourself! Leave them good memories and a lot of war stories to tell the grandkids—that's what I'm doing. So how's this detective business going?"

I told him what little more I'd found out about Dorcas Wilcox.

"Is she knocked up, Jack?"

"Why do you ask that?"

"Hey—it happens in the best of families." He looked at me closely. "By God she is, isn't she? She really is!"

Reluctantly, I nodded. "Her employer, Mrs. Gannet, says so, anyway."

"Margaret and the admiral know?"

"I haven't told them."

Tom nodded. "Yeah. They're worried enough." He stared away across the heads of neighboring diners. "So why'd she run off? Why didn't she get her parents to help out? She's got to know she's going to need a hell of a lot of help."

"That's the question, isn't it?"

"Jack, you think she's been killed?"

"I don't believe so. I think she's run somewhere. At least I hope that's it."

"Yeah. Kids running off. Happens all the time, don't it? I wish to hell mine would run off—they keep running back." He waved away my attempt to pay the check and initialed the slip, leaving a large tip for the waitress—"I pay them minimum wage; nobody can live on that." We stood a few minutes in the sunshine of Orange Avenue. I watched the traffic and the palms and the tourists crossing from the Hotel Del. The moment was a flashback to some similar moment before so much had happened to Tom and me and all the others. We had been standing on this same corner talking about something—running, college dreams, surfing—something. Now I was back. As Tom had said, sooner or later, everybody comes back to the island even if only to see it again. And Tom was right about something else: there weren't many places better.

"Listen." Tom leaned toward me and spoke under the chatter of the clutch of tourists nosing the shop windows. "In the restaurant business, I make a lot of contacts. I have to if I want to keep making money, you understand? So if you need help, Jack, just give a jingle. I'm really glad you're back. I mean that."

CHAPTER

I didn't have to settle in Coronado after retirement, and neither the admiral nor Tom had to take me in. But they had and the place was beginning to feel almost like home. Jenny and the admiral had asked me over for lunch, but it had conflicted with Tom's invitation. So after I left him, I drove the few blocks to their house before heading downtown. Jenny met me at the door and offered coffee. The admiral came in from the backyard and peeled off a pair of cotton gloves stained with garden soil. We sat at the kitchen table and I told them what I'd found out last night.

"None of her old friends knew anything about her?" Jenny offered a slice of pastry that I declined.

"Not that I spoke with. Do either of you know anything about David Gates?"

The admiral shook his head, frowning into memory. Jenny said, "That name . . . Oh!" Then, "You remember, Dalton. That poor child who died. You know—the picnic."

A grunt of recognition. "I was TAD to Norfolk when that happened."

"It was tragic, Jack. Dorcas felt so guilty. Margaret had to send her to a psychologist for a while after that."

"Did it happen before or after she ran away from home?"

"I don't know . . . I didn't know she'd run away until you told us the other day. But the accident happened in the spring-time . . . early March, I think."

The admiral sipped at his cup. "Do you think it has any bearing on this disappearance?"

"I don't know, sir. Probably not. But there might be a pattern in her behavior."

"You think she's running from something now?"

"It's a possibility we should consider. Is there any chance she'll get in touch with you if she's in trouble?"

"By God, I hope so."

"Maybe, Jack." Jenny lightly pushed her coffee cup handle with a forefinger. "I wish I could say yes. But Margaret and I—well, I don't know what it is, but my daughter was always . . . independent of me. I think Margaret sensed that I really never did like children, Jack. Not even my own daughter. I tried. With Margaret, with little Dorcas. But some women . . . suffer children rather than welcome them. I'm one of those kind." She looked up to catch my expression. "That's a hard admission to make, but I've come to realize it now. And to accept my blame for the way Margaret is now."

The admiral shook his head. "I think you had too much responsibility too early, Jenny." He turned to me. "You know how hard the service is on wives, Jack."

I knew Eleanor had never resented our daughters. But neither did I know all there was to know about Jenny's life or her daughter's.

"I tried very hard to make amends with Dorcas for my failure with Margaret. And for a while it was easier—I don't know why the friction's so much less with a grandchild. Maybe because we know we don't have to be responsible for them all the time." She sighed and touched the glass to her lips. "But in high school Dorcas began to grow distant—she developed her own circle of friends. She had to establish herself on her own, of course. It's to be expected."

"Is there anyone at all you can think of that she might go to if she needs help?"

Jenny slowly shook her head. "Besides us? No—not in the family. I don't know her other friends, now."

"You keep saying 'if she needs help,' Jack. Is she in any trouble? Have you found out something?"

I shook my head. "I don't have any evidence, admiral." And no information I was at liberty to tell them.

As I headed across the sweeping curve of the bay bridge into downtown San Diego, I studied the ripple of low headlands on the bay side of the Strand. I thought I could make out a distant gray dot that might have been my house. Even if it wasn't, I was beginning to feel a sense of belonging with this landscape. The points of reference that had been based exclusively on memory were coming to be based on the present. And with that new basis, I felt the beginnings of order in a life whose old frames of reference, emotional and geographic, had been torn away before I was ready to let them go.

Face it, Steele, the real reason Fairfax had been "home" was not that soft and green Virginia landscape that felt so easy on eyes and spirit. It was because Eleanor had lived there. And was buried there. The nearness of her grave had brought some comfort. But now it was a continent away, along with the places we had last visited together. What I was gradually discovering, and what Jenny's confession brought to light, was that my move to the West Coast had generated a sense of betrayal to Eleanor's memory. What I had to realize was that she couldn't get any farther away than dead.

The offices of Windsor, Blake, and Vengley filled a corner of the tenth floor in a high-rise back from First Avenue. The receptionist, efficient in a blue suit with a modest touch of color at the neck, nodded and pushed the intercom when I told her I had an appointment with Mr. Vengley. "He'll be right out."

He was, curiosity masked behind a polite smile and a dry,

perfunctory handshake. He led me to a corner office whose windows looked one way toward the busy flicker of traffic on the San Diego Freeway, and another toward the Embarcadero and the black hull and bare spars of the *Star of India* maritime museum. A sprinkle of bright-shirted tourists moved here and there across the old ship's decks.

"You mentioned something about my son, Mr. Steele?"

I explained about Dorcas Wilcox. "I understand she and your son were friends in high school."

"High school was several years ago. I don't remember the Wilcox girl. Certainly, Dwayne hasn't mentioned anyone by that name recently."

"Your son lives in the San Diego area?"

"As of the last I heard from him, Mr. Steele. Dwayne doesn't make much effort to communicate with me."

"So you don't really know if he's been in touch with Dorcas Wilcox?"

Vengley's frown said he didn't like to be caught in a contradiction. "That would seem to follow, wouldn't it?"

"Might he have told your wife? Does he communicate better with his mother?"

"My ex-wife. And no, I doubt that he's told her, either. Dwayne is emancipated, Mr. Steele. He has been for some time. I'd hoped that he would apply for law school after he graduated college, but he's still in the process of—ah—'finding himself.' "

"That's Occidental College in Los Angeles?"

"Yes. He graduated over a year ago. But since then he hasn't discovered just what it is he's looking for." The man rocked forward in the blue chair. "I suppose that's not abnormal. But sometimes I think Dwayne luxuriates in a lack of commitment to any responsible future."

"Was he a philosophy major?"

"Philosophy? No—art history. I tried to convince him to major in something a bit more realistic. But Dwayne, like his mother, has a penchant for doing the opposite of what I suggest." Vengley's hand strayed to a stack of papers on his desk and he lightly thumbed the pages. "So now he has a degree for which the demand is, to say the least, quite limited."

"Is it possible that he knew Dorcas Wilcox or a girl named Shirley while he was at Occidental?"

He looked up. "Did they go there? Then, yes, it is possible—the school is small. That's one of the reasons Dwayne chose it."

"But he never mentioned either of them to you."

"No." He glanced at a clock on the wall. "Mr. Steele, I wish I could assist you further. But there's nothing more I can tell you. And my next appointment is waiting."

Far be it from me to cut into the attorney's billable hours. I asked for Dwayne's last address and thanked Mr. Vengley. He walked me to a different door, one that opened directly on the hallway around the corner from the suite's main entry. "Naturally, if there's anything I can do—"

My smile was equally sincere. "Thank you."

The address was on the east side of downtown in a section that urban renewal hadn't yet reformed into condos and boutiques. Heavy traffic funneled off a nearby freeway and hissed and squealed among warehouses and shops to leave a film of dust and diesel soot along the naked streets. I found a parking place in front of the barred display window of a liquor store. Its sale prices were higher than the suburbs, but it did most of its business in Ripple and Thunderbird, anyway. I walked back along the trash-strewn sidewalk to the three-story house. It stood like a broken tooth between a brown-brick building whose sign advertised electrical repairs, and an open lot whose weeds were cut by sandy trails that glittered with broken glass. Sprayed over the shops and walls and spilling onto the apartment house, graffiti formed designs and cryptic messages. More names and drawings, among them a "666" and a cartoon of Satan, marked the warped porch boards that creaked under my shoes.

No one answered my knock. No one challenged as I pushed

past the rusty screen door into what used to be a formal entry. Apparently no one cared. There was little reason why they should. A heavy, scarred door blocked off the old living room. Down the hall, other doors were shut against intruders. A dented and splintered stairway led up to the second floor. Dwayne's room was near the landing. This hallway smelled a bit less of urine, but similar empty bottles and scraps of newspaper and brown bags were kicked against the chipped baseboards. A large hole in the plaster showed the laths beneath, and the ceiling sagged with water stains. The door I rapped on was also scarred. A ragged smear like old blood splashed down the lower panel. I waited. From somewhere on the floor above came the jangling, repetitive beat of heavy rock. In the walls, water gurgled briefly down a pipe.

"Dwayne? Dwayne Vengley?"

"Who's it?"

The voice was female and sleepy.

"A friend of Dorcas Wilcox. Is Dwayne Vengley here?"

A heavy bolt slid back, a hasp grated, another lock clicked. The door opened to show a length of chain and a young Negro woman's eye and cheek. "Who you a friend of?"

"Dorcas Wilcox. Does Dwayne Vengley live here?"

"Never heard of no Dorcas. What you want with Dwayne?"

"Are you Shirley?"

She shook her head. "Why?"

"I owe Dwayne some money."

The eye stared at me. A heavy, sweet odor of incense or candle wax seeped out through the crevice.

"Dorcas gave me some money for him. Is he around?"

"You can give me it. I'll give him it."

"I don't know . . . Dorcas told me to be sure and give it to him in person and get a receipt." I smiled. "Is he around?"

"Was he around, he be at the door now."

"Do you know where I can find him?"

"His mamma sent you, didn't she?"

"Why?"

"Why? 'Cause she always doing shit like that!"

"When will he be back?"

"He gone. Been gone." The eye, a black iris surrounded by a white so bloodshot that it looked rheumy and brown, glanced down to my shoes and then up again. "You ain't a cop?"

"If I was, I'd have a warrant and a badge. What I've got is a check." I tapped my jacket pocket. Her eyes stared at the cloth as if they might see through it. "It's a lot of money. But he has to sign for it in person."

The eye blinked. "Dwayne, he owe me some money. Left without paying his share of the rent."

"How much?"

"Four hundred. Two months' rent."

"He's been gone two months?"

"Yeah. That's what he owe me."

"And if you knew where he was, you'd already have that money, right?"

The eye blinked again. "Shit—you ain't from his mamma. And you ain't got no money for him. Get on away from here!" The door closed and I heard the series of locks snap into place.

Back in the car, I twisted my way through one-way streets to the main post office on E Street. The fee brought a shake of the clerk's head. "No address card on a Vengley at that address."

"How about any other address?"

Another shake. "Sorry."

Sorry didn't get Henry's two dollars back this time. Apparently the main post office had a no-rebate policy. On a hunch, I stopped at the pay phone near the entry and thumbed what was left of the ripped telephone book. Vengley was an uncommon name, but there were five listed: one Roger, an attorney with home and office numbers—and I guessed that might be Dwayne's father; an A. L. Vengley, followed by Barbara Vengley, Sherman Vengley, and Stanley Vengley. No Dwayne. I started feeding quarters into the slot and was uncharacteristically lucky with the first one, A. L.

"Yes," said the woman's suddenly nervous voice. "I have a son named Dwayne. What's happened to him?"

"Nothing that I know of. I'm trying to locate a missing woman who may be a friend of his. I'd like to interview him—find out if she told him where she might be." The word "interview" was softer than "talk to" or "ask a few questions." Those phrases sounded like police.

"He has an apartment on Island Street. Downtown."

"I was just there. He moved out a couple months ago. I wonder if you know where he went."

"Two months ago?"

The line was silent and I sensed the woman about to hang up. "Ma'am? Can I come over and speak with you? It's very important for me to find this young woman—her parents are very worried about her."

With some hesitation, she agreed. I verified the address. The condominium was out past the furry green hills of Balboa Park and perched on the face of a mesa in University Heights. The sand-colored units stepped up the side of the canyon. Each balcony overlooked the twisting roads and roofs and occasional swimming pools below. The "A" stood for "Annette," the "L" I didn't ask about, and the relationship with Dwayne's father was sore.

"We've been divorced for three years, Mr. Steele. And I should have left that bastard long ago."

I nodded. The woman's anger at her ex-husband showed in tense gestures that accompanied the words.

"He's one of the most self-centered, materialistic, and greedy people I've ever known. And a hypocrite—egotistical and manipulative. He had a hundred ways of imposing—" She caught the bitterness in her voice and said sweetly, "But those are virtues in an attorney, aren't they?"

That was one way of looking at it. I nudged her further in

the right direction. "He didn't like it that Dwayne wouldn't go
to law school?"

"Roger didn't like anything that contradicted his wishes."
She looked down at the Kleenex fraying in her hand and then
out the balcony doors to the view of neighboring ridges with
their own condominiums. "It's no wonder our child has . . ."
Again she caught herself, lips clamped against the words. "You
say he moved out two months ago?"

"That's what I was told. Do you have any idea where he
might have gone?"

"No." She dropped the tissue into an unused ashtray. The
room was crowded with furniture designed for larger space and
with knickknacks collected over a lifetime. They were, I
guessed, her part of the settlement. "He's been looking for
work for a long time, I know that. He's had job offers, but they
aren't exactly what he wants. God knows what he's living on—
he stopped asking me for money when I couldn't give him as
much as he wanted." She sighed. "I've tried to tell him: take
any job just to get started, build up a work record. But he won't
listen; he doesn't want to start where everyone else does. And
then he moved into that horrible place. I tried to convince him
to at least live in a decent part of town—he refused to live here.
I tried—" She fell silent.

"And he told you to get lost."

Surprised, she looked up at me, then smiled wryly. "You
have children, I see."

"Two daughters."

"My friends say they're as much trouble as sons." Another
deep breath. "You said you were looking for a missing woman.
One of your daughters?"

"Not mine. Dorcas Wilcox."

"Wilcox? Dori Wilcox is missing?"

"Has your son been in touch with her lately?"

"They went to high school together. And college."

"Did he speak of her often?"

"No—they were friends, but I don't think they were dating.

You know, not a girlfriend-boyfriend thing. But on vacations they'd go out to movies or see other college friends."

"Can you give me the names and addresses of some of these people?"

She mentioned a few, including Stacey Briggs and Kimberly Overstreet. There was no Shirley. I noted the new names and, when Mrs. Vengley couldn't remember addresses, the areas of San Diego where she thought they lived.

"Do you know when Dwayne last saw Dorcas?"

"No. I'm sorry. Do you think . . . something may have happened to her?"

I shrugged. "All I know for certain is that she's disappeared. Did she or Dwayne ever mention any friends in Colorado?"

Puzzled, the woman shook her head. "Not that I remember. Is that . . . do you think that might be where Dwayne went?"

"Wouldn't he say something to you before moving that far away?"

Her teeth nipped at a spur of dry skin on her lower lip. "Not any more. He thinks I've already meddled too much in his life." The anger was gone, now, replaced by a weary sadness. Her voice was flat as it stated fact. "His father's turned him against me. It started long before the divorce. But since then, since he's come back from college, it's been worse. No matter how much I try—"

Again she cut herself off. I couldn't figure out if she didn't trust me with what she thought, or if that was her technique for hinting at deeper meaning while demonstrating grace under pressure. I wrote my name on a slip of paper. "If he does call, would you get in touch with me?"

That wry smile again. "If you'll do the same for me."

CHAPTER

Steven Glover, the first of the names provided by Mrs. Vengley, didn't answer his telephone. A recorded, cheery jingle was happy to sing me another number where he could be reached. It turned out to be a real estate office out near La Mesa. A man's voice said Glover was showing homes—if I wanted to talk to him, I could leave a message. Better, I should come out and see what the Sueno Grande Estates had to offer.

A flag-bedecked model home served as the sales office. Automobiles crowded the curbs of a winding street that had baskets of plastic flowers dangling from its name plate, "Pulga Vista Avenue." A large sign announced "Starting at only $250,000." Smiling salesmen in white shirts and striped ties squired couples from one lot to another. Glover was tall with butter-colored hair and a slender build. He had a firm handshake and a straight, honest gaze. "Yes, sir—good to see you again!"

I explained that it wasn't again and told him what I wanted. The white, perfect teeth disappeared. "Dwayne? Come to think of it, I haven't seen him for a few weeks now." He led me outside, distant from the handful of sales people shuffling papers on the folding work table that, with a few equally foldable chairs, furnished the empty living room. "Dwayne. I guess he could have moved. I wouldn't know."

"You went to Occidental with him and Dorcas Wilcox?"

"Yes."

"Do you know where Dorcas might be?"

"Dori?" He shrugged. "Last I heard, she was living up around Julian. You—ah—want to tell me why you're looking for them?"

"She seems to have disappeared. Her parents are worried."

"I see. Well, I wish I could help you, but like I say, I haven't talked with either one of them in a long time."

"Are she and Dwayne involved with each other?"

"Involved? Like going together?"

I nodded. For some reason the young man wasn't comfortable talking about them.

"I don't know. I don't think so. All the time I've known them, they've been just friends. We're all just friends. But I haven't talked to either of them in months. I didn't even know Dwayne had moved."

"Has Dorcas mentioned anyone she's serious about?"

"No. But like I say, I haven't seen her in a while, so who knows?"

I wrote my name and number again on another slip of paper. If I went into the detecting business full-time, I'd have to get business cards. But what kind of business would the card list? Retired Spy-Catcher? Tracer of Runaways? "If you hear from either of them, would you give me a call?"

He looked at the slip. "Sure."

"Do you know if Dwayne found work?"

"Work? You mean a job?

"His mother told me he was looking for work."

"Oh—his mother. I guess he wouldn't have told her. Dwayne and his mother didn't get along too well." He shrugged again. "I think he's working as a salesman, but I don't know where."

"Can you tell me where Shelley Aguirre works?"

Glover's blue eyes blinked and the uneasiness increased. "What do you want with her?"

"Maybe she's heard from Dorcas or Dwayne."

"Yeah. Maybe." Glover didn't add anything.

"I have her home address. But I could save time by talking to her at work." I studied his face. "There's no reason why I shouldn't talk with her, is there?"

"No! It's just I don't think she knows where they are either. I mean if Dwayne wouldn't tell me something, he wouldn't tell Shelley. Dwayne and I are closer," he added lamely.

"I still should talk to her. Do you have that work address?"

Reluctantly, he did. It was a graphics firm not too far away in the Encanto section. In the rearview mirror, the young man stood and stared after the car as I pulled away. Then he turned and walked rapidly toward the sales office.

The graphics building was a brick box that faced a blank wall to the street. A receptionist directed me to a long, low-ceilinged room. A line of six drafting tables ran under large windows on the north side. Work tables littered with T-squares and papers formed a parallel line under bright fluorescent lights along the other wall. Many of the desks were empty, but a few people bent here and there over their work. Shelley Aguirre seemed to be looking for me, and as I approached, I could see the fright in her eyes.

"Did Steven Glover call to say I was coming, Miss Aguirre?"

The small woman's brown eyes widened "yes" as her cropped pale-blond hair shook "no."

"All I'm trying to do is locate a missing girl, Shelley—a friend of yours, in fact." She didn't say anything. I looked over her shoulder at the sketch she was working on. An elongated woman leaned back in a tense arc to stare toward a roughed-in square. The figure echoed Aubrey Beardsley and the turn of the century. "Nice work," I lied.

"Thanks." She lied, too.

"You were an art major at Occidental, right?"

". . . Yes."

"And had some classes with Dwayne Vengley."

"How did you know?"

It wasn't too hard to guess—studio majors and art history

majors shared a number of classes. But I let the question hang. Sometimes a little mystery works for you. "Come on, I'll treat you to a cup of coffee."

She didn't really want to go. I didn't give her a chance to hold back. Her arm was like a thin stick in my hand as I guided her toward my car. "Where's a good place? I'll have you back in twenty minutes."

The good place was a fast-food restaurant, one of those brightly colored boxes that sit on every corner in a business district. This time of the afternoon, only a few people were scattered among the booths and tables. I set the Styrofoam cup in front of her. "Were you and Dorcas friends in college?"

She stared at the cup. "We knew each other."

As I leaned forward to hear her soft words, I tried to study her eyes. But she kept them focused on the steaming coffee. "When did you first meet her?"

"In our freshman year. She . . . she was a suitemate."

"So you saw a lot of her."

"Yes. I guess so."

"And that continued through school?"

". . . yes . . ."

"And Dwayne Vengley, too? You saw a lot of him?"

"No—I mean I did. But I didn't really know him that well."

"Did he and Dorcas date?"

She shook her head. "They were friends, but it wasn't like that—not dating or in love. Just friends."

"How about Steve Glover? Did you see a lot of him?"

"Yes. I guess so. We dated."

"And you still do?"

She nodded.

"And Shirley. Did you know her?"

"Shirley Norris?" The Aguirre girl frowned. "She left school after her sophomore year. The sophomore slump, I guess."

"You haven't seen her since?"

"No."

"Why did Dorcas leave school that time?"

The girl's startled eyes looked up from the coffee cup and her voice was even fainter. "When?"

"Winter quarter of her junior year. The time she ran away and went to Lake Tahoe." I sighed. "You know about it, Shelley. Steven knows about it, too."

"He said so?"

"I just want to find out what happened. Look, people— runaways—tend to act in patterns, and what happened then might be a clue to where she is now."

"It was after Jerry . . . committed suicide. Jerry Hawley?"

I nodded as if I was familiar with the name.

"She had to get away. She liked him, I guess. I mean, we all went around together—Jerry, Dori, Steve, and Dwayne. And me. And then that happened. It really freaked us all out, you know? Dori took it real hard; she said she just wanted to be by herself and think things out." Shelley shrugged. "So she went off."

"Did she tell anyone she was going? Dwayne? You?"

"Maybe she told Dwayne, I don't know. She and Dwayne and Jerry, they were close. But she didn't tell me. I remember people came and asked if I knew where she was—somebody from the dean's office—but there wasn't anything I could tell them."

"Do you know if anything's happened lately that might have caused her to run away again?"

"No."

"Do you know if she has a current boyfriend?"

"No."

"Do you know where Dwayne might have gone?"

"No."

"You realize her parents are very worried about her?"

"Yes. I guess so."

I stifled a sigh and wrote on a scrap of napkin. "Okay, Shelley. I have the feeling you know more than you're telling me. But I don't know why you want to keep it a secret. All I want to do is find out if Dorcas is all right; I won't and can't make her do anything she doesn't want to do." I glanced up. "You are keeping something back, aren't you?"

Her head quivered no. "Why should I?"

"I don't know, yet. If I have to find out, I will, of course. And, eventually, I will find Dorcas. I just can't understand why you don't want to help your friend, especially when you know how worried her mother and father are." I waited, but the girl only stared at her untouched coffee. "Okay, Shelley, come on— I'll take you back to work."

On the silent ride back to the graphics firm, she folded and refolded the scrap of napkin that held my name and number.

It wasn't terror, it wasn't love. If she didn't, in the depths of her heart, know differently, she would call it hypnotism. But it never had been that, either. She remembered when they had messed around with that in junior high. She remembered telling Dwayne she couldn't keep her arm from lifting when he commanded it, and she had told herself, too; and the arm really had lifted of its own will—light, effortless, floating away from her side like Dwayne's voice told it to. But even when her body lay like a board between two chairs, one under her neck, the other under her heels, revealing a strength that she could never obtain without hypnotism, she knew what was happening. She wasn't out; she wasn't unaware. She just knew that her flesh was strong enough to do what his soft voice told her and that if he told her to do things she did not want to do, her watching self could take over and resist.

So this wasn't hypnotism, because there was no watching self. Brainwashing, maybe. But maybe not. She didn't know anything about that, but in the movies it took all sorts of physical gimmicks—flashing lights, isolation cells, sleep deprivation and instruction—and there was none of that. So it probably wasn't brainwashing. Maybe it was exactly what he called it: the Bond. And the absolution brought by the knowledge of Power.

Curiosity, too. She had been curious about his journey, his discoveries. For a long time they had been talking about the fringes of things—the edge of consciousness, that which lay just beyond sensible knowledge, that rim of awareness of the spiritual realm. The doors through and the glimpses of the Other Side. He had been into it far more than she. In fact, at first she had avoided him. But he was always there on the edge of vision: reminding her, demanding that she remember the Bond, and everything that had made up the Bond. Then he offered a reprieve from guilt through the worship of power. The guilt and her own weakness, the curiosity, were equally persistent.

She could say it was the PCP or LSD or whatever designer drug she finally accepted. But that was later, after she had already found herself drawn back again to an older and more sexually mature and even frightening Dwayne. Before, in junior high school, when they had touched and explored each other it was with the excitement of daring the forbidden. In high school, it became not just the innocent pleasure of discovery, but the grown-up awareness of fulfillment. They weren't playing the kid games but doing the real thing, and you could feel the difference between you and those who hadn't yet crossed into that knowl-edge. It was in your walk, it was something in your eyes, it was in the unworded understanding between those who had and those who hadn't, and it was a secret that even the other members of the Four never guessed. And even in college, somehow, the fear gradually faded and the excitement was brought back and it was made all the more fulfilling by rituals. After a while, Dwayne talked a lot about the conjuration of lust but she didn't really understand what it meant and finally she asked him to show her, and she'd asked without drinking or dropping so it wasn't any of those outside forces that drove her to it. That was it: she wasn't driven to it, she had embraced it willingly, and, with a tiny chill deep in her chest, she admitted that the decision was hers alone— she willingly joined the all-encompassing evil force that ruled this insane and death-plagued earth. Earth is the anteroom of hell, Dwayne said; the spirits who rule it are not—could not be—the benevolent gods of familiar religions. No god with any sense of righteousness or love could allow things like the Holocaust, or a crippled and suffering child, or cancer, or the feebleminded like—he reminded her—David. All those pains were manifestations of a vast realm of evil. Satan rules. The Beast rules. And she herself had discovered his power in her, his mark in her own psyche.

But not without rebellion. Even if the Beast ruled, she had still felt shock and loss and a sense of emptiness when that frightened and struggling figure suddenly disappeared into blackness beyond the cliff. It had been a game. He told them it would be a game and no one even thought about David getting hurt. When he shoved him, Dori's eyes saw but her mind couldn't believe. Later, when belief came and brought with it the stifled moans and shuddering, the uncontrollable tears from all of them, Dwayne was there to tell them what to say: An accident. We're all in this together. A bond of death. An accident. Say it was an accident or we all go to prison for murder.

And a bond of shame which she didn't face until the next morning when she woke in the bed that had once been so safe. When the warm sunlight, patterned on her bedroom wall through the softly curtained windows, suddenly congealed into a stifling iciness as she remembered: oh, my God in heaven, what did I do?

Then she ran.

For all the good it did, because the guilt kept pace and the degradation of the streets only reinforced her sense of worthlessness. The people at the shelter in Los Angeles where she finally washed up gave her a look at what was waiting for her. They told her what they could do—which wasn't much—and what they couldn't do, and left her to make up her own mind. But she didn't deserve any better than the streets—she knew that. The streets were her punishment and what she deserved. But she didn't even have the courage for that. She was afraid. And that was why she went home, still bearing the guilt, still knowing what she merited and the cowardice that denied it. And she took it with her to college because there was no other direction or place that would make any difference. Kimberly and Stacey seemed to have stifled any feelings about it; they avoided Dwayne and Dori, and, in effect, the Four were no longer together. There was too much in each other's eyes. Margot, who didn't understand, was angry. Was still angry when Dori went away to Occidental where Dwayne, too, had decided to go. Dwayne, who later told her about the absolution of power. About the willful rejection of guilt. About the assertion of self against all that would destroy it.

CHAPTER

The dean's office of Occidental College didn't want to talk to me about Jerry Hawley, and I wasn't surprised. If I'd driven up there and asked in person, I might have learned a little more. But then I might not. The woman to whom my inquiry had finally been shunted sounded pretty tough over the telephone. She said that the very unfortunate matter was closed as far as the college was concerned and that any further information would have to be obtained from other sources. You, Mr. Steele, could direct your inquiries to relatives of the victim—and she couldn't divulge that address—or to the appropriate police agency. I hope that helped you. Good-bye.

No, thinking back over the terse conversation, I was decidedly glad I hadn't wasted time and gas. However, as public agencies, police departments were another thing. This taxpayer spent the tag end of the working day on the phone with various clerks and officers. Finally I ended up with the homicide office of the Pasadena PD. They had been called in as the nearest agency equipped to investigate suicides and other unnatural deaths on campus.

"Yeah, Mr. Steele. It was a suicide, no question. The boy hung himself with the belt of his bathrobe. Tied one end to the bathroom doorknob, noose in the other end, slung it over the top of the door. Stepped off a chair." The world-weary voice added, "Wasn't one of these sex thrills—you know, accidental hanging while masturbating. Kid just did it." He asked, "You really think this's got something to do with that girl you're looking for?"

"It's a long shot," I admitted. "I'm just trying to fill in a background for her. Maybe one thing will lead to another."

"Yeah. Way these things usually work. But I don't know—suicide, anymore, it just seems like the thing to do. She a high school girl?"

"No. She was in the same college class as Hawley."

"I see. Not as likely to be a suicide, then, statistics-wise." He added, "But God knows it happens. Well, that's about all we got on it. Like I say, trace of chemicals in his system—some kind of designer drug, the pathologist guessed. Not enough to cause hallucinations just prior to the time of death, though. Looks like he was popping something a few days before, but that's it. No alcohol, no previous brain damage. Hell, who knows what makes a kid do it?"

"And you have no record on a Shirley or a Dorcas Wilcox or a Dwayne Vengley?"

"Nope. Names aren't in our computer." And, the voice implied, he'd done enough for public relations.

I thanked the officer and hung up, aware that though the information was nice to know, it didn't seem to lead anywhere.

Which was also where my attempted interviews with the last two names given by Mrs. Vengley had led, too. The girl, Melodie, had moved to Portland a year ago. The man, Tim Gifford, had moved maybe six weeks ago. The post office records had a forwarding address for him: a box number in Santa Fe, New Mexico.

Rubbing my burning eyes, I totaled up the expenses and dialed Henry's number. Margaret answered and with the carefully controlled enunciation of a self-conscious drinker told me that Henry was still at the office and wouldn't be back until around eleven. "Have you found out anything, Jack?"

"Not yet. These things take time."

"I know. It's just . . . I was hoping maybe you could find out something by now."

"It's only been forty-eight hours, Margaret." But she was right: forty-eight hours with nothing to show for it. I was unhappy, too. "Let's not give up too soon." To buck up my courage as well as hers.

"Yes, of course. Do you want Henry to phone you when he gets home?"

That would probably be a good idea, but the woman sounded as if she might have trouble remembering that I had called, let alone what I'd told her. "If he can. If not, I'll get back to him."

Henry still hadn't called by the time I returned from my run along the beach. I checked my watch and drove up the Strand into Coronado. Jenny and the admiral had asked if I could drop by for an evening drink, and I left home early enough to follow the thought that had crossed my mind as my heels thudded on the hard, wet sand and the spray from the incoming surf salted my lips. Exercise always seems to help thought—increased blood flow, maybe, or just getting away from the issue to let the half- or even un-conscious wrestle with it while the surface of my mind focused on the running. Or maybe it's the reward for earning my bread by the sweat of my brow. Whatever, an answer to one question had suggested itself. With a little luck that answer might lead to others.

The early-evening traffic was light on Orange Avenue. Since the bridge had been built, Glorietta Boulevard siphoned off most of the cars headed for the Strand. And Fourth Street— leading to North Island—had been widened to accommodate the other major traffic flow. Turning off Orange, I found parking next to the municipal tennis courts beside the town library. An elderly couple in white tennis togs played a vigorous game marked by the twang of rackets and the squeak of rubber soles. Out of those sounds came the name Patty Denard—one of the girls I dated in high school. It had been one of those relationships that were strictly friendship and never developed into any kind of romance. I couldn't remember why. She was attractive in a pert, athletic way, and we'd played on these same courts in the long twilight of cooling summer evenings. Had a good time together, too. But neither of us had wanted more. Our minds were on what we would be doing after graduation, and tennis was the only game we were interested in. Still, I wondered where she was now, and hoped that she and so many other freshly remembered names were happy.

Across D Avenue loomed the dark bulk of the high school. I stood a few moments to study a shadowy front that had been remodeled in contemporary drab. At least the WPA façade of a few decades ago had offered an attempt at stateliness. The stiff figures in a dated bas-relief had carried a sense of the past. Now, that sense was my own memory of images and faces— and not a little comedy, some of which still held the bite of mortification. Thomas Wolfe was right, and maybe it was best that way. With a sigh, I turned away from the ugliness of the building and went under shaggy palm trees into the reading room of the library.

The newspaper file was limited, but the *San Diego Union* and *Los Angeles Times* back issues were on microfilm. I searched through the columns until I found the article buried among items of local and regional news in the *Times:* "College Student Commits Suicide." Under the small headline, the story said that Gerald Hawley, twenty, a student at Occidental College, had been found dead the night before, an apparent suicide. Police sources said the young man died of strangulation after hanging himself in his room on campus. The fully clothed body was found by a neighbor who came in to ask Hawley to turn down the volume on a stereo set. Hawley's friends were at a loss to explain the death. "He didn't seem depressed or worried," said Dwayne Vengley, twenty-one, an acquaintance. Other sources stated that Hawley had been looking forward to skiing during the upcoming winter vacation. Hawley's parents lived on Mulholland Drive in Los Angeles.

I made a photocopy of the article and drove the half dozen blocks across town to the admiral's. My eyes were on the road and its sequence of stop signs. But my mind was on that name that kept cropping up: Dwayne Vengley.

Neither Jenny nor the admiral recognized the name. The David Gates affair had taken place five years ago, and even their original knowledge of it had been limited only to its effect on Dorcas. Jenny described her role as more of a hand-holder than a confessor. "I didn't want to ask too many questions, Jack. It was such a traumatic time, and there really didn't seem much point in making Dori go over it again and again."

The four of us sat in the large, quiet living room: myself, the admiral and Jenny, and Megan Wells—introduced by Jenny as "one of our favorite young people." A tall woman somewhere in her thirties, the widow of a naval aviator, she had a natural beauty that called for only the slightest touches of makeup. I wasn't surprised when Jenny said that Megan had been a model before she married.

"It was a very brief career," she smiled. "I found I had neither the talent to pose nor the patience to learn."

But if she lacked patience, she did have the other attributes. It was a thought I kept to myself because it was painfully evident to both of us that Jenny was playing matchmaker. I should have guessed it would happen sooner or later, but was surprised it came so soon. A lot of women—and even some men—insist that single people should be mated as quickly as possible. The idea had infected a number of acquaintances in Washington who, after a suitable period following Eleanor's death, had begun introducing me to their eligible friends. But I was certain both my daughters were more secure without a mother than they would have been with just any new one, and I wasn't looking for companionship. I didn't feel either incomplete or lonely as a widower. The memory of Eleanor still filled any emotional yearnings, and my marriage to my job was as yet unbroken. Of course, all of the Washington matchmaking efforts came to a screeching halt when the congressman surfaced.

Apparently Megan felt the same unease, murmuring as we had been introduced, "I didn't know Jenny had invited anyone else."

"I only stopped by for a few minutes," I apologized. We shared a sense of relief as the admiral assured me that I certainly had time for one drink.

"And this young man who committed suicide—you think that's what made Dorcas drop out of college?" The admiral fidgeted with an unlit cigar.

"That's just a guess."

"But you sense a pattern in Dori's behavior," said Megan.

I nodded, watching the woman frown at her glass.

Jenny asked, "If it's a pattern, what's she running from now?"

"I haven't discovered any recent deaths among her friends," I hedged. "And the idea of a pattern is only one more guess among many."

Megan asked, "Was she dating Jerry Hawley? In love with him?"

"They were friends. I don't know how close."

"She seems to have had more than her share of tragedy," she said quietly.

Jenny nodded. "I've sometimes wondered if some people don't draw bad luck."

"Nonsense." The admiral finally lit his cigar, waving out the long wooden match through a cloud of smoke. "We all get our share, maybe some more than others. But no one's handing it out to us and keeping a tally." He snapped the match stick and set it in the ashtray. "Luck is what you do with what happens to you. And I'm not all that sure Henry doesn't do the worst. If there's bad luck in that family, that's where it comes from."

"Oh, don't listen to him, Megan."

She sipped at her drink. "Henry seems to do quite well for himself, admiral."

"You know him?" I asked.

"He's my cousin. It's how I met Margaret's parents."

Which explained the openness with which the admiral and Jenny had talked about Dorcas. "Small world."

She smiled. "Not that small, thank God. Henry goes his way, and I have gone mine."

Which was as fine an exit line as I could ask for. "And I'd better be going mine—I still have a couple of phone calls to make."

Both Jenny and the admiral wanted me to stay longer, but I wasn't lying about the telephone work. Megan offered a polite good-bye, and I went down the front steps, my sense of relief tinged with the melancholy of a mild and insincere regret. She was an intelligent woman, attractive as well as pleasant. But I wasn't in the market. And neither was she.

The distant telephone bell rattled half a dozen times before a man's voice said, "Hello?"

I said who I was and what I wanted. "I realize this is a painful subject, Mr. Hawley, but it might help me locate Dorcas. Her family is very worried."

"I don't see how it can help. My son died almost two years ago, Mr. Steele."

"I grant the chances are pretty poor, but the only two leads I have are slim and none. How well did your son know Dwayne Vengley?"

A long pause. "Is he involved in this?"

"I don't know. I haven't been able to locate him yet. But his name keeps coming up." Which, in another setting for work like this, had been prima facie cause for suspicion.

"I never did like that kid. I never could see why Jerry wanted to hang around with him."

"Care to amplify a little? Anything you tell me will be confidential, of course."

"I don't give a damn if it's confidential or not. I said at the time Jerry died, and I'll say it again: I think Vengley knew more about it than he told the police."

"Are you suggesting your son's death wasn't a suicide, Mr. Hawley?"

A deep sigh. "No, no. The police were convinced it was a suicide. Jerry's hands weren't tied and there was no sign of a struggle of any kind. It's just that Jerry had no reason to do what he did. There was no reason for it at all!"

I pushed the issue. "I still don't see what that has to do with Vengley."

"I'm not sure myself. It's just that Jerry . . . changed. After he met that Vengley kid." The line was silent and I waited. "He got moody, and for no reason. He was on the soccer team and quit. I mean, Jerry loved playing soccer. But when I asked him once how his team was doing, he said he didn't have time for it anymore—he'd quit."

"Mr. Hawley, might that have been a prelude—a warning—that your son was contemplating suicide?"

"Looking back, I suppose we should have paid more attention. But it wasn't that intense. Or persistent. It came and went. Sometimes—most of the time—he was his old self: outgoing, happy, full of life. But the more he saw of Vengley . . ." Another sigh. "It's just something I felt, Mr. Steele. I don't have any evidence of anything at all. But when you mentioned Vengley's name, it brought back all those feelings. And now you tell me he's mixed up with a missing girl."

" 'Mixed up' might be a bit presumptive. I think he knew her. That's all."

"He knew Jerry, too."

That was true. "Did your son ever mention Dorcas Wilcox?"

"Not that I recall. His first year, he had a number of friends and brought several of them home on weekends or saw them over vacations. By his last year, he didn't bring anyone home. The only one I knew about was the Vengley kid, and that's because he stayed here a couple weekends with Jerry."

"Did you see the police report on your son's death?"

"Yeah. I insisted on seeing everything. I wanted to know why. But I still don't."

"The autopsy report mentioned a trace of drugs. Did Jerry have a history of drug use?"

"No. He was clean." The man amended. "He was clean as far as I knew, anyway. But who knows what kids do when they're away from home? They can be led, Mr. Steele. And I wouldn't be surprised if it was by Vengley."

I thanked Mr. Hawley for the information and sat staring at the evening sky over San Diego. The lights reflected in the calm waters of the bay as shimmering dots of white and green and red. Among other thoughts, I remembered the view from this same spot a few decades past, before the houses had been built and the boat slips dredged. The low spit of sand and grass had been known as the Hog Ranch. Under the nearly dark moon its gently shelving beach had been one of the favorite spawning sites for grunion. I could still recall the flash of silver catching the starlight as the sardine-sized fish came in with the tide to burrow into the wet sand. Then they skittered frantically back into the next small wave, their mating over until the next full moon. Perhaps up the Strand on the undisturbed sands of the Amphibious Base, the grunion still ran. I hoped so. It was good to think that, beneath the growth and building and change, the rhythms of an ancient life still went on.

The Hog Ranch. The grunion weren't the only creatures to practice springtime mating rituals on these sands. Some evenings, the domes of car roofs scattered under the moonlight had rivaled the swell of dunes. And I could still remember one of the "luaus" we'd organized on a summer night—driftwood blazing to take the chill off the ocean wind, langosta pulled from the sea just below the Mexican line, fruit juice fortified by a bottle of rum traded in Tijuana for a few lobsters, and the whole feast smuggled across the border in sweaty guilt. Which made it taste all the better. And more people invited than there was food to serve. So we came down early to fish some sand sharks from the bay and, wrapping them in wet newspaper and seaweed, baked them under the fire's hot coals. To be served proudly as ocean flank fish. I'd have to ask Tom what name the restaurants called it now. Mako-mako, perhaps, or Pacific whitefish.

God only knew what the sharks had fed on in San Diego Bay. Half the Pacific Fleet dumped its sewage into the waters and the ecology movement was somewhere in the future. Still, we had been lucky; no one caught cholera, no one died, no one got hung up on the drugs that, even then, were surfacing in the high schools. Luck. Perhaps some common sense, though I doubted that. There was too much evidence of its lack in a lot of things we did. We just happened to get away with them. What happened to those who didn't get away with it? They were among the damaged, the crippled, the dead. Time thrust us all forward inexorably to survive or to fall aside, and, despite the admiral's dictum, a lot of the outcome depended on luck alone, good or bad.

I poured the rest of my beer into the glass and imagined Megan Wells's wry reaction to my talking like the closing paragraphs of *The Great Gatsby*. Every soul born walks this earth under a death sentence, and there's no profit in lamenting what can't be helped. What I had to do—and here I stirred my legs to fetch the telephone directory and begin scanning names— was apply myself to those things that could be helped.

CHAPTER

10

Smiling politely, I stood in the porch light and introduced myself to the large-boned girl whose dark hair was pulled back in a curly ponytail. But Stacey Briggs wasn't overjoyed to make my acquaintance.

"I told you on the phone I don't know anything about Dori or where she is."

"This is about Dwayne Vengley—the Dwayne I mentioned earlier."

Her eyes widened slightly. "Who?"

"A high school friend that you and Dorcas and the rest of the Four Femmes ran around with your senior year. Margot Hoyer remembers him; I'm sure you do, too."

Now she did. "Oh, that Dwayne. I haven't seen him in such a long time . . ."

"I see. Did you go to Occidental with Dorcas?"

"No. Sweet Briar."

"In Virginia?"

She nodded.

"That's a very nice school—and a long way from home."

"It's what I wanted. I wanted to get away from home for a while. Is there something wrong with that?"

"Nothing at all. My own daughters had the same idea. May I come in?"

She finally turned from the door and led me into the cramped living room. A plaid couch almost filled one wall. A work table and electric typewriter turned another wall into a small office space. The breakfast shelf marked off the kitchen from the dining area, and drapes closed what must have been sliding glass doors leading to a balcony.

I glanced over the papers scattered on the desk. "What work do you do, Stacey?"

"Account executive." She mentioned the television station. "Why?"

"Just trying to be friendly."

"Well, don't try! I've already answered your questions once, and I can't understand why you keep bothering me."

"Don't you want your friend to be found?"

She didn't answer at first. Her mouth clamped shut and she frowned at the coffee table in front of the sofa. "What makes you think she's really lost? I mean, couldn't she have just gone off somewhere for a while?"

"Sure. That's one of the things I'm trying to find out. Is there someplace she might have gone? Some place her parents don't know about?"

"Well, I certainly don't know. I haven't seen her in ages. I told you."

"When did you last see Dwayne Vengley?"

"What does he have to do with it?"

"Maybe nothing. But Dorcas had a letter from a Dwayne, and now he seems to have disappeared, too."

"Well I haven't had anything to do with him in a long time. A real long time."

"Did Dorcas ever mention Jerry Hawley?"

"Who?"

I repeated the name. "He committed suicide a few years ago. When Dorcas was at college."

The young woman shook her head, face blank.

WHEN REASON SLEEPS • 91

"Apparently he was a good friend of Dori and Dwayne and a few others up at Occidental."

"I wouldn't know."

It was obvious she was hiding something, and equally obvious she didn't want me to learn what it was. "Stacey, the only thing I'm trying to find out is whether or not Dorcas is safe. I'm not the police; I'm not going to haul her back to her parents if she doesn't want to come. I won't even tell her family where she is if she doesn't want me to. But she does have the responsibility to let them know she's unharmed—if that's the case."

"I don't know where she is! Can't you accept that? It's God's honest truth—I do not know where Dorcas Wilcox is!"

"But you do know something that might lead me to her."

"No!" She stood with both arms tensely along her sides, hands curling into fists, and glared at me with a mixture of anger and fear. "I want you to leave—I don't want to talk to you anymore!"

Mrs. Steele's little boy knew a hint when he saw one, and even though I wanted to ask about the death of the Gates boy, Miss Briggs was finished answering any more questions. "All right, Stacey. Here's my telephone number. If you do want to tell me something—if you change your mind—please give me a call."

She didn't say yes or no; but she didn't throw away the slip of paper, either. At least not while I was there.

Henry's voice waited for me on the answering machine, saying it was sorry to have missed me and asking me to call any time no matter how late.

I did, telling the man what I'd found out about Jerry Hawley and Dwayne.

Henry asked, "That letter you showed me—that was from the same Dwayne?"

"I'm not sure. It read like someone who knew her pretty well—someone she'd talked with over a period of time. And so far, Vengley is the only Dwayne that fits."

"And he's missing, too?"

"I can't find anyone who knows where he is."

"Do you make anything of that, Steele?"

"Just that it may or may not be coincidence."

"So what the hell have you really found out?"

"About as much as I can without having police powers."

"Police powers for what?"

"For the name and address of that Colorado telephone number. For a warrant to search Vengley's last-known address. For access to the confidential files on the Hawley death. These things seem somehow all mixed together, but I'm just a civilian, Henry. I don't have the authority to run a formal investigation."

He got the point. "You're saying I should go back to the police with what you've told me and see what they'll do?"

"I think it's worth a try."

He didn't say yes, no, or thank you. "What do I owe you?"

CHAPTER

I jogged along the early-morning beach, telling myself I'd done the right thing in advising Henry to go back to the police. Ahead, down the gentle tilt of sand and foam, a cluster of seagulls lifted heavily into the wind as I neared. Through the pant of my breath and the thud of heels on the wetpack, the headset of the Walkman interrupted the morning news to tell me what the weather was going to be. "High today in the low seventies, low in the mid-fifties. Light and early fog along the coast." A weather report that hadn't changed since I was a kid waking to the same forecast on the clock-radio so many times that I could repeat it from memory.

Admiral Combs hadn't been as phlegmatic as Henry about my stepping back from the case. When I told him about it, the telephone had been silent for a long count before he grunted and said he wished I hadn't done that.

"Well, admiral, I've reached an impasse. The police can do a lot more than I can now—they have access to information that I don't."

"I realize that, Jack. And I understand your reluctance to waste any more time on this." Still, the pause told me, he didn't like it. "I've been tossing all night, wondering what might have happened to make her run again."

"We don't know for certain that there is a cause."

"Yes, yes. Damn it, I understand that. But you did point to a pattern in her behavior starting with the David Gates thing, and that has me worried."

David Gates.

That was the loose thread that all day yesterday had tugged at my attention. Now I regretted not asking Stacey about it.

"That happened in springtime," the admiral went on. "Then that boy's suicide and she ran again—another spring. Now it's springtime again and she's gone. Something must have sent her off, Jack. And I'm damned worried for her."

Vengley dead? Suicide? Accident? And Dorcas running from that knowledge?

The chill and foggy haze down the shoreline matched the vague outlines of my thoughts. I replayed my short conversation with the admiral. The thump of my running feet, the one-two of my breathing in pace with my strides, seemed to echo the names, as well as the questions that came with them.

I hadn't told the admiral I would do anything more. But as I stretched my legs in a closing sprint down the street and hung gasping at the front door to catch my breath before entering, I admitted to the irritable feeling of not having done enough. The Gates death was an avenue I hadn't pursued as well as I should have. And shoddy work—especially mine—bothered me.

Nonetheless, I'd advised Henry to see what the police could do. That advice was sound. I told myself that as I rattled pots and pans in a kitchen designed, like so many new California homes, for couples who didn't want or couldn't afford children. And, I repeated as I pulled silverware from the dishwasher and stacked it away in the cupboards, Henry had not been upset to see me drop the case. But Henry, my self responded, had not been the one to ask for help in the first place. It had been Jenny and the admiral. And none of them knew Dorcas was quite probably pregnant.

What the hell, a few telephone calls and then I could go back with a good conscience and tell the admiral that I'd tracked down the loose ends.

Margaret answered, her voice creaky and dull as if talking or even thinking this early in the morning were an effort. "Henry told me what you told him, Jack. He made an appointment. Somebody in the sheriff's office. Do you want him to call you afterwards?"

"I would like to know what he finds out." And there was something I wanted to find out. "Margaret, what can you tell me about David Gates?"

The silence was long and when her voice came back it was tense. But she only asked, "Why, Jack? Why do you want to know?"

"The name came up when I talked to Margot Hoyer's brother. He told me about the beach party and the accident."

"What did he say?"

"Nothing. What else is there to say, Margaret? Who was Gates?"

"A child—a young boy . . . He went to high school with Dorcas." With a clutch of breath, she added, "I don't want to talk about him—I don't want to hear any more about him!"

"Why, Margaret?"

"Because people are vicious—they lie and they're vicious!"

"Margaret—"

"No! I don't care what anyone says, it was an accident. The police investigated and it was just a terrible, terrible accident, and Dorcas had nothing to do with it!"

"Margaret—"

But she had hung up.

Newspapers would offer a start. But reading months of the *San Diego Union* without a clear idea of the date and with a victim whose name wasn't famous enough to be indexed wasn't that much of a start. There might be another way, and I tried it.

The efficient-sounding receptionist put me through to Tom's office.

"Jack—don't tell me, let me guess: you need a favor."

"How'd you know that?"

"Figure it—you're not calling so soon to ask me out for a beer; that usually waits a week or so. Plus you're working a case in new territory. So you need somebody who's got contacts with the natives. Am I right or am I right?"

"You're a hell of a lot better detective than I am. Ever hear of David Gates?"

He thought a minute. "No. What's he do?"

"Not much now. He was an accident victim five or six years ago. Out on Point Loma."

"San Diego Police called in?"

"I'm sure they had an investigation."

"I got your man. Give Lieutenant Tony Broadbeck a call. SDPD. I don't know his office number, but the switchboard can give it to you. Just tell him I said you need help."

"I owe you, Tommy."

"Hey, I won't forget it, either."

He might not, but if I asked for another favor, Tommy would be willing to help again. He was one of those people who feel genuinely good when they can provide help to a friend. Maybe the foundation of that feeling was the man's ego, his increased sense of importance. I'd always felt that about Tommy. But if that was a fault, it was a minor one. For whatever reason, the man delivered. When I finally reached Lieutenant Broadbeck and told him what I needed and who recommended him, the policeman agreed to meet me for lunch.

"David Gates." Broadbeck was a lanky man with a shaggy mustache that showed streaks of white among the black. His hair was unstreaked, though the sideburns were gray. His brown eyes held a guarded look as if they had been forced to see more than they wanted to. "I wasn't on that one, but I took a look at the file after you called. Kid. Died falling off the edge of a cliff on Point Loma."

"When was this?"

Broadbeck named the date and it agreed with what Jason and Jenny had told me: near the end of Dorcas Wilcox's senior year in high school.

I pushed a tomato slice around my salad plate and half-heard the chatter of other diners who filled the small restaurant near police headquarters. A lot of them seemed to be summer students from City College a block or so away.

"Was he alone or with some other kids?"

The brown eyes studied me. We had introduced ourselves by talking a little about Tommy. Broadbeck asked how long I'd known Jenkins by way of verifying whatever the man needed to verify. But the cop still didn't know that much about me. "You working on this? You a PI or something?"

"More a something." I explained a little bit about my own military experience and Admiral Combs's and his missing granddaughter. "So I wondered if Duane Vengley's name came up in the Gates case."

Broadbeck nodded and wiped a french fry through the sandwich juice that puddled on his plate. "It's a name you don't forget—especially since his old man's a big-time lawyer in town. He was there and three others besides the Gates kid. They were trespassing at night above Sunset Cliffs—you know how kids do. A little night partying, probably some booze, maybe dope. Anyway, Gates fell over the edge, almost a hundred feet, and was killed."

"No question of foul play?"

"Not in the coroner's report, anyway. The other kids' families swing some weight around town, too. But even so, there wasn't anything in the autopsy to suggest homicide, so, accidental death."

"Any chance of my seeing the file?"

The lieutenant shrugged. "It's a public document, and you're one of that endangered species, a taxpayer. Here's the case number."

I thanked him and we spent a little more time talking about military life and Viet Nam. Then Broadbeck showed me where to find the records office in the white halls of the sprawling police administration building. A sign quoted the per-page fee for documents. A clerk ran off a copy of the coroner's thick report, took my money, and, without asking, handed me a receipt. She probably thought I was a leg man for a defense lawyer.

The focus of the investigation, naturally, had been the victim, to ascertain the cause of death and the possibility of any suspicious contributions to it. The pathologist's statement made up the bulk of the pages, revealing, among the myriad technical details of breaks and lesions, that Gates was a Caucasian male, nineteen years old, with a history of mental retardation attributed to Fragile-X Syndrome. The probable cause of death was a crushed skull. Some seawater was found in his lungs which indicated breathing after impact. The injuries were consistent with a fall from the cliffs above and impact on the rocks.

The responding officer's and the investigating officer's reports, as well as the statements of four witnesses, formed appendices to the document. The witnesses had signed their statements: Dorcas Wilcox, Kimberly Overstreet, Stacey Briggs, and Duane Vengley.

They all said the same thing. They had sneaked out to the cliffs to have a party. Gates had wandered away from the group into the dark near the cliffs. He apparently stepped over the edge. None of them saw it happen, but they heard a noise and looked for him. When they couldn't find him, they became worried. Stacey Briggs returned home to call the police while the other three remained to search some more.

Nothing in the official file indicated any blame. No charges were brought.

And a lot, it seemed, was left unsaid.

Downtown San Diego still has a compactness that belies the growth which has made the city one of the nation's largest. The main library is only half a dozen blocks along E Street from the police building. I was directed to the microfilm section and scrolled back through reels of the *Union* until I found the right date. Then I scanned the print until I located the item: *Youth Dies at Sunset Cliffs*. The reporter's story was similar to the police report, but made more emphatic the point that no criminal charges were being sought against the other unnamed juveniles accompanying the victim. A final paragraph spoke to the city's efforts to improve pedestrian safeguards and barriers at the popular spot.

I made notes on what few items were different from the police version. Then I dialed the police administration building once more. Officer Mason, the investigating officer for the Gates case, was no longer employed. He had moved to the Houston Police Department three years ago—I would have to try that agency for any up-to-date address.

That left only Gates's family. I called first, then headed north once more to La Jolla.

"As I said, Mr. Steele, I don't know what more I can add to the information you already have." The woman spoke mildly and looked mild, too. Her graying blond hair was cut shoulder-length and curled under at the ends. It reminded me of a wholesome female lead from a 1950s movie—June Allyson or Doris Day. Her slightly plump body was wrapped in a brightly flowered dress akin to those sported by matrons on the Alexandria tea circuit. Even her gestures, as she invited me in and indicated a chair in the large, light-filled living room of the old brick mansion, were modulated by propriety. "May I offer you coffee or tea?"

"No thank you, Mrs. Gates. I understand your son was . . . handicapped?"

She smiled gently. "Mentally retarded, Mr. Steele. But emotionally, he was a very loving, kind, and generous boy." Her glance went to a framed photograph that sat alone on the baby grand piano. The picture, perhaps a graduation portrait, was of a youth who smiled stiffly. His face was slightly askew, large ears off-center, lower than normal, I decided—and the smile didn't match eyes that looked both hopeful and defeated at the same time. In fact, there was something in the mixture that reminded me of Dorcas's gaze when she was a little girl.

"But he went to the same high school as Dorcas Wilcox?"

"In the Special Education program. He was in one of the first groups to be 'mainstreamed' as they called it."

"So he knew Dorcas and the others—the ones who were with him that night?"

"Not really. He knew Dwayne—Dwayne was very kind toward David. One of the few, I might add." She explained, giving facts without rancor. "The program was supposed to enable greater socialization of the Special Education children; they were to make friends among the regular students, attend the dances and sporting events with designated peer tutors; in short, to become part of the community."

"It didn't work?"

"Not immediately—certainly not that year. I understand that later, after the students became used to the . . . F.L.K.'s—the funny looking kids, as they called them—then the program was effective for some of the children. But not all, Mr. Steele. And that first year was very difficult. David was very lonely."

It sounded like another of those bureaucratic plans that look good on paper and even better on the account sheet. The kind that hurt people who don't fit the profile. Even though the misfits become statistically expendable, the school district saves enough money to give the superintendent a glowing report and another hefty raise. School administration seems to be a minor-league training ground for the major league of Sacramento or even Washington. "But Dwayne Vengley was his friend?"

"Thank God for him, and how tragic David's death was for him, too." She was silent a moment, looking down at her hands clasped lightly together in her lap. "Dwayne used to come by and take David out for a soft drink and a pizza at a place where the young people liked to gather. It was the high point of David's week. Of his life, perhaps."

"But he didn't know the girls—Dorcas, Kimberly, Stacey."

"I'm sure he'd seen them at school. But of course there was nothing of a relationship between them." She smiled. "David used to pretend he had a girlfriend—he'd come home and talk about 'Sandra' and how they had arranged for a date for the movies. Dwayne would even tease him about his girlfriend—in a gentle, not a vicious manner—and David enjoyed that very much. It made him feel very grown up."

"But there was no Sandra?"

"No. Just an imaginary girlfriend. But very real to David, of course."

"How did he happen to be with the group that night?"

For the first time, a small frown creased her forehead between carefully outlined eyebrows. The gentle, refined manner revealed an air of sadness. "Dwayne invited him to a beach party. David had never been on one—not with the other young people, the normal ones. He was so excited. He wore his favorite pullover." She shook her head and tried to keep her mind focused on the question. "It was a rather large party, Dwayne told me afterwards. And David wasn't really comfortable because the others made a point of ignoring him. They can be cruel, you understand—unintentionally, perhaps; but as I've said, David was a very sensitive and loving child. He knew when he was being slighted." She looked up at me. "So many people used to try to console me by saying that at least David was too dull to realize he was retarded. But that's ignorance, Mr. Steele. David knew. They all know they're different from the normal, no matter how hard they try not to be. And they suffer that knowledge. After all, they're reminded of it every day."

"I understand."

"Anyway, Dwayne and several others—the girls—decided to have their own party away from the group. So they went out on the point. They shouldn't have, of course, and Dwayne was very remorseful about choosing the cliffs. He blamed himself for the accident, and I can still see him at the funeral." Another smile, this one not quite so gentle. "David had more school friends at his funeral than he had in life."

I hesitated, but I had to ask, "And there's no question that it was an accident?"

She stared at me a long moment, shock and a deep hurt mingling in her eyes. "Of course not! What a horrible thought!"

"I'm sorry to ask that, but I don't know much about what happened."

"It could only have been an accident, Mr. Steele. David would never have killed himself—in fact he was afraid of heights. And no one in the world would have wanted to harm the child. Certainly not Dwayne, who was David's only friend that year in school." She shook her head again, positive. "No. It was a tragic accident, but an accident nevertheless."

In my car, I made a few notes and then drove slowly down the curving and tree-guarded streets past the large homes and out to an overlook that showed the sparkle of the Pacific. A distant, looming rise marked Point Loma, almost invisible in the sea haze down the coast. In the soft sunlight, the vast bowl of earth between La Jolla and the Point showed a long, curving strip of sand with tiny white streaks of surf and hundreds of dots of bathers. Two or three miles of beaches that, at night, would offer a vast alternative of other sites for David's party.

From the coast, I gazed out at the sea and the distant horizon where the glimmer of a sail marked a boat hull-down over the curve of earth. Clean. From this distance, and despite the steady, tiny restlessness of traffic on avenues and drives, the coast and sea looked pristine. Balboa chose the right name for the glorious stretch of blue and sunny ocean that had spread at his feet in a vista of beauty and emptiness and peace. But Balboa—like the rest of us—knew that any ocean can darken, that the peace of every sea is transitory, and that in its depths swim things that belie the calm and happy surface.

CHAPTER

The Wilcox home was only a few minutes away. I took Prospect Street and turned onto the now familiar curving lane of quiet shade and private walls and hedges. The soft chime of the doorbell echoed on the other side of a door carved with ornate Spanish motifs. No answer. I rang again. The hiss of sprinklers beyond a hedge in a neighboring yard made the silence deeper. Finally the latch clicked and Margaret, bleary and moving with exaggerated control, squinted to focus her eyes on me.

"Jack? . . . Why? . . . Henry's not . . ."

"I need to ask you a few questions, Margaret. May I come in?"

"Come in?" She backed up reflexively to let me enter. Then she raised a hand. "Why? No . . . I don't—"

"It's about David Gates. And Dwayne and Dorcas, Stacey and Kimberly."

She stared, but I wasn't all that certain it was me she saw. I closed the street door and guided the stumbling woman to a chair in the cool living room. A flash of scarlet bougainvillea wound up beside one of the windows. The patch of private, manicured lawn outside showed a rock fountain that splashed a steady, bright chuckle.

"I've looked at the police file on David Gates's death, Margaret."

"You can't . . . You have no right . . ."

"The police listed it as an accident. No question. There's nothing—not one thing—in the file that implicates Dorcas or anyone else. No suspicion of foul play, no possible charges against your daughter."

"It was an accident. I told you that!"

"That's what puzzles me, Margaret. You keep insisting when there's no reason to. Who said anything to the contrary? And what did they say?"

Now I knew she saw me. Bloodshot and watery blue eyes bulged with fear in their net of puffy flesh.

"It's the reason Dorcas ran away in her senior year of high school, isn't it? Was she the one who told you it wasn't an accident? Was it Dwayne? Who, Margaret, and what did they tell you?"

The woman leaned away, an arm groping behind to brace against the upholstered chair. I could see thoughts tumble over themselves behind her eyes, and a widening terror that she struggled to resist. "A drink . . . Jack, I need a drink . . ."

She tried to stand. I pressed her gently back into the chair. "Tell me, Margaret. Who said what?"

"This is my house! You can't push me like this in my own house!"

"David Gates. What happened to David Gates?"

"Oh, God!"

"What did Dori tell you about David Gates?"

"Shut up! It didn't happen!"

"Tell me, Margaret. You really do want to tell someone. Tell me!"

The wrinkled lips worked, pinched between her teeth.

"Tell me, Margaret. I want to help you and Dorcas."

Gradually, brokenly, the woman began to talk. What's wrong, Dori? That's what she'd asked her daughter. The girl was numb and distant, depressed. Understandably so—who wouldn't be after something like that? The doctor advised Margaret to get Dori to talk about it. "Let her talk it out," he said. "She's feeling guilt and needs to know she's forgiven." Guilt. For an accident? Foolish—yes. They had been foolish to go along those cliffs at night, especially with that retarded boy. But children did foolish things, and it had been an accident— terribly painful for David's parents, of course. She was a mother, she could understand their loss. But Dori didn't have to ruin her life with remorse for something that wasn't her fault. That's what Margaret explained to her daughter. Dori, it wasn't your fault. That's what she said: you just acted unthinkingly. Going to a dangerous place like that was a foolish thing to do, but you can't torture yourself about it anymore. You've suffered enough. It was an accident and you mustn't blame yourself. "My fault," she had said. Two words and silence. "No, it's not! It was an accident—it could have been you or Kimberly, any of you. It just happened to be David. God help us, Dori, but if it had to be anyone, it's best it was that poor boy. He probably didn't even know what was happening to him."

"Goddamn you, Mother, it was my fault! Mine!"

And then, word by shaking, torn word, Dori told Margaret and even now she couldn't make sense of it. Couldn't understand all Dori was telling her. A game. Some kind of game they were playing with David Gates about something named a Place of Calling. A ritual to open some kind of gates and the boy's name and his innocence all tangled in a sobbing, convulsed swarm of words that didn't make any sense at all. An invocation. A springtime sacrifice to Beelzebub.

"Dorcas, stop it! That's not true—you know it's not true! You didn't do anything like that—you know it!"

But she wouldn't stop. Margaret couldn't make her stop, now. The words tumbled and spewed incoherently as she fought between crying and breathing and nothing Margaret could say would make her daughter shut up.

Finally she screamed at Dorcas, "You didn't sacrifice him— stop saying that word! I forbid you to say that word!"

Dorcas, wet mouth open and eyes and nose red, stared at her mother as if suddenly aware she was not alone.

"Dorcas, stop saying things like that. People—some people—may believe you."

"A sacrifice, Mother. David was a sacrifice to Ninib, to the Zonei and the Seal of the Seventh Gate. And I helped—I helped kill him."

"Stop, do you hear me?" It was from fear that she slapped the girl, not from hatred or rejection. Fear. Dorcas was raving, tipping into some kind of insanity brought on by the shock and her always overactive imagination. And all that anyone who overheard would have to do would be to call the police—an anonymous tip, rumor, and Dorcas's life would be ruined forever. It was those movies the girl had gone to—those Gothic things with ghosts and devils and special effects that brought terrified giggles and screams. Dori used to laugh about them, but obviously they'd done their damage—subconsciously burrowing into her imagination until now, faced with the trauma of a real death, the engraved images surfaced to confound reality with movie lies.

"A murder, Mother." Dori's voice had steadied and her eyes were intent now. The white flash of her hand on her daughter's cheek was turning to an angry red, but the girl didn't rub at it or cry or even seem to notice. Instead she stared at Margaret with a fierceness that made her eyes look a little insane as she whispered, "A sacrificial murder!"

"No—you didn't do anything like that! You're sick, Dori. That's what's wrong. This whole affair has unbalanced you and you need help. And your father and I will get it for you. Now take these pills—they'll help you sleep. You need sleep and rest; the doctor said so. And for God's sake don't say one more word about sacrifice or . . . or murder. People wouldn't understand, Dori."

The next morning, her daughter had run away.

I picked through the disjointed phrases, the convoluted sentences, fragments that had no clear subject. The woman's slurred words wove back and forth over the nightmare that had haunted her for so long, and gradually the phrases and ragged pieces of conversation began to build into a picture. Even as I watched, she seemed to slide back from the present into that time when the world's orderly foundation had changed for her. And she had discovered she lacked any strength to compensate for that loss. Then, increasingly, she had sought an alcoholic refuge where nothing could bring more harm.

"Does Henry know about this?"

"Henry? . . . Henry? . . ." She lurched to her feet and waved an exhausted arm against my chest. "Sleep. I'm tired. I need sleep."

CHAPTER

Kimberly Overstreet's married name was Goddard, I remembered. I checked the number Henry had given me against the listing in the telephone book. Then I took Nautilus Street inland past the La Jolla High School and up Soledad Mountain to a small lane that wound into a canyon. The pretentiousness of the homes in this pocket challenged those overlooking the sea, but they hadn't shouldered that pretension for as many decades. They were stark, shoehorned onto smaller lots, and their landscaping accentuated façades rather than complemented them. A curving drive led to the front of a gray-and-white colonial. Three-story columns rose up from a semicircular porch and hinted of the White House. A heavyset Latin woman in the black nylon uniform of a maid answered my ring. Her voice had the singsong inflection of memorized English phrases.

"Come in, please. I will see if Mrs. Goddard is at home."

The foyer where I was asked to wait was floored in large brown tiles. Beyond, a light-filled living room stressed natural colors and materials and a furniture whose fabric emphasized pleats. I stared at the large still-life that faced the dressing mirror and coat rack on the other wall of the foyer. It was a harshly colored, semiabstract painting of fruit in a basket. The artist's black signature filled the lower left corner and rivaled his subject in prominence. The squeak of rubber soles on slate brought a young woman wearing a white tennis suit. She dabbed irritably at perspiring temples with a monogrammed hand towel. "Yes? Who are you and what do you want?"

"Sorry to interrupt you, Mrs. Goddard." I smiled and told her who I was and that I wanted to talk about Dorcas Wilcox and the time in high school when she ran away from home.

She did not smile back and she was not pleased. "All that happened a long time ago, Mr. Steele. Like I told you on the phone, we don't see each other anymore, and I don't know where she is."

"You also told me you didn't know anyone named Dwayne. But Dwayne Vengley ran around with the Four Femmes in your senior year."

She didn't show fear at the name, just more irritation. "I didn't remember that Dwayne. And I haven't seen him since high school. Which is why I didn't remember him."

"What about Shirley Ellman? Do you remember her?"

"Sure. But I heard she died in a car accident three or four years ago."

"I see." From somewhere beyond the windows, a woman's voice said something in Spanish and a man's Spanish answered. "Mrs. Goddard—may I call you Kimberly?—when you were in high school, did you and your friends play any kind of ritualistic games? Dungeons and Dragons, for example?"

"No."

"Or perhaps dabble in the occult?"

"No, I didn't. And I really don't see what any of this has to do with finding Dori now."

"She apparently had an interest in metaphysical questions. She majored in philosophy in college."

"Well, I majored in communications."

"And she seems to have corresponded with some kind of Eastern religious group."

"That's her problem, isn't it? I mean, that kind of stuff really is juvenile, isn't it?"

I agreed. "But it can lead to very adult crimes."

"What's that mean?"

"Some people might get their thrills with a ritual sacrifice. Of an animal. Of a human."

"I don't know what you're talking about."

"It's possible that Dori's caught up in some kind of cult."

"Oh. Well, like I said, that's her problem."

"When you did happen to meet, did she ever mention any cults or talk to you about any religious movement she was interested in?"

The woman dabbed again with the small towel. "She did say a few things now and then—you know, talking about est or TM. And for a while she was hung up on Tibetan prayer wheels or crystals or something."

"Did she ever mention Vengley's name when she talked about these things?"

"Not that I remember." Her shrug said none of it was worth talking about. "I'm just not into that kind of stuff."

"And never have been?"

Her defenses came up again. "No."

"Not even with David Gates, Kimberly?"

"No! That was an accident—a tragic accident that I've been trying very hard to forget. And it was a long time ago, too, and nobody can say one thing different. Now you listen, Mr. Steele or whatever your name is, I don't have to put up with this. My husband is an attorney-at-law and if I tell him you've been harassing me you will be in deep shit!"

"I'm just trying to find a missing girl who's a friend of yours."

"She's not a friend anymore—I haven't seen her in a long time and I've got other friends now. Important ones! I don't know what you're trying to do, but you're bothering me and you're in my home. Now get out. Now!"

I did, thanking her politely for her time. She slammed the door on my gratitude.

In my car, I let the steering wheel guide itself back down the mountain. Kimberly was right about one thing—she didn't know what I was trying to do because I wasn't all that sure myself. Cults and ritual sacrifice—thrill murders and mumbo-jumbo. I was going by guess and by God, and more the latter than the former. What I groped through were not facts so much—there weren't many of those—as feelings and intimations. And the feeling that kept returning had to do with Dorcas's relationship to Vengley. As well as the feeling of shadowy ties between Vengley and several of the people I'd talked to in the last couple of days.

Steven Glover and Shelley Aguirre, for instance. There was something there. Probably to do with Jerry Hawley's suicide. Certainly there was a parallel between that and David Gates's death. As well as between the defensiveness of Kimberly Goddard and Stacey Briggs, and that of Glover and Aguirre. Patterns. You looked for patterns and then you used your reason and worked with the probabilities. In many ways, I had occasionally thought, my work for the last twenty years had been a lot like the skin-diving trips we went on as kids: short-lived plunges into alien waters looking for patterns. The coastal rocks Tom and I and the others would dive around had no patterns. There was only the swirl and tangle of currents, the chaos of fallen rock, sandy lanes of seabed. When you saw a pattern it meant something: the sinuous parallel lines of a moray, the spidery fan of a langosta's legs, the mossy half dome of a clamped abalone shell. In the chaos of life's events, too, you looked for patterns: repeated methods of operation, similar occurrences, familiar behaviors. Such as Dorcas's running away following each death. Such as deaths whose causes were unnatural. Even the time of the year. And you had faith that out of the matrix of chaos, patterns would emerge that, with care, would lead to meaning.

But what of the larger chaos? The cosmic meaninglessness that Dorcas apparently struggled to define? Job had stopped asking for meaning and submitted to faith. The aged Ben Franklin said he expected to soon find out about questions of faith. Not as safe a response as Job's in an Age of Faith, but practical and appropriate for the Age of Reason. But in a different age, one where faith was ill-defined and reason was suspect, how did one answer? Some wanted a return to blind faith as the only alternative to fallen reason. Others answered that life's absurdity in the universe left no room for reason, faith, or any other god. Yet belief in absurdity, like belief in reason, was an act of faith itself. Monsignor Kaufmann's response to Sartre, perhaps drawn from Kierkegaard: all humans are condemned to live by faith whether we want to or not. So Kaufmann chose that which promised best and which people far wiser than himself had chosen: belief in Christ. Others—perhaps like Dorcas—might accept any meaning to the cosmos instead of the emptiness of no meaning at all. But perhaps for her, traditional religion and cultural values no longer held conviction. Perhaps she sought meaning in beliefs that came from different roots—Hindu, Zoroastrian, Loa, Baha'i. Perhaps she and others explored ideas that challenged traditional Judeo-Christian prohibitions: Hare Krishna, Jamatkhana Agakhan, Higher Harmony, Ridway, Ramawhosis. There were also those, reluctant to go too far from tradition, who would follow charismatic leaders, who would devote labor and savings to their glory: Jim Jones and the People's Temple, the PTL Club, Oral Roberts, Swaggert, Tammy and Jimmy, Guru Ma. The names went on and on. For an age that was supposed to be faithless, there were a lot of people so hungry for it that all reason was lost. And there was an unending number of charlatans to offer spiritual security. For a fee.

The search for spiritual meaning had long been combined with different kinds of sacrifice. Children offered to Baal, burnt offerings to Yaweh, sacrificial lambs. "This is the body and blood of Christ . . ." Sacrifice as a symbol of transcending the restrictions of the flesh. Sacrifice as an actual transcendence. Either way, sacrifice was an ancient means of intensifying emotion and hallowing ritual. And religious intensity had been bred into America from the beginning: witchcraft trials, the Great

Awakening, Millerites, nineteenth-century revivalism, Shakers, camp meetings, Mormons, Jehovah's Witnesses, Father Divine, the Pentecostals, Hasidim.

I pulled the car into my garage and sat a few minutes before going into the house. Why should that search for intensity of religious experience cease now? Obviously, it hadn't—a flip through the television channels showed that. I could even remember one of my field trips for a Stanford class on comparative religion over twenty years ago: an isolated and run-down farm in the wet and rugged hills up near San Gregorio. The leader called it a religious commune, and himself the Master of Souls. Chubby, bearded, rumpled, he looked like the town drunk. And the man's grin was a mixture of leer at the visiting coeds and surprise at being taken seriously by a university professor and his class. But the four or five silent, middle-aged women who worked the farm and obeyed his commands took him seriously enough to call themselves his wives. And even, I recalled, resented the intrusion of outsiders into the world they had created with their faith. Yet if those women truly believed, it was because they willfully stopped their noses to the odor of deceit and mendacity.

What else was it that now stirred in memory . . . ? Several years back . . . talking with someone . . . a bar—an officer's club bar. Okinawa—that was it! The air force base at Kadena. One of the flights from Atsugi to Honolulu that had been interrupted by an overheated engine. A twelve-hour delay, and killing time listening to a Protestant chaplain drink mai-tais and bitch indignantly about the U.S. Army's recognition of the Church of Satan. It had recently become an official religion. Its military adherents now had the same rights to holy days and ceremonies as Protestants, Catholics, and Jews. The chaplain was a short, soft-faced man with rimless glasses and almost colorless pale hair. He'd talked about *The Satanic Bible*'s popularity among young people. All they wanted, he said, was approval to pursue the sins of the flesh. And they hypocritically called that filth a religion. "Turning from the Word of God to the word of Satan—that's not what the Founding Fathers meant by 'freedom of religion.' "

Tommy Jenkins was able to help again. "The cult and ritual murder people. That's who you want to talk with, Jack."

"The what?"

"I read in the paper a few months back. SDPD, like a lot of other PDs, they set up this special team to study cults and rituals. Cattle mutilations, chicken heads, crap like that. You know these random killings? They think some of them are tied to Satanists and witches. Christ knows, I believe it; I mean it's California, what else can you expect? If it's going to be any-where, it's going to be here. Give Tony a call—he'll tell you who to get in touch with."

I did. Lieutenant Broadbeck was cautiously reserved until he found it wasn't his time I was asking for again. "Detective Sergeant Shaughnessy is the man you want to talk to. He took the FBI course in cults and rituals. Wait a minute, I'll get his extension for you."

The man was on the street. I left name and number with the officer who answered the telephone, but it wasn't until almost five that the sergeant called back. I told him what it was about.

"Does this have to do with any particular case?"

"A missing girl." I added, "Maybe a couple deaths a few years back, but that's only hypothetical." It sounded pretty farfetched as I told it, and I apologized. "I really don't have any evidence; it's just a vague possibility that I'm checking out."

"Yeah?" Shaughnessy was interested—anything to do with occult crime interested him, he told me. And the possibility of ritual murder interested him more. It was an area the police were only now mapping out. The more he dug into it, the less surprised he was at what he found. In fact, a lot of what turned up came from informants who weren't really sure of what they were reporting, only that they felt something was wrong, or

they'd heard a rumor, or somebody had bragged about something. "Maybe I can help you."

I asked, "Buy you an early dinner?"

"Hey, why not?"

Detective Sergeant Shaughnessy was a few years younger than
me and about three inches taller. He had a flattened nose, a
long, square jaw that looked as if it could handle a hard punch,
and, over blue eyes, a little scar tissue that said it had. "Ninib?
That's what she said?"

"That's what it sounded like. She also said something about
a sacrifice to open the Seal of the Seventh Gate. There were
some other phrases, but I couldn't make them out. It—ah—
sounds like a lot of pretentious crap to me."

Shaughnessy wasn't interested in my opinion of it. "It could
be The Book of Entrance. From the *Necronomicon*. A lot of
kids have been reading that." He leaned against the back of
the captain's chair the fish restaurant provided and stared at
the harbor. Outside the plate-glass window and past the private
boats rubbing their moorings, points of restless sunlight spar-
kled on the water. "A lot of those conjurations and rites call
for blood and flesh offerings."

"Human?"

"The book doesn't say it has to be. But with some of these
people, who knows?" Frowning, he twisted a wad of pasta on
his fork and jabbed at a shrimp. "My guess is, human sacrifice
happens."

I shouldn't have been surprised. Halloween movies, late
shows on television, all the lighting effects of a smoky devil
worship were there for anyone who could push a button or turn
a dial. But that was Hollywood. "That's hard to accept,
Sergeant."

Shaughnessy shrugged. "A lot of cops who should know better don't accept it, either. But my experience tells me any weird
shit somebody can think of sooner or later shows up on the

street." He shrugged again. "But a lot of times, bones from a grave will do, and we get a whole slew of grave robberies every Halloween. I haven't had a case of human sacrifice yet, but I do think it could happen."

"Who might be a lucky candidate?"

"It would vary with the ritual. But usually you want somebody whose soul hasn't been corrupted by the world."

"A moral innocent? Like a retarded person?"

"I haven't heard of that. But anything's possible. The best is a victim that's unborn." He looked up. "They're truly innocent—haven't even been in the world, so they're the purest. Plus, the Bible describes children as closest to God, so that kind of sacrifice insults God more."

"Unborn babies? Fetuses?"

"The best is a third-trimester fetus offered at a certain moon phase or especially in late April or early May, depending on the cult."

"So a cult would go after pregnant women?"

He nodded and took a long drink of his wine. "There's an information network on crimes with satanic elements. It reported a fetus sacrifice a couple years ago near Aberdeen, South Dakota. We found out only because the mother died from the abortion."

"They forced her to have an abortion?"

"She volunteered. She was part of the cult." He added, "Some cults, you're supposed to have human sacrifice to become a priest or priestess. Best if it's a kid of your own. If not, someone else's will do."

"A man fathers a child or a woman gets pregnant knowing they're going to use it for sacrifice?"

"Hey, remember Abraham and Isaac. It's the ultimate test of obedience and faith."

The man was entirely convinced, and I felt a prickle of flesh at the nape of my neck. "This woman really thought she was a witch?"

He held his hand palm-down and wagged it above the sea-blue tablecloth. "Witches claim they practice white magic. Run around naked in the woods and sing chants to nature. They don't like being called Satanists. Like I say, the victim was found dead, so it was harder than hell to interview her. And not too many people were willing to talk about it, either. This was South Dakota. There couldn't be any Satanists in God-fearing South Dakota." He snorted.

"Yet you've found it here in San Diego."

"But not human sacrifice—not yet."

"Do you know the Satanist cults here?"

"Hell, they're in the Yellow Pages." Shaughnessy leaned forward, intent. "I'm not one of those who believe in a widespread organization of Satanists. There are some international groups: the Order of the Golden Dawn, started a hundred years ago in England. And the OTO—Ordo Templi Orientis, started in Germany about the same time." He shook his head. "But they're not highly organized structures. They have a post office box, write letters to each other, trade porno films. That kind of thing. What we've got in California are a bunch of splinter groups: the Brotherhood of the Ram, the Process Church of the Final Covenant—Son of Sam was supposed to belong to that one. LaVey's Church of Satan. Now there"—his finger emphasized the point—"is what I'm talking about. Out of LaVey's group come a bunch of splinter groups: the Temple of Set, the Church of Satanic Brotherhood, the Satanic Orthodox Church of Nethilum. Everybody wants to lead their own cult, you see, and that works against a rigid organization."

"All these people practice sacrifice?"

"No evidence of it. Public Satanists are too high-profile. If they break the law, they might lose their tax break for being churches. Thing is, their message is do whatever you're strong enough to get away with. People read that shit and think they'll try to show how really powerful they are. The really dangerous ones are the sociopaths, the unaffiliated Satanists. They'd probably be out killing someone anyway, but Satanism gives them an excuse. And sometimes the trigger."

Between my fingers, I twisted a sea-blue matchbook bearing the restaurant's name: The Blue Crab. "But even they can get followers?"

"Hey, there's Charlie Manson. People—kids especially—want to control their world. Magic promises that. The whole appeal of magic is that the mind can control matter and there's nothing random in the universe; everything has meaning and correspondence. If you know the secrets to that meaning, you can manipulate the world. And if you don't do it, some other magician will. What you do is convince a thirteen-year-old kid you've got power and can pass it on to him. Then you've got him."

I dredged up a distant memory of the appeal magic had when I was a kid—not just the fun of entertaining and mystifying my friends and relatives with the Magic Handkerchief or the Tibetan Steel Rings. It was the promise that, for a few dollars, I could learn secrets that would let me influence the mysterious currents of the universe. Ads in comic books marketed the ancient wisdom of the Rosicrucians, complete with the drawing of a man who radiated power from a triangle in his forehead. A genuine and unexpurgated copy of the *Book of the Dead* would reveal timeless wisdom. A special sale price on the *Egyptian Guide to Spiritual Power*. In a way it was as escapist as the comics themselves, and—very quickly—just as unconvincing. But I had to admit the appeal had been there. As a college student I had taken a series of comparative religion classes from Professor Spiegleberg. I was searching for universal truths, yes, but also for hints of the more arcane and perhaps enabling knowledge of the book of Atharva-Veda or the Upanishads. I had finally decided that strength like that had to come from within and not through the help of texts. But what of those who failed to discover that?

"You're talking kids, what, around twelve? Early teens? What about adults who practice Satanism? Like those people down in Matamoros who killed thirteen victims?"

"That was Palo Mayombe—the black magic side of Santeria,"

Shaughnessy said. "A lot of people in the drug trade practice that—Jamaicans, Haitians. Santeria's a mixture of Catholicism and African religions from all over the Caribbean. What they do is make offerings to some god or saint for protection or favors, and Palo Mayombe grew out of that." He leaned his elbows on the blue tablecloth as the waiter took away the empty plates and brought coffee. "I got called in on a drug bust a month ago down in National City. The arresting officers found this guy's basement rigged up with a goddamned altar. Had about a hundred of these perfumed red candles burning all over the place—hotter than hell and smelled like a French whorehouse. Had a crucifix on the altar—pure silver—stuck in a bowl of water, a bunch of daisies, an unopened bottle of rum, and a wooden cross with a couple white feathers tied to it. Had a bowl full of blood and chicken guts on the floor in front of it. And all sorts of food offerings, too. Cockroaches you wouldn't believe." He added, "They weren't part of the ceremony."

"Santeria?"

"Yeah. White's the color of Obatala, father of all saints, source of purity and wisdom in Santeria. But either the guy didn't make the right offering or he didn't listen when Obatala told him to knock off the dealing, because we busted his ass with two keys of pure. But that wasn't black magic—it was the guy's religion. Just like some Catholics have a little shrine in the backyard or give gifts to saints for special favors. Now, if the guy thinks Obatala's not strong enough medicine, next time he might start practicing black magic—Palo Mayombe."

"But what about the sociopaths? The ones who do practice human sacrifice?"

Shaughnessy's head wagged. "They're like the weather—everybody talks about 'em, nobody does anything about 'em. Reason is, there's not that much evidence. Full moon, certain high unholy days, you get all sorts of rumors. But there's no evidence of an organized underground. Like I said, it's a bunch of small groups or individuals making up their own ceremonies." He drained his coffee cup. "They're the ones to be scared of—they're nuts. Others use it to frighten kids; I know a couple cases where satanic rituals have scared children into doing what pornographers wanted and then keeping quiet about it. You read about them: the day-care trials. But I don't class that as cult activity. They go through the motions, but they don't really believe in it—it's just a way to control the kids."

"But isn't that what it's all about—control?"

"Yeah." The detective nodded. "You got that right. For the adults, especially. The few I know about firsthand were in it for sex, money, and power. That's where you're likely to get the drug use, too. Some guy—or woman—recruits a kid, gets him into rituals, he brings in a few of his friends, pretty soon you got a cult. Whether it turns murderous or not can just be a matter of luck."

Outside the restaurant, we paused by the locked gate leading to the private dock and its moored boats. "Do people stay involved in these cults for a long time, or do they just sample it and move on?"

"Depends on the individual. I've heard there are satanic families; parents who raise their kids up as Satanists instead of Lutherans or Catholics or whatever. But they don't broadcast what they're doing. And despite the Satanic Church they don't have an organization. At least I don't believe they do. Some people think different."

"It's conceivable a teenager could start out practicing Satanism and stay with it as an adult?"

"Hell, till he died of old age, I guess. Again, I've heard about—but I haven't seen—grimoires that go back four or five generations."

"Grimoires?"

"A book of satanic rituals and prayers for a person, family, or cult. Supposed to be covered in human skin. Has the rituals to be practiced and when, the names of their victims and spirits they control. There's a Book of Shadows, too. It's a kind of diary of what the member or cult did and when. That way the

member or even the next generation can see the correspon-
dences and know what rituals and prayers work."

I watched the opaque, green water bob along the hull of the
nearest moored boat. It hadn't been scraped in a while. At the
waterline, fingers of black scum swayed gently. "The girl I'm
looking for may be pregnant."

"Oh? How far along?"

"Probably in the second trimester now. Maybe more."

"I see. And she's involved in a cult?"

"I think she was. I don't know if she still is." I added, "Before
she disappeared, she said the baby was a bond of some kind.
A bond of life."

The detective, too, watched the uneasy boats. "A bond of
life . . . That doesn't sound like Satanism. Death, maybe, but
not life. Still, you're right to be worried. Beltane is coming up."

"What's that?"

"Spring unholy day—last of April, first of May. A time of
sacrifice."

"Jesus . . ."

Shaughnessy fished in his wallet for a business card before
heading for his car. "Look, I got to get home. But here's my
number. You have more questions, you need any help, give
me a call. Anytime."

CHAPTER

I had a lot to mull over, not the least of which was this glimpse into dark crevices of human behavior. I didn't think of myself as naïve; I knew Satanism wasn't confined to films and television. But neither did I envision it as something intruding into the lives of people I knew, people like the admiral and Jenny or even Henry and Margaret.

Spying, betrayal, espionage—these I knew firsthand. The motives behind these acts were money, political conviction, or a combination of the two. But to justify abortion or murder with inflated jargon and comic-book incantations defied reason. It was hard to see it as even a throwback to some primitive yearning. Instead, it was self-delusion, willful surrender to irrationality. That was it: it was a sleep of reason that didn't merely free demons but created them and gave them power. Anyone in their right mind would laugh at such fantasies. And if he weren't in his "right mind"? Was madness so widespread? Was the creature beneath the depths of Balboa's sunny ocean truly so vast, truly so close? Had I truly been so blind?

The trip home across the tall, sweeping bay bridge went unnoticed. It wasn't until I was in my living room and jotting down the information Shaughnessy gave me that I remembered my intention to call Henry. And it wasn't until I reached for the telephone that I remembered to check the answerer for messages. There was one: "Mr. Steele? This is Ralph Goddard. Please call me this evening anytime before ten," followed by the number.

Goddard was polite but firm. "My wife tells me you made certain insinuations about her, Mr. Steele, that are both damaging to her reputation as well as emotionally unsettling. If you try to contact her again, or if you in any way publicize your allegations, you will be sued for damages. Do I make myself understood?"

"I asked your wife questions about David Gates's death, a case in which she was involved. She chose not to answer."

"That case was thoroughly investigated by the authorities and closed with a finding of accidental death. The tenor of your questions challenges that finding, Mr. Steele, and has considerably upset Kimberly. Moreover, any suspicions you have are entirely unfounded and without basis in fact."

"I don't have enough for suspicions, Mr. Goddard. Only for a few ideas."

"Then keep your ideas private—and away from my wife. If your unwarranted intrusion into our lives creates the slightest problem for either Kimberly or myself, I assure you, Mr. Steele, you will—I repeat, will—be subject to litigation." Click.

Henry was less combative but almost as abrupt. "I told the sheriff's officer what you'd found out, Steele. He said nothing points to foul play, and everything points to Dorcas willingly going somewhere. He further said Dorcas was over twenty-one and had a right to go anywhere without telling anybody."

I wasn't surprised; that was my reading, too. "What did he say about investigating the Hawley death?"

"He said he'd look at the reports, but he wasn't very eager about that." Henry cleared his throat. "I understand you came around to talk to Margaret this morning."

"What can you tell me about David Gates's death?"

"Goddamn it, that case is closed! I don't know what Margaret told you—she was damned near incoherent by the time I got home. Pie-eyed. But Dorcas has nothing—not one thing—to feel guilty about. Everyone—the police, Dorcas, Mrs. Gates herself—said it was an accident. We've suffered enough over that incident and it's closed!"

"Did Margaret ever tell you about Dorcas's statement that it was a sacrifice to Beelzebub?"

"That's sheer nonsense. She mentioned it and I told her it was nonsense! Dorcas was upset. God, who wouldn't be? She was saying things without any idea of how they sounded. Of course she felt guilty. Who wouldn't? They knew they shouldn't have gone out there with that handicapped boy in the first place, and they didn't keep an eye on him once they were there. Christ, you know how kids that age are. But it was an accident. Dorcas . . . well, Dori just let her imagination get the best of her. None of that sacrifice nonsense happened. It just didn't happen, and I thought Margaret had all that crap out of her mind long ago."

"You don't even think it's possible?"

"No! Of course not! I do know my own daughter. I know what she's capable of and what she would never under any circumstances do. She's a loving, caring person. She still cries, for God's sake, when a dog gets hit by a car. I saw her. That's not the kind of person who would murder another human being!"

I tried to imagine one of my own daughters participating in a sacrificial rite, one not even involving a human, and I could not. The only image of Karen or Rebecca was their disgust at the idea. "Do you want me to keep looking for Dorcas?"

Henry sighed. "I'm sure she's just gone off to be by herself for a while. Why, I don't know, but I don't think it's nearly as serious as Margaret's parents do."

"Is that a yes or no, Henry?"

He finally spoke. "I'm sending a check for one thousand dollars to you to cover expenses."

It must have been a yes. "You might not like what I turn up."

"Just turn up the fact that she's alive and well. Any nonsense about Beelzebub or sacrifices is mere hogwash and I'm not worried about anything like that."

CHAPTER

15

Neither Jenny nor the admiral wanted to hear anything about Dorcas being involved in Satanism.

"I can't imagine it, Jack. I just can't imagine anyone doing that kind of thing, much less Dori!"

"I don't know that there's any truth to it, Jenny. But Margaret's lived with the suspicion for a long time. It's eaten away at her."

"And she never said a thing to me about it! All this time . . . I'll call her as soon as I hang up, Jack."

"Do you know anyone who might give me information about Satanism in the local high schools? Especially when Dori was there?"

"You might talk to Megan Wells. She was a counselor in one of the area high schools before she married. Perhaps she can think of someone."

She gave me Megan's home and work numbers and asked if I thought Dorcas's disappearance was related to Satanism.

"No," I said cautiously. "I don't think so. But I do feel she's still interested in religions. She apparently received books from an ashram or religious commune."

"Oh, Jack, not one of those awful cults!"

"There's no real evidence of that, Jenny."

"There doesn't seem to be evidence of much at all, does there?"

That was true, and didn't leave much to say. Jenny hung up to call her daughter; it was still early enough to catch Megan at work. I dialed that number. She was surprised to hear my name, and I caught a note of reservation in her voice. "Don't tell me you're calling for one of our seminars."

Her business was a new service answering to the increased demand for private instruction in business and industry. She advised companies on whether they should develop their own specialized curriculum and instructors or hire outside agencies. She offered guidance for establishing those schools, as well as providing speakers and short courses and even arranging the location and catering if necessary. She had told me some of the challenges of finding speakers on a wide variety of topics and at a wide range of fees. It was, she had smiled, private enterprise in public education, and a lot of work for a one-woman office.

"Not unless you have a speaker on Satanism."

"You're serious? I think I could find one. Satanism and cults or just Satanism?"

I could see her start to scan through a Rolodex or, more likely, the subject files on a computer. "Whoa—I'm not serious about a speaker. But I do need some information if you have it." I explained why and she said she might be able to tell me a little about it. We agreed to meet at the Mexican Village on the lower end of Orange Avenue.

A lot of things had changed at this end of Coronado, too. The old ferry slip was now a small park surrounded by condos. The busy street traffic that used to jam into lines to wait for the boat ride across the harbor was no more. A few lost tourists wandered up from the new cluster of shops at the passenger ferry dock; a car or two hissed past in the soft evening light. Even the curbs were empty so parking was free.

Still, not all was changed. For generations the Village had been the closest and loudest watering hole for navy pilots on liberty from North Island. The girls who sought to marry them still made fragrant weekend crowds in the dark and low-ceilinged bar that sprawled away into dim corners. I was grateful that it was a weeknight and free of the hustle of liberty hounds. Megan looked around with a wry smile at the shadowy booths and tables of black wood. "Larry brought me here once—he thought I ought to see the top guns at work."

"Flyers from his squadron?"

"The women shooting them down."

She told me a bit about her husband—factual, brief, and unsentimental. She had loved the uniform and liked the man. But even as the navy chaplain finished the ceremony and they'd rushed out under the uplifted swords of Larry's fellow pilots, she'd had reservations about marrying. Not that it made any difference. They hadn't had enough time together to really know if it had been the right thing to do. In the two years of their marriage, the squadron was always flying to different bases for two- and three-week training sessions; then they went on sea duty, and about halfway through that tour Larry, practicing night landings, had crashed into the end of the bobbing flight deck. Megan came to terms with her guilt on the grounds that they might have had a good marriage after all. And that at least Larry never knew they might not have.

I told her about Eleanor, showed her pictures of Karen and Rebecca when she asked to see them, and sprinted through the thoughtful, if not awkward, silence that followed show-and-tell. "Did you ever run across any cult or satanic problems as a counselor?"

"Not directly, no. But the district provided a workshop for counselors on cults and what we should look for. And we did hear stories of grave robberies in Chula Vista. But none of it ever came to light as Satanism."

"And nothing at La Jolla High School?"

She shook her head. "I worked in the Encinas district. We wouldn't have known about La Jolla." Behind her, in an icy light that gleamed up the rows of bottles and glasses, the bartender was busy with an order of margaritas for diners in one of the back rooms. "The workshop was on cults and devil worship. It was in the newspapers at the time, and parents were worried. As I remember, girls were supposed to be more attracted to witchcraft or white magic than to Satanism. But I wouldn't be surprised to learn that Dori dabbled in it."

"Why's that?"

"She always has been a very lonely girl. And neither Henry nor Margaret is the most communicative parent in the world." A swirl of Megan's glass. "She fits the profile they gave us of likely joiners."

"But neither Henry nor Margaret expressed any worry about her?"

"Not to me."

"Even with the Gates death?"

"No." Megan sipped at her margarita. "The things parents might notice—changes in eating and sleeping patterns, heavy alcohol or drug use, erratic grades—these can have other causes, too. Causes that come to mind more readily than Satanism."

"What about symbols and videos and music—the worship of violence?"

"I suppose it would depend on how much fascination the child showed with violence. I'm not an expert at this, Jack, but I think a lot of that is natural curiosity and even bravado. Moreover, a lot of parents—and I think Margaret and Henry fit this—don't really want to know if something's wrong. They think if they ignore it, junior will grow out of it by himself."

She searched her memory for the checklist of things that might indicate Satanist or cult activity. Nothing she could recall indicated Dorcas's involvement. Still, the images that had haunted Margaret all these years had, Megan said, a ring of truth. She also gave me a sheet that she'd printed from one of her files before leaving work. It listed mailing addresses that offered more information on cults and the agencies that combated them. She explained, "Something starts making headlines, and someone will call up wanting a program on it."

In the chill air outside the restaurant, there came another of those slightly awkward moments. "I'd like to thank you with a dinner when this is cleared up," I said.

She smiled and held out a hand. "That's not necessary."

"I wasn't thinking necessity, Megan—I was thinking pleasure."

She gave that a long moment's thought and finally said, "I'll look forward to it, then."

Like Megan, Sergeant Shaughnessy had given me the names of a few books on Satanism, some of which were in the small Coronado library. A few others I found in the New Age section of the bookstore at the other end of Orange Avenue. The clerk, a girl with thick glasses, smiled a bit too brightly as she wrapped up copies of the *Necronomicon* and LaVey's *The Satanic Bible*. I felt her relief as I went out into the light traffic of early evening. I could have said "research" or "for a friend," but I didn't. She wouldn't have believed me anyway, and besides, it was kind of funny. But it also gave me a hint of the ego gratification that could be found in a public admission of one's dalliance with the occult. The girl had not been afraid of me, but she was certainly wary. That kind of effect on others was, in a way, an exertion of power. It commanded their attention—it made them behave in a way I dictated. Perhaps people caught in a world blindly careless of their feelings found in even that small taste of power a promise of far greater sweets to come.

My evening was spent reading. The appeal for immature readers of *The Satanic Bible* and the *Necronomicon* was evident in prose styles that were juvenile in inflated self-importance. LaVey's strident voice reminded me of bull sessions I had with teenage friends: the challenges to established churches, the heavy sarcasm caused by hypocrisies among famous adults, the mixture of nervous laughter and bravado in discovering that "dog" is "god" spelled backwards. In another light, LaVey's appeal was the same heavy-handed irreverence of *Mad Magazine*. The *Necronomicon*, also, insisted too loudly on its power and ancient mystery. Symbols, rituals, chants—all attributed on its own authority to pre-Christian cults of the Middle East—were presented in a language that, even with my limited linguistics background, was amateurishly artificial.

But it, too, played on the appeal of the forbidden and the mysterious. It threatened danger to all but the most careful practitioner—that is, to everyone but you, dear reader. And it promised power.

Yawning, I finally closed the last book and lay in bed to stare at the dimness of the ceiling. The truly wondrous thing was that people actually believed. They hungered for some kind of certainty. They hurt so much from fear and the vision of nothingness that they gave themselves in belief to nonsense like this. Hard to accept, perhaps, but I could think of at least one religion, strong and growing, whose documentary basis was equally immature and questionable. And Hitler's appeal had been hard for outsiders to accept, too. In the jerky black-and-white newsreels, Der Führer seemed a comic madman with his absurd mustache and high-pitched ranting. But millions of people supported him with their faith and with their lives.

"Hitler could not have caused such a magnitude of evil without the action of the Devil." I tried to remember the name of the Jesuit priest who had argued that idea. For him, the Devil had been an active fact: the spirit world existed, and the Bible was revealed truth; the Devil was of that spiritual world, and the Bible said God created the Devil for His own inscrutable purposes. The priest had pointed out that worship of Satan did go back almost as far as the Catholic Church itself: Knights Templar, Black Masses, Madame La Voison. And he had cited an Italian priest who was currently writing on the role of exorcism and its even greater need in contemporary society.

From the library texts, names and dates floated through my sleepy mind as I stared at the ceiling. On the other side of the fragile neck of the Strand, the incoming Pacific beat with a steady pulse. I didn't believe then and I still doubted the priest's argument. To assert Satan's biblical genealogy wasn't the same as establishing his presence. And using the logic that God exists and therefore Satan exists seemed fallacious on at least two counts: an unwarranted expansion of human reason to govern God, or the restriction of God's powers to humanity's comprehension of them. Miracles may exist, and I wasn't prepared to deny the possibility of a spiritual world. But I wouldn't presume to define it, either. If there were any physical evidence for a Demon, it might be found only in Satanism's practitioners and in the results for humanity of those practices. At any rate, there is where a Satan would be combated, and that made the question of his independent existence irrelevant. Long ago my work had carried me into the ethical swamps of conflicting political ideologies and recurrent questions of ends justifying means. I'd managed to find the firm ground of a pragmatic belief that life was more valuable than death, and that which made human existence better was more valuable than that which made it worse. I'd seen problems come when people—on our side or theirs—substituted for "life" a political code or an individual man: communism, Mao, capitalism, Stalin . . . even, with the self-defined patriots, the President. And now it looked like I'd run across a new combination of politics and personality cult—Satanism.

Once more, it was the surrender of reason to the romantic appeal of the irrational. But, ironically, that was an empirical truth I also believed in—the irrational, the Dionysian escape into ecstatic states, religious or secular. It did provide a source of knowledge that wasn't encompassed by the realm of reason, or Nietzsche's Apollo. The irrational is both those things, isn't it? An escape from the pressures of life as well as an avenue to some different kinds of knowledge. As an artist, Eleanor had helped me tap that side of the psyche. It was chaotic and formless, but it was also unbounded possibility. Freedom from the restrictions of society, of family, even of reason. But not freedom from the self and those basic responsibilities that always devolve on the self. The irrational doesn't have program or structure, and that's the source of its illuminations. To channel its energies into a structure would not be to follow its illuminations but to supplant it with an exercise of reason—perverted, perhaps, or based on a fallacy, but a form of reason, nevertheless. Thus the cults' insistence on highly structured priesthoods, their reliance on elaborate ritual, their own repeated logic of punishment and reward, of concordance of magic act and resultant effect. Their psychic energy may be drawn from the power of the irrational, but their form and purpose are a kind of perverted rationality. The force and power of the irrational was used to support a twisted reason based on the worship of death.

And that is what I was faced with: not only the sleep of reason, but more importantly its perversion.

So what weapons would be effective? What kind of defenses would I need? How to take arms against the ghosts in other minds while recognizing their existence in my own?

CHAPTER

In the bright overcast of morning, I vaguely recalled my final thoughts as I had fallen asleep the night before. I had been trying to clarify a transcendental dimension to the hunt for Dorcas. But this morning, those thoughts and ideas had lost any clarity or outline. There was only the fact of the missing pregnant girl, the thoroughly nontranscendent demand that something be done quickly, and the lingering odor of a spreading malignancy.

By the time I finished my run and a light breakfast, the hour wasn't too early to call Jerry Hawley's father again.

"A cult? You're telling me Jerry was involved in some kind of cult?"

"I'm asking if that might have been the case, Mr. Hawley. You said earlier that he became moody and stopped playing soccer for no apparent reason. At about the same time, did he seem more secretive? Did he start ignoring old friends or stay away from home for longer periods?"

"He was at college. We wouldn't see much of him at all except on vacations." The voice paused. "He did stop coming home so much on weekends, but he said he was studying . . . we didn't think anything of it."

"How were his grades?"

"Not very good the fall quarter. That's why we thought he was studying so hard that winter."

"Was your son interested in religion?"

"You mean like the Moonies or something?"

"Religion in general. Did he read a lot about other religions or did he seem to be searching for a faith?"

"I don't know. It's not the kind of thing we'd talk about. I mean we sent him to Sunday school as a kid, but I guess from junior high on, it was pretty much up to him whether he went to church or not." Hawley added somewhat apologetically, "Neither his mother nor I were regulars at church. We just didn't make time to go. But it's helped a lot since . . . well, it's given us some strength."

"How much did he tell you about Dwayne Vengley?"

"Very little. I met him one time when Jerry brought him home. It wasn't too long after they met, I believe. I wasn't too impressed with him, but I made it a point not to say anything bad to Jerry about his friends."

"There were others you didn't approve of?"

"Not then, no. But all his life Jerry would pick the damnedest people to be friends with. In grade school he just about worshiped this one kid who was one of the toughest little imps imaginable. And in junior high he got into a little trouble following the lead of a kid who later ended up in jail. Not serious trouble, thank God; just some vandalism—a broken store window, some spray painting. But he was thoroughly remorseful; he earned his own money to pay his share of the damages. Still, even in high school, he was always bringing home people with safety pins in their noses." A sigh. "We even talked to a psychiatrist about it; he said Jerry was apologizing for his affluent background. But he didn't have one thing to apologize for—I by God got where I am fair and square, and I never once pressured Jerry into doing anything he didn't want to do."

"And you saw his friendship with Vengley to be of this sort?"

He thought about that. "No. Vengley had plenty of money,

for one thing. Occidental isn't cheap, and his father's a well-known attorney down in San Diego. I really don't know what it was about him that attracted Jerry . . . maybe his attitude—he had this superior attitude. Not that he'd say anything snotty, but you could just tell he was looking down his nose at you." His voice implied that he should have thought of it sooner. "It really was the same attitude some of his punk rocker friends had—as if they were sneering at you, your house, your beliefs. But you knew damned well they'd take every penny you gave them."

"Do you think he supplied your son with drugs?"

He didn't answer immediately. "I don't know—you can get that stuff almost anywhere. So I suppose they could have done drugs together. Whether he was a pusher or not, I don't know." The voice shifted, bringing in a certain weariness. "Mr. Steele, I know I said I didn't like Vengley. I still have very serious reservations about that young man. But it's a pretty subjective feeling, and I certainly don't think he led Jerry into any kind of cult. My son had a good head on his shoulders; he wouldn't have let himself be manipulated by some charlatan. I've seen those people, Mr. Steele—running around with their robes and sandals and banging drums. Jerry wasn't that type."

I hadn't been thinking of that kind of cult, but it would do the boy's father no good to explain. Besides, the man had told me what I wanted to know. "Thank you, Mr. Hawley. I don't think I'll need to bother you anymore."

I watched the girl look up, puzzled. The supervisor bent across her desk to say something. Then she looked my way and her eyes widened. At first I thought she would not leave her desk, but she did. Nodding absently at something the supervisor said, she walked numbly toward me. I was someone she hadn't expected, and someone she didn't want to see again.

"I hope you don't mind giving me a few more minutes of your time, Shelley."

She did, it was obvious. But all she said was something about the supervisor who wanted people to take care of personal business on their own time.

"I talked to him already and explained why I'm here." I smiled. "He said you could take an early lunch break with me."

She looked around as if she wanted to call for help. None of the figures bending here and there over drafting tables or staring intently at computer screens looked our way. I put a hand under a bony elbow and guided her toward the door.

"Why?"

"We need to talk, Shelley. About Dori, about Dwayne."

That was her only question. I led her to the car in the visitor's slot. We pulled into the pulse of traffic that marked the coming noon hour.

This time Steven hadn't called to warn her that I was coming. As the car weaved among others filling the lanes, I sensed her struggle to organize her thoughts, to anticipate my questions. "Why are you so tense, Shelley? You seem almost afraid of me."

"No! . . . I mean I don't know. I mean I wasn't expecting to see you . . ."

"I hope it's not an unpleasant surprise. Is it unpleasant?"

"No. I just . . . I already told you everything, that's all."

"You like Chinese food?" I guided the car toward a restaurant with rearing dragons at the eaves and a sign for kosher Chinese tacos.

"It's okay, I guess."

"If you want something else, just say the word."

"No—it's fine."

We parked and I walked around to open her door. She hesitated, but there was no sense sitting in the car. Face blank, she finally slid off the seat. A brisk Chinese woman led us to a small table at the room's far end. She handed us menus decorated with red tassles and pictures of a high-arched, ornate bridge.

"I'm going to have something light. Age and heavy lunches don't go together. You order whatever you want."

I don't think she knew what she ordered. She seemed surprised when a plate of food was set in front of her. None of my banter about my daughters or trends in California cuisine made her relax. Questions about her job, her family, herself, were answered with a terse yes or no or just silence. Finally I pushed my empty plate aside. "You're not eating much."

"I'm not really too hungry."

"And I suspect you wish I'd get to the point. All right, here it is: I want you to tell me why Jerry Hawley committed suicide."

Her head shook before the words came out. "I don't know."

"You, Dori, Jerry, Steven, and Dwayne—and a few others. You ran around together. You saw a lot of each other. And you did some things that maybe you don't want to think about now."

"I don't know what you mean!"

"Sure you do. Dwayne organized things, didn't he? He led the rituals, didn't he, Shelley?"

I spoke as if I knew all about it. She stared at me with eyes shocked wide enough to let me gaze into her very soul.

"Didn't he, Shelley? The rituals. Were they incantations? Conjurations?"

Slowly and still staring, her head nodded once. I resisted the urge to lean forward.

"The conjuration of lust?" I smiled.

She nodded again, eyes staying on mine.

"Of destruction?"

"Yes."

"What about compassion?"

"After."

"After Jerry died?"

"Yes."

"So that his soul would rest?"

"No. So his power would help us. Jerry's a Prince of Satan now—he's a god in the Kingdom of Darkness."

She was using the present tense. I did, too. "And now his spirit is called on to help you?"

Her brown eyes looked back at me with an innocent, unsettling conviction. "He's there."

I completed the thought. "When you want to call him."

"When the High Priest calls him. A High Priest or Priestess has to call him."

"Dorcas was a member of your grotto at Occidental?"

"Kabbal—we call it a Kabbal. The others"—her hand moved in dismissal and I heard the first note of assertion in her voice—"the grottos, they're just dabblers."

"But Dorcas had joined before you did."

Shelley nodded. "She quit for a while. She and Dwayne, I guess, did some workings in high school, but then Dori dropped out before coming to Occidental. But Dwayne said she should come back in, so after a while she did." The girl's dark eyes frowned slightly in awe. "Dwayne's like that—he just gets people to do what he wants them to. It's because he's a Brother of the Inner Circle."

"You joined because he wanted you to?"

"No. Because Jerry joined. Dori dated Jerry for a while our freshman year and then they broke up, so he asked me out. And Dwayne was always around—he knew Dori—so he and Jerry started going around together. I didn't know anything about the Kabbal or Dori being in it before. I mean she didn't say a thing to me, and we were best friends, you know? It really blew my mind when Jerry told me what Dwayne told him. I asked Dori and she didn't want to talk about it at first—she was afraid, you know? But finally she did, and then Jerry and Dwayne . . . well, I joined and then after a while we brought Dori back in. Dwayne brought her back in."

"And Steven?"

"I met him later. I dated him for a while and then we brought him in."

"What about Tim Gifford?"

"Dwayne already knew him. He was in the Kabbal when I joined."

"How did Jerry commit suicide?"

"He . . . he hanged himself."

"Why, Shelley?"

She shook her head, staring at her plate.

"Was it a ritual suicide?"

"We didn't . . . the Kabbal didn't hold a ceremony. I didn't know about it until it was all over."

"But Dwayne knew about it."

She nodded.

"Did he help Jerry do it?"

"No. Not exactly. He said he helped Jerry decide. They talked a long time, I guess, before Jerry did it. I don't know, maybe all night. A day and a night, maybe. And he and Jerry finally decided it was the thing to do. Dwayne said he promised Jerry a conjuration of compassion and . . ." She clamped her mouth shut.

"And what, Shelley?"

Lips tight, she shook her head.

I studied the suddenly closed face and wondered what additional admission could frighten the girl. "Was it a sacrifice? Did Dwayne tell Jerry he would get a soul to accompany him?"

She stared at me a long moment. "Slaves. He would send Jerry slave-souls."

"Did he do it? Dwayne?"

"Not then. Later—one year after. I wasn't there but I heard about it. I've never been to a High Sacrifice. Only people who are Prince or Princess, Priest or Priestess can go to the High Sacrifice. And members of the Inner Circle."

"Do you know who the Chosen One was?"

"No. Only the High Priest knows that."

"The sacrifice was a fetus, wasn't it?"

"It was an innocent. A pure soul. That's all they told me."

"Where did they get it?"

"I don't know!"

She answered too quickly. I tried to read the dark eyes. "Do you know where Dori is now, Shelley?"

She shook her head again. "She dropped out after Jerry

crossed over. She left school for a long time and when she came back, I didn't see anything of her. In fact, I didn't even know she was back in school until Steven told me."

"Dwayne didn't like her leaving?"

"No. But he didn't make a big thing of it. He says that's what the Kabbal is all about—liberating people so they're free to do what they want."

"Do you feel free in the Kabbal, Shelley? Do you do what you want to?"

"I guess. Yes. It was my choice to join. Now it's my choice to . . . obey. The Kabbal is freedom; my wishes are theirs and together we are free."

The answer had the rhythm of incantation and not the slightest nuance of irony. What I was staring at across the tatters of egg roll and hot sauce was a True Believer. "Where's Dwayne now?"

"In . . . some place in Colorado."

"Why?"

"I don't know. Maybe the High Priest sent him."

"Dwayne's not the High Priest?"

"No—he's a Brother of the Inner Circle. That's just one step below High Priest."

"Who's the High Priest?"

The energy she had shown while telling me about the Kabbal began to withdraw. I saw the small woman almost shrink as caution and wariness pulled her away. Even her hands began to fold closer to her body.

"Shelley?"

I had asked more than I should have. Now she was afraid she had told me too much. "I want to go."

"Something may have happened to Dori, Shelley. These things you're telling me might help me find her."

"I want to go."

That was the last thing she said and all my urging was met with silence. On the ride back to her office, a worried frown pinched her dark eyebrows together. She gazed straight ahead into the midday traffic that glittered and swirled in the hot sunlight. I wasn't new to people clamming up, but I'd never seen it so literally. A shell seemed to clamp down around her and in my mind's eye she almost curled into a fetal position. She answered none of my questions, refused to nod at any comment; she focused on something inside with a stillness that froze even the blink of her eyes. When she left the car it was without a glance backward. The building's door closed off her small, silent figure.

At home, I telephoned Detective Betts of the Pasadena Police. When the division secretary said Betts was on the street, I left my name. Then I settled into a canvas chair in the shade of my cramped deck and opened a bottle of mineral water. It was the kind Tommy drank. A beer would have tasted better, but it couldn't cut the thirst that came from the salty Chinese food. And which was intensified by the fidgety worry that had grown as I listened to Shelley. I watched a small ketch work its way out of a slip across the channel. Using only the jib in the light breeze that came from the ocean, it glided silently toward the open, sun-sparkled waters of the bay. There, the crew—a man and woman wearing matching hot-pink bikinis—hoisted the main. The boat heeled a bit and quickly disappeared behind a row of homes.

I hadn't yet heard from Rebecca, which didn't surprise me. A week for the first letter to get there, and chances were she had planned a trip over the long spring vacation. She mentioned visiting Portugal sometime soon. That could take another week. Then, if she wrote to the old Fairfax address, it would take additional time to be forwarded here. And where else would she have written? I hadn't known my new address until less than ten days ago, when I'd bought this house, which the realtor told me had been on the market for what—four hours? I had the house because I had cash in the bank—the money from the Fairfax sale plus the investment and savings accounts that had been building for twenty years. The insurance settlement for

Eleanor's death had been dumped into a separate account and ignored. It made a nice emergency reserve in case the girls needed it. Or it would make a large addition to my own insurance when I died. As for me, with care and modest expenses, I could get by pretty well on my retirement.

There was even enough for a boat to ride against that empty dock. It was an extension of the narrow boardwalk that ran from the deck and across the patch of grass that was my new backyard. Its vacant water and empty cleats had been filled with an imaginary ketch from the moment I saw the home. The *Eleanor* out of Coronado, California . . . no, she wouldn't want that; too lugubrious, she'd say. Or, laughing, how would my next woman feel sailing on a boat named after my first wife? Things we would joke about lying head by head on a single pillow. Serious jokes, of course—neither of us had wanted the other to be alone if one died. But neither of us was planning to die. It was all just talk.

A deep breath pushed all that to the back of my mind. In the four years since her death, the pain had gradually ebbed. But I still had a habit of talking things over with her. Personal things, things about the girls. Nothing about my work. Even while she was alive, the demands of security had kept me from talking with her about that, and I still heard her slightly bemused question, "I wonder how other women manage without talking to a husband about his work?" But we could talk about Eleanor's work. And there were always family issues, things like the choice of wedding caterers for Karen, what college for Rebecca, the name of our long-dreamed-of boat. But why this resurgence of sadness and nostalgia now? This concern with death that came like a dark furrow in the soft blue California sky? Why the nagging vision of Shelley's dark eyes staring at me with a mixture of terror and denial?

Maybe a name combining Karen and Rebecca. They'd like that and so would Eleanor. *KaReb? Ren Reb? KaBec?* The *Ship Rek?* I washed those names out of mind with another swallow— it might be harder to name the damned thing than to buy it.

But wouldn't Karen and Chuck have fun sailing! Or how about me and Rebecca taking it down the Baja coast to Los Cabos? Hell, with enough provisions, a two-week sail to Hawaii and points beyond! Thirty, thirty-two feet. Seaworthy at that length and not too cramped for two people. Walk out my own back door, hoist sail, and be away on a clean and vacant sea that ran all the way to China.

I sipped again and tried to envision the nameless yawl or ketch tied up to the pier. Ample deck cabin amidships. A sturdy, squared-off hull designed for strength and comfort rather than speed. In my imagination I outfitted the boat and tinkered with the cabin layout, the rigging, the electronics, the auxiliary diesel. Tommy Jenkins had his contacts in the boat business. It could happen, and I tried to hold on to that bright possibility against the tug of Shelley Aguirre, Dwayne Vengley, Dorcas Wilcox. And two deaths so far—two deaths that I was certain of.

It didn't work. The vision of the yacht faded and the insistent names and puzzles and relationships took its place. If the high sacrifice occurred one year after Jerry's suicide, it would have been when Dorcas had just returned from working in the Sierras and Dwayne was about to graduate. She probably wasn't a part of that. Shelley said she didn't even know Dori was back in school. That meant she wasn't involved with Dwayne's group at that time. But Dwayne had kept in touch with her—the signature on the letter indicated that. And, once before, he had managed to pull her back after she left.

I drained the bottle and heaved out of the canvas deck chair to wander back inside. The soiled scrap of letter in its envelope of clear plastic, Dori's fascination with the power of crystals, implied that the girl was still searching for whatever spiritual enlightenment she might find. And that Dwayne was still offering his version of an answer. A Dwayne who, according to Shelley, was still very active, even a leader, in the Kabbal. Shirley. "Shirley was all twisted up about it at first . . . but she's into it now . . ." Did that refer to a ritual? To another

Kabbal somewhere else? Was Dwayne looking for a sacrifice? Another unborn slave-soul to send to Jerry Hawley on another anniversary of his death? It didn't sound like that—the Shirley mentioned seemed alive and participating in something ongoing.

The ring of the telephone interrupted my tangled thoughts; Detective Betts's voice said he was returning my call.

"Do you remember what Jerry Hawley's room was like?" I asked.

Betts thought a moment. "Like? You mean the location of windows and doors and all?"

"Not the floor plan, the decorations. Were there any candles around? Or graffiti?"

"You're thinking ritual suicide? Occult crime?"

"I've found out he was involved with a group that practiced Satanism." I gave the detective a short version of what Shelley had told me.

The man at the other end of the line grunted. "Well, now. That's interesting. He did have a few posters—weird things, you know: Day-Glo pictures of hell and fiery towers, pictures of naked women being tortured, that sort of thing. I thought at the time he might be into occultism, but there was no reason to follow up the idea; he was dead and it was definitely a suicide."

"Do you remember if he had any tattoos or ritual scars?"

"Not that I saw. And I don't remember any being noted on the autopsy report."

"Did you have any missing-persons reports come in one year after his death?"

"Why?"

I explained.

"A sacrifice? Jesus, no. I'll check the records, but I don't remember anything turning up like that. If it was a fetus, there probably wouldn't be any record anyway."

"Unless the mother died, too."

"Yeah, there's that. I'll check."

"Do you know of any Satanist groups in or around Occidental?"

"Not offhand. But I'd be surprised if there aren't some. We can't keep records on that kind of stuff—First Amendment restrictions. Devil worshipers find out we're spying on them, they get the ACLU all over us."

"Do you have an occult crimes section?"

"Person. But she's called in only if there's a crime. We have to be real careful about violating their civil rights, Mr. Steele. All police agencies do. That's why a lot of departments don't even want to hear about occult crime; and if something does go to court, the DA better not breathe a word about ritual or ceremony, or it's a First Amendment walk."

"Just focus on the criminal act itself?"

"You better believe it. Forget motive, just present the evidence."

I thanked the man. The detective said he'd give a call if a search of the missing-persons records showed anything happening on the anniversary of Hawley's death.

A rattle at the mail chute came as a welcome interruption to my restless wandering. I thumbed through the envelopes. Three were form letters from Sacramento—replies to my inquiries about Dorcas. She had not gotten married in the state, no death certificate in her name, no traffic violations. The last, from the Motor Vehicles Division, also listed her insurance company and coverage. But a call to that number told me she hadn't changed any address. In fact, the agent was a bit worried. "Do you think she moved out of state?"

"Not permanently. But she is missing."

"Her policy's paid up for the rest of the period. She made a lump-sum payment in April."

"And you have no recent claims on the policy?"

"No, sir. But if you hear from her and she's planning to move, would you ask her to drop us a line? Her payments might go down in a different state."

Or, more likely, up. "Will do."

A smaller envelope held a bill from Shell Oil which puzzled me until I reread the address: Dorcas Wilcox with my street address. It was from the check I'd sent a few days earlier. The company's computer had quickly updated her address from the cabin to mine. They weren't going to take a chance on a debtor moving beyond their reach. I spread out the small stack of receipts. Most were from Brown's Full Service in Julian. But two others were different. The dim purple carbon named gas stations in St. George, Utah, and Grand Junction, Colorado. The dates were after she'd disappeared.

The winter rains fell steadily outside the window; the heavy gray of the late, overcast afternoon made the room colder and gloomier. She watched the rain, one of those endless, persistent California drizzles, drip off the long, sad curve of eucalyptus leaves and down to the soggy lawns of the quadrangle. A pair of students, huddled under the glistening black of an umbrella, walked quickly toward the white box of the library. Japanese, probably; they liked that kind of umbrella and they were always first in line when the library opened Sunday afternoons.

She should go to the library, too. Goldman's term paper was due in another couple of weeks, and she still hadn't finished her first studio project. But it was hard even to think of going. It was hard to keep her mind on anything, really, and all this—the outside world, school, her studies and deadlines, they all seemed so unreal. More and more, the only life that had any meaning was what she found with them. It was as if she only really woke up when she was with them, and the rest of the time she sort of drowsed through the hours. Her father had noticed it over Christmas break, wondering why she was so irritable, why she spent so much time alone in her room, why she didn't do more of the things happy families were supposed to do at Christmas.

"Just leave her alone." Her mother's thick voice drew on her

nerves like a knife blade across a taut wire. "Leave her alone if she wants to be alone."

"Well, I'd like to see a little of her!" Her father's voice rumbled angrily down the hallway from the living room, accompanied by the jingle of holiday music on the stereo. "Goddamn it, it is Christmas, after all, and it's not only depressing, it's damned bad manners—my mother was very hurt when she wouldn't even come out of her room to say hello."

Her mother's voice muttered something that her father didn't bother answering. She heard the icy tinkle of a drink and then he snorted something. "Boy troubles. It's probably boy troubles. Be damned glad when she grows out of this stage."

It wasn't boy troubles and she didn't grow out of it. It was simply that she hadn't felt alive without them and she had been counting the days and hours before vacation was over and she would be back with them and away from the guilty memories held by this room, this house, by her mother's unfocused eyes.

Last night she had felt truly alive. A lot of it was a blur now, and hazy with fragmented memory and the frayed consciousness that had come with the Potion. Warmth and chanting. The glare of candles and fire. The pale glimmer of flesh as she gazed down between sweaty, taut breasts at the gold chalice resting on the flatness of a stomach. Then, her body had seemed distant and she could watch with eyes that belonged to someone else as if the altar was the flesh of another person. And when she was brought back to her body it was with the relief of timelessness— there was no future, especially no past. There was only what Dwayne had promised: the Now. Intense, all-encompassing, blissfully exclusive. The Now! Reborn into the Now by the close deliciousness of caressing hands that stroked her body with slowly increasing yearning and fervor, spread the gentle Oil of Anointment and, with soft persistence, touched the hot smoothness of her skin; dallying, edging closer, the dozens of hands, male and female and exciting not to know which was which, teasing themselves and her and focusing their hunger on her, surrendering her sense of self to them; she, the center of that energy, a goddess to fulfill the dreams that made them moan and writhe and twist out of their own robes to press their arms, their chests, their lips against her with more heated urgency until she again moved away from self to become their instrument and gasped and lifted spreading thighs with want, oiled breasts aching and mouth hungry to unite with the smooth, scented flesh that closed around her, lifting her and obliterating her on the surging thrust of communal yearning and fulfillment.

But with the gray sky and the chill rain, last night's memory seemed distant, and into that distance went the intensity and anonymity of being the center of others' desire. If the soreness in her groin was hers, so was the sated, turgid feeling that made the day seem cushioned and muffled. Last night, it had seemed to go on forever and she didn't want it to stop. But of course it had; all of them had finally slept until the thick, suety candles guttered out in that heavy odor of rotten sweetness they had. Jerry was right; like him, she had awakened to feel completely, totally at rest. Like a rock on the earth, he had said, with no burden, with no guilt, with no hungers. And it was true. She hadn't wanted to move, had no reason to move.

But the night had passed, and today she woke to the rain.

CHAPTER

Gliding from beneath the airplane's shiny aluminum wing, the wrinkled and thrusting earth lifted abruptly from the yellow and red and brown of desert. First shadowy valleys and then snow-gleamed faces of pale blue rock slid silently past. Dark pines patterned the massive slopes, ridges ran in every direction. Above timberline, the paler green of tundra looked soft and pristine against the snow. Cliffs of a thousand feet dropped sharply from the edges of sun-filled meadow, and fingerlike spires jabbed upward from the heads of snow-clogged canyons. Close enough to the airplane to reveal blue shadow and winking glitter, snowfields lay under the shelter of wind-scoured rocks.

I turned from a study of the achingly bright mountains below and began gathering up the plastic remnants of the flight meal. The stewardesses hurried the serving cart up the aisle, a final sweep before landing. A nasal squawk from the speakers told us that the temperature in Denver was seventy-two, and reminded passengers meeting connecting flights that they should proceed immediately to their boarding areas.

Henry had not hesitated when I telephoned to tell him about the gas receipts.

"Grand Junction? In Colorado?"

"My guess is she was heading for Kremmling. That's a small

town about a hundred and fifty miles west of Denver. But it's only a guess."

Henry remembered. "That's where she made that long-distance call to?"

"Right. But the number's been disconnected, and Colorado's a big state. Don't get your hopes up."

"Well, a place like Kremmling can't be that big a town, can it, Jack? Can you go there? Look around, see if she's there?"

"It's not much of a lead."

"But it's the only lead we have, isn't it? I'd go myself, Jack, but I can't right now. You know how upset Margaret's been—especially since you asked her all those questions. Look." He governed the impatience in his voice. "You know how important it is to have someone on the ground asking questions. I can't go. Period. I'm willing to pay you to do it—I want to pay you. You'd probably do a better job than I would anyway; it's not my line of work, after all. And if you can find out something, maybe Margaret can get a grip on herself . . ."

We both knew there was nothing keeping me in San Diego. But only I knew the urgency that would have sent me to Colorado even if Henry had not authorized the trip. "If I can locate her, what do you want me to tell her?"

Henry hadn't thought that far ahead. "I suppose find out if she's all right—if she needs anything. Money, whatever. And we'd like her to call us. If that's where she wants to be, fine. But tell her to at least call home and tell her mother she's all right."

If I found her. And if she—and her unborn child—were all right.

The car-rental agent drew a map of the quickest way from Denver to Kremmling: I-70 west to Dillon, north on State 9 to the town. Depending on the traffic, she added, figure about a three-hour drive. The interstate, a double band of concrete lanes, rose steadily from the shallow bowl of prairie that held Denver. Then it arced between faces of harshly blasted rock and up valleys into the cool pine forests of the Divide. Cross-continent traffic was heavy. A steady line of laboring semi trucks blocked the climbing lanes to the snowy Eisenhower Tunnels. But I made good time and enjoyed seeing a part of the country I hadn't viewed in years. Denver had been a frequent stop— to change planes, to attend seminars or conferences at one of the military installations along the Front Range. But there had been little time to get into the mountains that formed the western horizon. Now, despite the worry, I enjoyed the views of peaks with their green bases and white crowns against the clearest and bluest sky I'd ever seen.

The road north from the tinseled and tourist-filled town of Silverthorne followed the valley of the Blue River. Picnic areas and camping grounds were spotted with parked cars and brightly colored tents. All but the highest ski areas were closed this late in spring, and low on the mountains, the steep runs cut through dark pines were beginning to melt to bare rock or still-brown grass and mud. New billboards advertised mountain bicycle tours and scenic chairlifts. Dude-ranch signs showed that the coming summer would have its own attractions. Gradually, the major tourist centers fell behind as State 9 led north into high desert and a broad, treeless valley covered with knee-high sage-brush and sinuous ridges of wind-packed snow. Traffic lessened, too. Most of the tourists sped far over the fifty-five limit on their way up to Steamboat Springs or back to the fun and games of Summit County. Working ranches replaced dude ranches. Scattered and windshaken, small factory-built houses staked out a lonely bare patch here and there in the sagebrush and grimy snow.

A sudden burst of colorful sails and cold, wind-chopped water marked Green Mountain Reservoir. A scatter of summer cabins made tiny dots on the distant shore. On this side was a flicker of yellow, blue, and red tents, and the glitter of vans and cars. A few sailboards were pulled up on the stony beaches, and dust plumes from dirt bikes blew along unpaved service roads. Then the empty sagebrush stretched north to a distant rise glimmering with white snow. On the eastern side of the valley, sandy benches hid all but the peaks of distant mountains. On the west, the jagged Gore Range looked cold and isolate and windy.

It was hard to believe, after the shoulder-rubbing crowds of Southern California, that there was so much space with so few people. I felt a kind of psychic expansion—akin to the feeling that came on an empty sea—that stretched the boundaries of self and at the same time made me aware of isolation and smallness. If I were in search of some kind of spiritual knowledge, it could be found in the emptiness and vastness and silence of these jagged mountain faces. And, unlike the sea, one could drive or walk to it. I hoped that clean feeling was the reason Dori had come here.

The strip of asphalt turned away from the Blue River. It climbed a treeless ridge to slant down again to the Colorado River on the other side. Here, the stream was about a hundred yards wide and rimmed with willow and cottonwood breaking into leaf. Just across the bridge Kremmling was marked by a sign saying "Elevation 7,364 feet." In other states, the town limits announced population figures; in Colorado, it was elevation. Scattered homes and businesses, a lumberyard, leafless cottonwoods that towered over almost empty lanes. I followed the state highway around to its junction with the town's main street, U.S. 40. A gas station attendant told me that the sheriff's office was in Hot Sulphur Springs, the county seat, about twenty miles east on 40. I headed that way. At worst, I would lose a little time letting the sheriff know I was looking for someone. At best, I might get some help.

"Well, Mr. Steele, you know you don't have any jurisdiction in this county." The deputy was a head taller than me and weighed half as much. Narrow shoulders, only a little wider than the large red ears that stuck straight out from the side of his head, made rigid, square corners under his western-style shirt. But what he lacked in bulk he made up for in wiriness. And in the weight of official rules.

"I don't have jurisdiction anywhere—I'm not a law officer and I'm not a licensed PI. I'm just trying to help a friend locate his missing daughter."

"How come your friend's not doing it himself?"

"He's looking after his wife—the girl's mother. Her health isn't good, and the worry's made it worse." It was close enough to be true.

"But this missing daughter's over eighteen?"

Despite the risks of stirring up bureaucracy, I had hoped there would be more benefit than loss in going to the sheriff's office. Now I wasn't so sure. But just as the deputy could not arrest Dorcas without cause, so he couldn't stop me from looking for her. "She's free to go wherever she wants. I'm just trying to find out if she's all right or if she needs help. I don't even know if she's in this county."

"Let me get this straight, now—" He had been getting things straight for the last forty-five minutes. I kept the mask of a smile on my face as he went over it again. "This girl, Dorcas Wilcox, her father just wants to know if she's all right. And the reason you think she's in Grand County is you got a disconnected phone number?"

"And some gas receipts that indicate she was headed for Colorado."

"Uh-huh. And you want this office to help you locate this person."

"I'm asking if you've had any report on her or her car—the white Mustang with California plates."

"Get a lot of California plates coming through. Don't remember that vehicle, though." He propped a narrow cowboy boot on the edge of his desk. "I don't know that we can do much for you, Mr. Steele. There's no warrant out on this person."

"I realize that, Deputy. But I wonder if you could find out who might have had the telephone number. It's a Kremmling prefix."

"Covers a lot of territory."

"That's why I'm here asking."

"Uh-huh." He glanced again at me and apparently made up his mind about something. Picking up the telephone, he punched in a series of numbers. "Let me speak to Mr. Richardson, please." Covering the mouthpiece, he explained, "He's the phone company's district manager. I need his okay to find out about numbers." Then back to the telephone. "Mr. Richardson? This is Gary Norris over at the sheriff's office. I need to know the name on a telephone number . . . right—just a minute." To me: "Is this an unlisted number?"

"Not that I know of. Just disconnected."

"No, so we don't need a warrant. But it was disconnected a while back. I guess the name of the last person is what we need . . . thanks." To me: "He's giving me somebody." We waited a minute or two. "Yes, Miz Glover. How're you today? That's fine . . . Yes'm. Well, here's the number I need." He told her and we waited another couple of minutes. Then Norris leaned forward to write something. "Okay, thanks, ma'am . . . yes'm, you, too."

Norris pushed the slip of paper across the desk. "Gaylord Pettes. Disconnected four months ago from a cabin up on Black-tail Creek Road. Turnoff's about ten miles up One-thirty-four. Probably near Radium—most of that's National Forest in there, except down near Radium."

"Do you know if Pettes left a forwarding address with the phone company?"

The deputy clamped his mouth into a tight line, peeved either at me for wanting still more or at himself for not thinking to ask. He dialed again. "Miz Glover? Gary Norris again . . . yes'm. Did Pettes leave a forwarding address?" He wrote again. "Thanks again, ma'am." Another slip of paper. "Moved to Ward, over on the eastern slope in Boulder County. Here's that number and address."

I had to be certain. Pettes could have turned his cabin over to Dorcas without a telephone. Or she could be living there without permission. There was only one way to find out. The drive along dirt county roads took me in a loop between the steep and wooded peaks of the Gore Range and down into warmer valleys empty of everything except a few cows and an occasional camp van parked in the shade of a pine. The deputy said the address was located in Township One South and Range 82 West. On the map, the area was a square of public land crossed by the Colorado River. At its center a small cluster of black dots marked the town of Radium. The cabin had a fire-fighting number—A 207—but it took me the rest of the afternoon to finally locate it. A two-rut track branched off Blacktail Creek Road and twisted down a steep mountain face to the creek itself. The cabin, several rooms of rambling logs nestled under tall aspen, was empty and apparently had been since Pettes moved out. No other tire tracks marred the pine needles in the turn-around. A film of powdery dust coated the painted boards of the porch. The padlocks on the outbuildings were rusty with disuse. I'd made certain.

Bumping the growling car back up the track to the county road, I turned south. Rattling over the washboarded dirt for mile after country mile, I finally swung with a relieved sigh onto the pavement of Highway 131 at State Bridge on the Colorado River again. In another twenty or so miles I picked up I-70 and headed east toward Denver, a hundred long miles away.

I made it as far as Boulder before night and weariness forced me into a motel. Henry answered the telephone on the second ring and I told him what little I'd found out. He told me he'd never heard Dorcas mention a Gaylord Pettes.

"I'll start again in the morning," I said. "I've got an address for him."

"All right. Keep us informed, please."

And a jolly good evening to you, too, Henry. I stood under the hot shower and let it beat stiffness from my back. At least the scenery was pretty, though my neck and shoulders said I'd seen enough of it. Colorado was, indeed, a big state, made bigger by steep mountains and jolting, unpaved roads.

CHAPTER

The morning sun spotlighted what I had dimly seen last night as I crossed a ridge into Boulder Valley: an abrupt barrier of foothills and, rising from their wooded feet, massive slabs of tilted, gray-green rocks that jutted out like the petrified plates of some ancient animal. Notches between the foothills gave glimpses of higher peaks ten, twenty miles west, whitened with a coat of snow against that cloudless blue sky. The narrow highway running north and south where the prairie met the mountains was crowded with cars. But the empty, pine-scattered foothills and the level sweep of farm and pasture to the east emphasized space. There was a feeling of light and volume about the scene that Eleanor would have studied with a delighted eye. As I drove, I tried to imagine what kind of vision she would have found in this landscape.

Ward was about twenty miles west and up a winding canyon. The old mining town sprawled over a steep slope under the junction of State 72 and Lefthand Canyon Road. Most of its buildings clustered in the bottom of a gulch whose snow had only recently melted. A few others scattered up rock faces marked with yellow mine tailings and black and rotting timbers from a century past. A lot of dirt roads led off into the trees. None of them had names or numbers. Some of the homes were new or newly rebuilt. Most were sagging frame structures that had rooms tacked on as the inhabitants needed more space. A few were empty. Through glassless windows, the scraped rock of the building's hillside excavation could be seen out the other side. Many cabins had cold frames or window boxes to extend the growing season for vegetables, herbs, and possibly something to smoke. Long stacks of split wood gave further hint of the length of winter. I wasn't sure what the population was, but the elevation was 9,253 feet. It didn't seem to bother the occasional jogger or bicyclist cranking up the mountain. Porches and front doors were a step away from the single paved road, bringing a reminder of European villages built before the automobile. A single post with stop signs on two sides marked the town's center. I pulled my car into a gravelly space behind a two-story frame building that crowded the paved street and bore a sign: "Ward Store."

A yellow dog sniffed at my cuffs as I stepped across the wooden landing and creaked open the screen door. Some light came through the small windows at the front. A woman with long, straight hair and a flowered dress reminiscent of the sixties stood reading behind a modern cash register. When I didn't wander down the narrow aisle of snacks and canned food, she finally looked up. "Hi, help you out?"

I told her the road I was looking for and Pettes's name.

"Don't know him. But Gold Lake Road's just about a quarter mile north on Seventy-two. Right turn. Just have to look for the mailbox and then sort of drive around till you get the right cabin. Do you know the fire-fighting number?"

"No."

"Too bad. Every cabin's got a fire-fighting number on it now. That's the only address for a lot of them."

I showed the woman the picture of Dorcas. "Can you tell me if this girl's come in the store?"

She looked at me and then at the picture, tipping her head back to use the lower half of her glasses. "Pretty girl." She handed it back. "You a policeman or a federal agent?"

"Me? Neither—I'm just trying to help her folks find her. She's missing."

"Runaway? Well, this might be the one came into the store two, three weeks ago. I think it's her but she wasn't wearing glasses. I haven't seen her since." The woman added, "Doesn't mean she might not still be around. You know much about Ward?"

"First time here."

A nod. "You'll want to look less like a cop. We got a few folks around don't like cops—holdouts from the Vietnam War, ex-bikers and maybe not ex. And some who moved up here because they just don't like nobody. Got a topo?"

"A topographic map?"

She poked a thumb at a shelf holding a selection of local Geological Survey maps. "Yeah. They got the logging roads and buildings marked. Can't hardly find cabins without one." She smiled.

"How much?"

She told me and I bought a sheet as well as some bottled water and sandwich makings. Then I followed her directions up the steeply climbing road and past some more houses clinging to the side of the mountain. The state highway ran down a ridge above town toward Gold Lake road.

The turnoff was gouged between banks of yellow sand and shattered quartz. I bounced past occasional clusters of mailboxes and pine trees with arrow shaped signs bearing last names and pointing down two-rut trails. None of the names was Pettes. About three miles in, the road dead-ended at a private-property sign and a peek at the oval of Gold Lake. It was a pretty scene, but I wasn't in the mood for postcard landscapes. Frustrated, I started back, driving in low gear and studying the mailboxes in case I missed the name coming in. A slow mile down the road still dusty from my passage, I saw a row of ten or so mailboxes. On one, stenciled in fresh white paint, was a name that had caught my eye coming in: "Shining Spirit Lodge."

Maybe. I remembered that book mailer with the religious

symbol for a return address. And this was the only mailbox without a proper name. Tracks curved off among dark pines on each side of the road. Flipping a mental coin, I took the north side.

It wound through trunks and occasional deep puddles that jolted the steering and creaked the car's springs. Fortunately, most of the cabins had their owners' names on the drive or porch. None were marked "Shining Spirit Lodge." Most were closed and silent. Once in a while, the sun sparked off a parked car, but none were white Mustangs with California plates. Signs warned "Posted—Keep Out" and "No Trespassing." The track led from lot to lot and finally curved in a long, irregular loop back to the main road. I pulled across to the south track.

It took another forty-five minutes of creaking, rocking travel to follow this rutted trail to its end. There were fewer cabins along this route, but the names I found weren't the ones I looked for. Those without names were empty and waiting for the weekend or the week or two that their owners would come from wherever—Texas, maybe, or Kansas. Finally, a chain flagged by a couple of bright ribbons closed the road. On an aspen that held one end of the chain, a fresh sign said "Shining Spirit Lodge—No Trespassing."

A faint circle among thick aspen trunks showed where other cars had turned around to head out again. I swung into the loop and killed the engine. Standing beside the car, I drew in the thin, pine-scented air that still held a reminder of last night's chill. Somewhere in the stillness, a crow called; above, an airliner made a brief, hollow whisper as it headed to San Francisco or Seattle. To the west, barely showing above the green fringe of forest, tips of snowy peaks sawed at the horizon. Through a thinning of trees, I could look east, downslope, along a valley that led to a glimpse of level, yellow prairie. If someone wanted privacy, she could certainly find it here.

A squirrel chattered angrily at me from high up a pine. The only other sound was the tick of the cooling engine. I walked around the chain and followed the road as it curved down a slope to make its rocky way across a shallow stream. Then it angled up a steep hill. I found myself laboring against the altitude, and where the sun lay heavy on the road, a film of sweat covered my face. In shady stretches, the moisture quickly evaporated to leave a gritty crust on my skin. It may have been a mile, possibly less—a new road always seems longer—before I reached a level meadow filled with mountain flowers. The road cut through the bright green grass toward a large lodge that sat at the edge of the clearing. It was another postcard scene. The first level and the chimney were fieldstone; the second level, topped by a steeply pitched roof of wooden shingles, was log. A few small outbuildings were scattered about, including a barn and a corral holding a pair of sleepy, drooping horses. A pickup truck sat near the stair leading up to a wide porch that shaded three sides. Gleaming in the sun stood a new metal swing set with a slide that led down into a large tub of water. No one showed.

I waited in the shade beside the road, studying the buildings and grounds. From somewhere behind the barn a hammer began knocking. I headed toward the building as the sound built in final crescendo, driving a nail home. Then it started again with a couple of taps. I called a loud hello and the hammering stopped.

I called again. From around the barn came a stocky man wearing jeans and a stained T-shirt. His pale hair was covered by a hunter's orange cap. When he saw me, he stopped for a moment and then came slowly forward without speaking.

"Are you Mr. Pettes?"

"No. Who're you?"

I introduced myself. "Will Mr. Pettes be back soon?"

A thoughtful pause. "He comes and goes." The man, somewhere in his forties and deeply tanned from the high-altitude sun, scratched at his chest with a stubby hand, three middle fingers curled under, thumb and little finger spread. "What you want with him?"

I showed him the picture of Dorcas. "I'm looking for a missing girl. Have you seen her?"

The hand took the photograph and the man's brown eyes studied it, then me. "Ain't seen her."

From the lodge came a brief clatter of crockery. I glanced that way. "Can I ask the person inside?"

"She ain't seen her neither." The man stepped between me and the lodge.

"How do you know?"

"Because ain't nobody like that been around." He bobbed the brim of his cap at the road. "You walk in here? Leave your car at the gate?"

"Yes."

"Get in the truck—I'll give you a ride back." He handed me the photograph.

"When will Mr. Pettes be here?"

"That's up to him. We just look after the place."

"So he doesn't live here."

The man said nothing.

"Can you tell me where he does live?"

After a moment's hesitation, he shrugged. "Denver. At the Temple."

"Can you give me the address?"

He did. I wrote my home telephone number on the back of Dori's photograph and handed it back to the man. "If you see this girl, will you give me a call? Collect."

The man turned the picture and read. " 'Mr. Steele.' I reckon."

The truck fired up with a clatter of loose valves and swung around in the grit parking area. Looking back at the lodge, I saw a curtain over a window drop quickly.

At the chain, I thanked the caretaker for the ride. He grunted something and watched as I pulled away.

I reached Denver by mid-afternoon and spent another hour locating the address the caretaker had given me. The Temple of the Shining Spirit was a cluster of painted brick row houses on a busy street in Aurora, the sprawling city that abutted Denver on the east. Primarily residential, the area's corners had changed to commerce—7-Elevens, neighborhood restaurants, used-book stores, beauty shops. And the Temple of the Shining Spirit.

A small arrow said "Parking" and led up an alley to the back of the pale gray buildings. Half a dozen cars sat nose in against a mesh fence bearing a sign that said "Parking for Temple Visitors Only—Violators Will Be Towed." I was a visitor; I parked. The high fence surrounded a sandy playground behind the converted row houses. Clusters of children ran or sat or swung in the sun-glared space. Another sign said "Shining Spirit Day Care," and a woman in a long dress sat on a concrete bench and watched the kids, her leg swinging idly. I asked her which of the several back doors led to Mr. Pettes.

"Pastor Pettes," she corrected me. "The last one on the left." And with a smile, "Welcome to the Temple."

"Thank you."

The door opened to a back porch converted to a vestibule that held a scattering of chairs. Another door opened to a desk where the kitchen used to be. I rapped on the door frame and called "Hello?" A few moments later the slap of loose slippers echoed in the silence. A young woman, many months pregnant and also wearing a long, loose dress, waddled into the room from a hallway. "Hi." She panted slightly with the weight of her stomach. "Welcome to the Temple. What can we do for you?"

I told her.

"He's in conference right now. If you'd like to have a seat?" A gesture toward one of the chairs in the vestibule. I nodded.

From there I had a view of the desk and part of the wall. A banner using intertwined flowers for letters spelled "Shining Spirit." A batik hanging showed a figure seated in the lotus position. The aura of its spirit formed a surrounding flame in the shape of an aspen leaf. A small table in the waiting room held pamphlets with a variety of titles. I helped myself to a sample: "Life Is Worth Living," "The Way to True Happiness," "What the Shining Spirit Is." I had questions about all three topics. The building was quiet and I could hear an occasional squeal from the playground.

For no apparent reason, the pregnant woman heaved to her feet. "Pastor Pettes can see you now. You're Mr.—?"

"Steele."

"This way, Mr. Steele."

I followed her slightly rolling walk. Her hair, a long braid down her spine, made a thick rope. It swayed between shoulder blades and pressed the thin fabric of the print dress. We passed through a short hallway under stairs leading to the second floor. She knocked at the double doors of what used to be the living room. Then she opened one and stood aside.

The room was spartan. The wooden floor gleamed with wax and ran almost empty to the blank white plaster of the walls. A narrow scarlet runner led from the door to a blond oak desk. Behind it sat a heavyset man whose neck was clamped between two massive, sloping shoulders. He wore a loose white robe with wide sleeves, faintly Japanese, and a pair of rimless glasses whose thick lenses magnified his eyes so that the blue irises seemed to fill the upper half of his large head.

"Mr. Steele." His voice was almost a whisper, lips scarcely moving. Yet it carried clearly. "Sister Rhona, a chair please."

I heard the pregnant woman stifle a puff as she carried in a rattan chair. I quickly offered to take it from her but she smiled and shook her head and placed it on the runner squarely in front of the desk. Then she bowed and backed out.

"She wanted to demonstrate the strength of her faith over the weakness of her flesh, Mr. Steele."

"Looks like walking does that. She must be due any minute."

"Four weeks." The florid face smiled. "Welcome to the Temple and what may I do for you?"

I took a copy of Dorcas's picture from my vest pocket. "I'm looking for this girl. Dorcas Wilcox. Do you know where she is?"

The magnified eyes glanced at the photograph as if confirming something. Then he turned back to me. "Why do you think I would know?"

"She was receiving mail from the Temple of the Shining Spirit." That was a guess. But the Buddha and his aura could have been what the mail person saw on the book mailer. "And I've traced her as far as Colorado."

Pettes studied me. The weight of meaty lips pulled his mouth into a pout. It wasn't the face of an ascetic. "And why are you looking for her?"

"Her parents are worried about her. She disappeared without telling anyone where she was going, and they asked me to find out if she was all right."

The head sagged further down between its shoulders to rest on a bed of chins. The oversized eyes blinked shut and for a moment I wondered if the man had dropped asleep. Then they opened. "She is here in the Temple."

I hadn't expected that. Outright denial, perhaps. Evasion or feigned ignorance, more likely. But honesty was a nice policy to run across now and then. "Can I talk with her?"

"She is over twenty-one. It's her right to go wherever she wishes."

"I'm aware of that. And her parents told me to tell her that they won't press for her return. They only want to know that she's in good health and needs no help."

A slight lift at the corner of those lips. "And you won't take my word for that?"

I shrugged. "I've come this far. Why not the final step?"

"Why not, indeed." The man's heavy arm moved surprisingly fast to pinch a small silver bell between thick fingers. It tinkled shrilly and the door opened behind me. "Ask Sister Dori to come to me, please."

CHAPTER

We waited in silence. Pettes apparently didn't believe in small talk, and my mind was on Dorcas. The hum and swish of passing traffic was muffled by thick walls and heavy drapes half-closing the shut windows. A faint creak from overhead marked someone's passage. Every now and then another squeal came from the playground. Finally there was a quiet rap on the door and it opened.

Wearing the loose dress and with her hair pulled back into a short braid, Dorcas entered and bowed to Pettes. She kept her hands in a prayer position and eyes properly downcast in front of the heavyset man. "May the Shining Spirit be with you."

"And with you, Sister Dori. We're sorry to interrupt your meditation, but Mr. Steele has been sent by your parents to make certain you are happy and healthy." His voice made a slight joke out of it. Dorcas turned to me for the first time.

There was a lot of her mother in her face. I saw the older woman's lost beauty especially in the girl's eyes and cheekbones. Henry's contribution was a stronger jaw that made her face longer and more balanced. The puzzled, aching hope that the camera had captured in her gaze had been replaced by serenity.

"I met you a long time ago, Dori—you were ten, maybe twelve years old."

"I'm sorry—I don't remember."

"I'm not surprised. How are you?"

"I am at peace."

A heave of flesh and robe from behind the desk. "I'm sure you'd rather talk in private, Mr. Steele. And I have other things to see to. Please use the room as long as you like."

Dori bowed deeply as the large man stood. I nodded my head. I long ago decided, as the saying goes, to bow to no one but God. Pettes, despite his voice and manner, hadn't worked any miracles I'd seen. The Pastor, eyes large and bright behind their lenses, nodded back and disappeared through a door behind the desk. I offered my chair to Dori. She shook her head. "It's our custom to stand in his presence."

"He's not here."

"But his presence is. It's everywhere his thoughts have been."

"You must spend a lot of time on your feet." I guessed the presence was enhanced by a tape recorder and microphone hidden in the filigreed bud vase on the desk. "Your father and mother are worried, Dori. They were afraid something had happened to you."

The smile of serenity she kept on her full lips tightened a bit. "I am in charge of my own destiny, Mr. Steele. They don't have any right, moral or legal, to make me do what I don't want to do."

"Of course not—you're legally emancipated. But when they hadn't heard from you and they didn't know where you were, they got worried. I'd worry about my own daughters."

Her head tilted a degree or two. "I was planning to write. But I haven't had time—the days go by so fast. But I was planning to write."

Shoes squeaking on the polished wood, I went over to the curtained window. Folding back the heavy maroon cloth, I looked out at the automobiles flickering past. "I can tell them you're happy here?"

"Of course!" Her smile, unforced now, reached her blue eyes, and there was no denying the pleasure that radiated from her. "These people are like family—better than family. There's none of the . . . the past that keeps hanging on and making everything so tense."

I raised the sash. The steady traffic noise filled the room. Then I leaned against the wall beside the window and beckoned her closer. "Has your mother been an alcoholic for a long time?"

The smile left her eyes and she nodded. "As long as I can remember. Dad pretends she isn't but she is."

"Since before or after David Gates's death?"

The question was like a slap and the young woman stiffened, poised on the edge of something. I wasn't sure if she was going to stay or run. When she finally spoke, it was after a long, tense stillness. "Before. Since I was a child. Then it got much worse." But her mind wasn't on her mother.

"What can you tell me about that, Dori?"

"He—it was an accident."

"You told your mother it was a sacrifice. And that you were responsible."

She didn't answer. Any animation that had brightened her face was gone now. "I thought you were looking for me. I thought Mom and Dad wanted you to find out if I was all right."

"That's true. But David Gates is part of it, isn't he?" I kept my voice beneath the background clatter of the cars and occasional motorcycle. If the room was bugged, the noise should bury our words. "Where's Dwayne?"

"He went back."

"To San Diego?"

She nodded.

"Is he coming back here?"

She nodded again.

"What did he have to do with David's death?"

"Please . . . that's over—it's over and we've found peace. Please!"

"You and Dwayne have found peace?"

"Yes! That's what's so wonderful about the Temple. About Pastor Pettes . . . this place is a refuge, a sanctuary. Everyone here had burdens, that's why they came. Now the burdens are no more!"

But David Gates was nonetheless dead, and the statute of limitations on murder never ran out. Even in California. I studied the girl for a long moment, unsure of the kind of person I looked at. Her mother had called her "delicate," and psychic bruises still lurked deep in the girl's eyes. But now she claimed to have found some kind of peace, some kind of denial or walling off of the past. "What about Jerry Hawley's suicide? What did Dwayne have to do with that?"

Her fingers twisted against themselves as she pressed her hands to her stomach. "I don't know."

"He helped Jerry decide, didn't he?"

"I don't know!"

"Dorcas, are you pregnant?"

"I'm Dori, not Dorcas! Please—I don't want to talk to you anymore. Leave me alone!"

"Wait—just a minute. Hold it, Dori. Please don't leave."

"You're upsetting me!" She closed her eyes and took several deep breaths, each a little longer and slower. "You're violating the balance."

"Take your time." I spoke to her as if talking to a frightened colt or a mind that teetered. "Take your time—easy, now. I'm not going to hurt you, Dori, or make you come back." I waited until she was back in control. "Dwayne told you he wanted to leave the Kabbal, is that it? That he wanted to get rid of his burden, too?"

Eyes closed and head tilted back, she nodded.

"And you believe him?"

She kept her eyes closed but there was no doubt in her voice. "Yes."

"He's the father of your baby?"

". . . Yes . . ."

"And the baby is your bond? Your commitment to each other?"

She nodded, the tension coming back in the taut cords of her neck.

I changed tack. "Did you visit the lodge near Ward?"

Her eyes opened, puzzled. "You know about that, too?"

"It's a nice place. Peaceful."

The smile of serenity came back. "Yes."

"Did you stay there long?"

"Just overnight. But Dwayne said—" She stopped abruptly, cautious.

"Dwayne said you could come back sometime?"

"Yes." She added, "I've always loved the mountains."

"That was where Dwayne told you to meet him? Where you drove to meet him?"

"Yes."

"What was he doing there?"

"Seeking. Like me. Like all of us, even you. Whether you know it or not."

I knew it. And now I had a pretty good idea what for. "He told you that Pettes and the Temple released him from his burden?"

"Pastor Pettes. Yes."

"Who's Shirley?"

Dori looked puzzled. "Shirley?"

"The girl Dwayne mentioned in his letter."

"His letter?" She frowned. "Oh, you found it in my cabin?"

"Yes. Looking for you."

"It's Shirley Graham—we went to Oxy together. She joined the Temple and moved up to the lodge before I came here. I haven't seen her yet."

"She's one of the caretakers up there?"

"Caretakers? Oh, you mean Sam and Darlene. No . . ." She halted and put two fingers to her mouth. "I said the word."

"What word?"

" 'No.' The Pastor wants us to think of all the times we say 'no.' All the times we deny ourselves and others and the world by saying 'no.' " She wagged her head. "I never realized before how much I was keeping from myself with that word."

"Shirley's not a caretaker?"

"She's a seeker, too. But she got to move up to the lodge—she was chosen to go on retreat."

I thought that over. "You didn't see her when you were up there with Dwayne?"

"No. She was on a trip. Back East to see her folks."

"Dwayne told you so?"

"Yes."

"Why do you trust Dwayne so much, Dori?"

"We've been . . . we've seen a lot together. We've shared things . . ."

"And you're sure he's no longer a Satanist?"

"Yes. He told me and I believe him. He has things—we both have things we need forgiveness for. We're both seeking . . . balance." She added in a rush, "We've both found the Shining Spirit!"

I tried to catch a hint of falsity in expression or voice, but there was none. Knowing what the answer would be, I tried anyway. "Will you come back with me?"

"You said—"

"It's just a question, Dori."

Her head gave a determined shake. "I'm happy here. For the first time in my life, I've found a place where I feel totally at rest. These people are my family now. My spiritual sisters and brothers. My spiritual family."

"And you don't intend to see your parents again?"

"Oh, yes! Of course I do. But I want to . . . to anchor myself first. I want to fill my soul with the peace and lightness and joy that the Temple holds." A gentle smile as her hands went unconsciously to her stomach. "Please tell Mom and Dad that I'm truly, truly happy. I'll call them—not right away; I don't want to start a hassle—it's too soon. I know exactly what my father would say if I called. But I will write."

"Can I tell them you're pregnant?"

Hesitantly she finally shrugged. "I don't want them to come see me. My baby—our baby—is a sacrament."

"A bond with Dwayne."

"Yes. A bond."

"I'll tell them."

She bowed over prayerful hands. "Good-bye, Mr. Steele. May the Shining Spirit bless you."

CHAPTER

I was certain Pettes had known who I was before I introduced myself. I couldn't imagine that Sam the caretaker hadn't telephoned from the lodge after escorting me off the ranch. Possibly Dorcas had been warned and rehearsed in what to say, too, though I was less certain of that. The catch phrases she spouted were shared by the group, and while she might evade, she didn't seem to be lying. Though I didn't know Dorcas well enough to be sure about that, I wanted to believe it. What I was surer of was Dwayne Vengley's hypocrisy. But what he was doing it for, I could only guess. And I didn't like what I guessed.

The question wasn't whether evil existed—we quickly discover it in others. The more honest discover it in themselves as well, and gain respect for its subtlety and persistence. But with Dorcas and especially with Vengley, the real question concerned its self-directed malignancy. It was an aspect which, like many, I admitted as possible but had a hard time believing in. I preferred to define evil as an absence: an absence of reason, an absence of empathy for others, of the Golden Rule. An absence, even, of self-respect. But just suppose that, rather than being the causes of evil, those absences were manifestations of an active force? What if that force did not merely fill voids but consciously assaulted the good? What if, rather than being self-deluded victims of empty magical formulae, the cult members did share the literal spirit of Satan—or, collectively, created that spirit?

The steady downward glide of the airplane made me yawn to relieve the pressure on my ears. Restless passengers craned toward the windows with the knowledge that they would be landing soon. I had telephoned the admiral and Margaret after leaving the Temple, telling them I'd located Dorcas and she seemed well and happy. The admiral didn't say much, but I heard relief in his voice as he told me he'd be eager to hear about it in detail. Margaret, voice only slightly slurred this early in the day, was ecstatic and said she would call Henry at work and give him the good news. She had a lot of questions, she said, but they could wait until I got back to San Diego.

I had questions, too, but I wasn't certain I would share them with anyone. Given the probability that Dwayne had lied to Dorcas, the obvious reason was to get her to the Temple. Why? Was the fetus to be used in the kind of sacrifice Lieutenant Broadbeck had told me about? The place seemed to be a home for pregnant women. Sister Rhona was almost at full term and it didn't seem possible they would abort a baby that close to delivery. But what if it were so? What if such sickening things were really happening? How to prove it? How to convince Dorcas of the danger she was in? How to stop it?

And what did I do about the Gates death? Easy enough to let it pass. Everyone, including the boy's mother, was satisfied he had died in an accident. Reexamining it would stir up tremendous pain for a lot of people, and accomplish what? The reassertion of an abstract sense of justice? That abstraction had value—I'd served and suffered for it and believed in it. But would the truth lead to justice? If so, what kind? And would it be worth the cost to those already victimized once?

Those and other questions made me as anxious as the rest of the passengers. But my anxiety wasn't resolved when the plane landed. It remained as I cleared the traffic around the airport and headed over the neck of Point Loma for La Jolla.

Nor did it go after telling Henry and Margaret about Dorcas and the Temple.

"Well," Henry walked me to the door, "the admiral said if anybody could find her, you could do it. I guess he was right." The man straightened a bit to look me in the eyes. "I want you to know I'm grateful, Jack. So is Margaret. You'll be sure to send me a list of the expenses and any additional costs you may have incurred?"

Behind us, Margaret stared at the lights of the swimming pool. Despite the sadness in her eyes, I had seen relief, too. Her daughter was alive. Even if she was still trying to find something that Margaret had been unable to provide, even if the emptiness that had been her own had been shifted over to her daughter and driven her to this . . . this cult called the Temple of whatever. At least she was alive. I had said her daughter was happy, too. Mixed news, that. Margaret's expression, loosened by the celebratory drinks, showed a conflict between joy at learning of her daughter's contentment and sadness and even resentment that the happiness was something Margaret had been unable to provide.

"There's a little more, Henry. I didn't want to say it in front of Margaret. Dorcas is pregnant."

"What? For God's sake . . . ! Well, she'll have to come home. That's all there is to it."

"She wants to stay, Henry."

"That's irrelevant! She's been brainwashed by those damned drum thumpers!" He sagged against the doorway. "How far along is she? Will she consider an abortion?"

"She wants to keep the child."

"She's too goddamned young to know what that means—"

"And she doesn't want to come back. Not right now, anyway."

His breath hissed through pinched nostrils. "Who's the father? Did she say who the goddamn father is?"

"Dwayne Vengley."

"Dwayne?" He blinked. "I thought she wasn't seeing him

anymore! Is he in this Temple thing? What about marriage? How in the hell—"

"I don't think they're getting married soon. But Dorcas sees the child as a bond between her and Dwayne and the Temple."

"A bond—Jesus, it's a bond all right. A hell of a lot more bond than that young lady realizes. It's goddamned obvious she's playing house and doesn't know what the hell she's doing!" He pushed away from the bricks. "But by God there are people . . . I've heard of people who—what do they call it?—deprogram. There are people who can take her whether she wants to leave or not."

"That's called kidnapping."

"What did Dwayne Vengley and those Temple people do? What did they do if it's not kidnapping?"

"Apparently invited her to visit, which she did of her own free will. And now she wants to stay." I let that sink in. "I suspect Dorcas doesn't leave the Temple very often, and then only when she's accompanied by others. And even if you did manage to kidnap her, my guess is she'd head right back to them at the first opportunity."

"Well what the hell am I supposed to do? What the hell do I tell Margaret?"

"You know better than I do how much you can tell her. As far as what you do, I'm not sure. Dorcas is an adult and she has a legal right to live her own life."

"Ruin it, you mean!"

That, too, but there was no sense saying it. "I asked you earlier about Dorcas and David Gates."

"What's that got to do with all this?"

"That's why she's at the Temple. She feels guilty about it. And she thinks Vengley feels guilty, too."

The man studied my face. "What are you trying to say, Steele?"

"It's possible that she and Vengley and the other girls were dabbling in the occult and that they killed Gates for a sacrifice."

"No!"

"That's what she believes. And if it is true, she could face a murder charge."

Henry groaned and pressed the back of his head against the wall. "If that did happen—and I don't believe it for one instant—but if it did, it wasn't her fault—she'd never even think of a thing like that!"

"If she didn't, perhaps Vengley did."

"Oh . . . oh, I see. Oh, shit." He stared away into the darkness where a distant, closed car passed on a quiet street. "Steele, I know I haven't been the kind of father I should have been. Sometimes at night, I've thanked God I only had one child to screw up." His hand wagged vaguely. "There have been reasons—it's not all my fault alone. But I've made enough mistakes. And there's no going back, is there? It's too late to do things over, isn't it?"

I said nothing; Henry had said it all.

"Is there any way we can convince her to come home?"

"I don't know. And if she does, she may have to find some way to compensate for the Gates thing."

"Well, we'll have to cross that bridge when we get there. If what you say is possible—if Dori believes it, anyway—Vengley's the last one she should be with. She needs our help, Steele." He paused at the doorway before going in. "By God, I'll see what I can find out about deprogrammers, too!"

I swung by the Combses' house after leaving Henry and made my report to the admiral. I also added my suspicions about Vengley and about satanic sacrifices.

"Jack." Jenny clutched her coffee cup with both hands and their quiver could be seen from where I sat across the room. "We have to get her out of there!"

"What about the police, Jack? We can ask them to raid that damned temple."

"Not without a warrant, admiral. So far there's no evidence of a crime, so no cause for a warrant."

"But they're goddamned Satanists—devil worshipers!"

"Protected by the First Amendment."

"Bullshit!"

"Dalton, listen to what Jack's telling us."

"The Denver police might be interested in the Temple. They might even poke around a little if the San Diego PD asks them to. But they can't do anything without evidence of criminal activity, admiral. Even devil worshipers have civil rights, provided they don't violate the law."

"Then what can we do, Jack?"

"I think the key is Vengley. If we prove to Dorcas that he lied to her about leaving the Satanists, I think she'll come home on her own."

Jenny spoke again. "But she's in danger—the baby . . ."

"Jack, we have to get the girl out of there as soon as possible. Even if this Pastor Pettes isn't a Satanist, you're right about Vengley—he lied to Dori. We may not know why, but we all feel it's wrong for her to trust the boy. We've got to find out what's going on, and she's got to be protected."

Everyone was stealing my lines. By the time I pulled into my garage, I hadn't come up with anything original in answer to the urgency of the situation. The only plan, if it could be called that, had to do with Vengley. But without police authority, I had no leverage—no threat of arrest, no promise of a deal—to coerce his friends into telling me where he was or what he was up to. The most likely informant was Shelley Aguirre. Yet even she had finally refused to answer any more questions. And it was possible she wasn't high enough in the Kabbal's organization to tell me what I had to know to convince Dorcas. If I pressed anyone too hard, Vengley might move again, taking Dorcas with him. But this time there would be no paper trail because they wouldn't make the same mistakes.

Preoccupied, I closed the garage door and went through the small kitchen, half-aware of the house's silence. The red light on the recorder blinked "message received." The playback only gave me silence as whoever called listened for a few seconds and then hung up. The blank spaces were repeated a dozen times. I figured anyone that eager to get in touch would call again soon. Upstairs in the master bedroom, I tossed my clothes bag on the bed and began to unpack. I had almost emptied the cloth suitcase when the reading lamp on the nightstand beside the bed tugged at my attention. I paused, studying it. The arm was tilted much farther down than when I had left. Its angle to the bed was changed, an angle I'd fussed over to get just right so that when I lay propped against the pillows, it avoided the page's glare yet didn't cast the shadow of my hand and pencil across the print. Stepping back, I surveyed the room and its tiny misalignments. One of Eleanor's paintings on the wall was at a slight but irritating tilt. The drawers of the dresser were unevenly closed. They were things that—in isolation—wouldn't be noticed. But when a person lived alone, the things in a room tended to stay at rest. And when they didn't it meant the rest-lessness of hurried, searching hands.

The two guest bedrooms showed less—an empty closet door hanging open in the unfurnished room, a wrinkled bedspread on the unmade mattress of the furnished room. Downstairs, I found a sign in the teakettle left on the cold burner with a splash of water in it. Apparently the intruder felt at home enough to have a cup of coffee while he searched. My habit was to empty the kettle of water and let it dry during the day; San Diego water tasted heavily of chemicals when it got stale. In the living room, the books sat in irregular lines as if someone had taken them out three and four at a time to look behind and then quickly shoved them back. The drawers of my desk, too, had been rifled. I had never been the most well-organized desk pilot, but I knew what was in the scattered piles of papers, maps, correspondence, and catalogues that littered its surface. Relying less on files than memory, I could find things when I needed them. But whoever went through my desk didn't know that. To them the piles were random and it was here that I saw the clearest evidence of a very thorough search.

But I could find nothing missing. A burglar would have stolen my television and stereo system, both portable because of my itinerant life. They weren't worth a lot, but they were quick to take and easy to sell. Spare checks would be taken, possibly, or the row of sterling silver shooting awards, to be melted into ingots. Certainly the pistols and target rifles. Their padlocked rack wouldn't keep out a determined thief who had the luxury of a little noise. So they were after something else.

A couple of possibilities: someone from the past who thought I was still in the game—that my "retirement" was faked or even that I had kept documents which might prove embarrassing to the agency or to someone still in Washington. That was the least likely; I had cleared my files and been checked through a very tight security. Moreover, the people with those kinds of suspicions knew no one would keep sensitive material where it could be easily found and burned. It could have been someone worried by my questions about David Gates's death. A possibility, but I didn't think I had frightened anyone that much, certainly not Kimberly Goddard and her lawyer husband. The only way that case could be reopened was with a confession from someone who had been there. That left Vengley and company. They might want to know how much I had learned about them or why I was asking. But my reason was Dorcas, and that they already knew. How much I'd found out about them was another issue, however. And what they had to hide was exactly the thing I was after.

I finished my survey of the rooms, the initial shock of anger subsiding into a feeling of violation and uncleanliness. Straightening the things that had been disturbed, I thoroughly rinsed out the teakettle and then surveyed the windows and doors for the point of entry. It was a ground-level window off the back deck: a pane of glass knocked out, the latch open. I thought I had left behind the old need for caution—the knowledge that no place was secure, that any door and every drawer could be opened. Now it was with me again, and I felt myself slip easily into the familiar habits of security as I looked at the doors and windows with new eyes and scanned the Yellow Pages for a glazier.

I made that call and then pulled my mail from the letter drop. Mostly people wanting to sell something to New Homeowner, but also the welcome handwriting of Karen. It was a hurried and chatty note that only a proud father would find interest in. I read the cramped pages twice, smiling at the understated, wry presentation of what were really notable accomplishments for a fledgling lawyer. Karen hoped I was enjoying both retirement and the new house. She and Chuck had been studying calendars and schedules to see how soon they would be able to come down and take advantage of a home on the water. She had received a post card from Rebecca sent from Lisbon, so it looked as if she made the Portugal trip. Said she would be back in Bordeaux on the fourteenth. Which, I noted, was today— yesterday, European time. Rebecca should have the letters now about my retirement and move. That explained the long silence from that young lady.

Other than that and a few other gossipy items, there was little new, according to Karen, and she had to rush to a meeting. I was to remember that there was such a thing as a telephone, and they'd be delighted to hear from me whenever I had time to call. Love . . . P.S.—why not think of coming up to Sacramento for a visit? Now that I was retired, I should have enough time to do the things I'd been talking of doing. Love.

I tucked the letter back into its envelope and gazed at the afternoon light glaring on the distant shore of the bay. What, I should write and tell Karen I was too busy hunting Satanists to make it to Sacramento right now? That I first wanted to find out who had broken into my new home? None of the above. I'd cite the refrain I always used: as soon as things settled down enough to allow me a few days free. It wasn't that I didn't want to see them—God knows I did. But I would feel like an intruder. Karen would go out of her way to make my visit happy and fun and busy. She'd give me time that she could ill afford to lose, and their routines would be totally destroyed. No, best if I waited until they could come down here on vacation when their routines and schedules would be upset anyway.

The telephone clattered and I flipped off the recorder as I answered.

"This is Detective Finch, SDPD. I wonder if I can come over and talk with you, Mr. Steele?"

"Sure. What about?"

"I'll explain when I get there."

He verified my address and asked a couple of questions about directions, then said it would take about forty-five minutes for him to arrive.

Finch didn't look like his name. Instead he was a heavyset man with a large, fleshy nose that looked almost purple from broken blood vessels.

"Can you tell me where you've been the last few days, Mr. Steele?"

"Colorado. Why?"

The man, solidly filling the chair as he rested a notebook on a crossed knee, ignored the question. "Doing what?"

"Looking for a missing girl."

The face turned quickly from the notebook. "You a rent-a-cop?"

"No. Just helping a friend."

Finch used his little finger to scratch at something just inside one nostril. "Want to tell me about that?"

I did. Enough, anyway. "Why all the questions, officer?"

"Want to give me this Henry Wilcox's address?"

I did.

"And you found this Dorcas Wilcox?"

"That's right."

"You got an address where she can be reached?"

"Do you mean can I prove I was in Colorado the last couple days?"

Finch nodded, lips stretched pleasantly and pale eyes studying me without expression.

"She's staying at the Temple of the Shining Spirit in Aurora, Colorado, on Fourteenth Avenue. I have my airplane ticket upstairs, if you want me to get it."

"Airline and flight?"

I told him and he made another note.

"You know a woman named Shelley Aguirre?"

"I've talked to her a couple times. She's a friend of Dorcas Wilcox. Has something happened to her?"

"Why'd you ask that?"

"You're here asking about her. It's pretty evident something's happened, isn't it?"

"Evident. Yeah." Finch scratched again as he gazed at me. "When's the last time you talked to her?"

"Three days ago. I went by her workplace and took her out to lunch. I hoped she could give me a lead to Dorcas."

"Did she?"

"Not directly, no. Just some background information on some of Dorcas's friends." I added, "She's involved in a cult of some kind. I had the feeling she was afraid to tell me too much about it."

"A cult?"

"Satanism, I think."

"I see." Finch's ballpoint pen made a brief scratch. "She's not involved in anything now, Mr. Steele. She's a homicide victim." He waited for my reaction.

The suspicion had already crossed my mind. Finch wouldn't be here unless it was something serious. But still it came with a sense of loss: she was someone I knew and now she was no more. "I'm sorry to hear that."

"You think one of these Satanists might have killed her?"

"I don't know. I'm just telling you what she told me." I asked, "When was she killed?"

"Sometime yesterday."

"How?"

"Stabbed. It could have been a burglar in her apartment, but we're looking at all the leads." For the first time, Finch smiled, folding his lips back to reveal widely spaced teeth that looked small and oddly dainty in his heavy mouth. "You're a lead. Her boss at work said you came and talked to her twice."

"I was a lead. If she was killed yesterday, I was in Colorado."

"Yeah." Finch's smile went away as he folded his notebook. "Okay, Mr. Steele. Thanks for your help."

I watched the homicide detective plod heavily down the short walk to his plain gray sedan. Swerving a sharp U-turn in the dead-end street, the car pulled away into darkness.

I wasn't surprised that the officer didn't ask more questions. I was a lead, not a suspect, and I had a good alibi. There was only so much time to spend on leads that went nowhere. But I also knew that Shelley had been afraid to tell me much about the Kabbal. Quite possibly she had been worried that she'd already said more than she should. But I could think of nothing she mentioned that would lead to her death. The cult members might not want publicity, but as I'd told the admiral, there was nothing illegal in being a devil worshiper and no reason to kill anyone who admitted to such a belief.

I rummaged in the refrigerator for something to thaw for supper, boiling up a pot of rice to go with whatever I dragged out. It took until halfway through the meal to decide, and even then I felt slightly foolish calling Shaughnessy. In fact, I was relieved that the officer wasn't on duty. Still, I left name and number and said it might have something to do with the Shelley Aguirre homicide. Please call.

CHAPTER

21

The call from Shaughnessy came the next morning when I was out running. Wiping sweat from my face, I telephoned back and was told the detective was in conference. By the time Shaughnessy called again, I'd finished breakfast and was trying to figure a way to deliver on my suggestion that Vengley could be the key to getting Dorcas back.

"You say you got something on the Aguirre case, Mr. Steele?"

"I said I might have something. Detective Finch interviewed me last night and I told him that Shelley was involved in a Satanist cult. He didn't seem too excited at the idea."

The phone was silent. "But you think something's there?"

"She was very hesitant to talk to me about the cult or the people in it. I think she was afraid of saying too much. But I don't know why she should. As you said, it's no crime to be a Satanist."

"Why did Finch interview you?"

I told him about questioning Aguirre and went into greater detail about my trip to Colorado. "Nothing in the Temple suggested Satanism. But for some reason Vengley lied to Dorcas to get her to the Temple."

"That's pretty slim."

"While I was in Colorado, someone broke into my house and searched it. I don't know who, or what they were after. I can't find anything missing."

"But you think it has to do with your search for the Wilcox girl?"

"Maybe it's coincidence, maybe not. But whoever broke in knew I wouldn't be coming home soon—they took time to do a long and careful job."

Shaughnessy hesitated. "The Aguirre case isn't mine, but let me do a little asking around. You going to be at this number for a while?"

"Yes."

It was several hours before Shaughnessy called again. "Can you come over to the police department?"

I could and did. The block-sized building had dark glass angled at a conventionally modern tilt, and its white concrete pillars gave the lower level an open and utilitarian appearance. The sergeant at the counter took my name and phoned upstairs for the detective. In a few minutes, Shaughnessy stepped out of the elevators and through the security gate.

"I got the okay to visit the crime scene—lab people are through with it, and they're ready to turn it back to the landlord, so no problem."

"And you want me to look at it?"

He nodded. "Finch is convinced it's a burglar killing—place was torn up by somebody looking for goodies, and he figures Aguirre came home at the wrong time." He led me to another bank of elevators that carried us into the parking garage under one wing of the building. "He doesn't buy the cult killing idea." There was no bitterness in Shaughnessy's voice, just stating a fact. As he had told me before, cult and ritual killings were foreign ideas to a lot of cops.

We said little on the way to Aguirre's apartment. Shaughnessy asked a few more questions about Dorcas and the Temple. That gave me the opening I'd waited for and I asked for help in locating Dwayne Vengley.

"What you want him for?"

"If I can show Dorcas he's still involved in Satanism, she might quit the Temple and come home."

"I'll see what I can do."

We turned off 94 onto the Dekema Freeway south, then into a tangle of side streets that led into the dry, brown arroyo of Paradise Hills. The apartment complex was a modest frame horseshoe, two stories high and built around the inevitable swimming pool and patio. Aguirre's rooms were on the second floor away from the patio. The door opened to a covered breeze-way. An orange warning was pasted at eye level. Shaughnessy worked the combination to the key-safe that dangled from the doorknob and then unlocked the door.

We stood in the stuffy, ripe air and surveyed the room. A chalk outline on the short nap of green carpet showed the girl's body. The source of the smell was a small but deep stain dried into a brown crust. From the small writing table that filled a far wall, papers lay scattered. The screen of the dark television set reflected tossed cushions from the sofa. An upturned waste-basket had spewed its litter. "Somebody was sure as hell searching for something," said Shaughnessy.

"Or trying to seem like a burglar. Can I look around?"

"That's why you're here."

I wandered through the several rooms. Living/dining, kitchenette separated by a breakfast shelf, bath, bedroom. Someone had looked in every conceivable place. Even the toilet tank lid was ajar and the medicine cabinet's contents tumbled into the sink.

"Did the autopsy show she was a user?"

"Why?"

I pointed to the toilet. "Looks like someone was searching for a stash."

Shaughnessy glanced at me and nodded. "The autopsy report's not available yet. I'll check when we get back."

The closet, too, had been ransacked. Clothes dangled from hangers and littered the cramped floor. I picked through dresses and blouses. Then, suddenly aware, I started going through the apartment again, this time with a sense of purpose.

Shaughnessy watched silently.

"It's not what is here," I told him. "It's what's not."

"Like what?"

"A ceremonial robe. Books on Satanism. Candles. There's not one thing to indicate she ever belonged to a cult."

The policeman looked around. "Not even a pentagram or an upside-down crucifix. You're right." He asked, "She admitted she was a Satanist?"

"Was proud of it. She even implied that LaVey and his people weren't true Satanists. Dabblers, she called them."

"Jesus."

I began another circuit. This time I sifted through the papers around the desk and the drawers of the nightstand by the bed. On the wall of the living room, I found what I was looking for: a rectangle of slightly paler wallpaper. "Something else not here: photographs of her boyfriend." I pointed to the small hole that had held a picture hanger of some kind.

Shaughnessy stared at the rectangle. "What boyfriend?"

"One Steven Glover. They went to college together and apparently have been dating since. She said he was in the Kabbal, too."

Shaughnessy jotted down the name. Then he looked at me again. "What kind of work you say you're in?"

"I'm retired."

"Military?" When I nodded, he said, "Yeah. You don't look old enough to be a retired civilian. What'd you do in the military?"

"Mostly intelligence operations."

"Ah." That explained a few things.

We spent another half hour poking around and then headed back downtown. At headquarters, the detective asked me if I wanted to wait in the lobby a few minutes while he checked to see if the autopsy was filed yet. When he came back, he shrugged. "The killing doesn't look like a ritual. One stab wound under the ribs and up into the heart. No other wounds, no defense marks."

"Did the blade have the flat sides to the ribs?"

"Yeah."

"And the tip was moved inside?"

Shaughnessy, eyes hooded, nodded.

"So someone knew what they were doing."

"And walked right up to her without a struggle."

Which didn't sound like a burglar. "Any evidence of dope?"

"Nothing recent. There was a little marijuana trace, a few days old, but nothing heavier."

I asked, "Do you go along with Finch? That it was a burglar?"

The detective took a moment before replying. "Evidence is what's there. Not what isn't."

I agreed. "Still, it's odd. Nothing tying her to the Kabbal, no pictures of her boyfriend. No old letters, no address book. Nothing that shows she had a personal life. It's odd."

"Yeah. But it's also not my case."

We both knew there were ways of working around that.

Shaughnessy cleared his throat. "I transferred into the department four years ago as a sergeant. Finch has been in the department twelve years. He just made sergeant last February."

I understood what the detective was saying. More, I realized he was breaching the line that separated cops from civilians, a line that usually enclosed and hid family squabbles from the eyes of outsiders. "He'd be upset if you nosed around his case."

"He'd pop a gasket. And if I mention Satanism, he'll scream burglary all the louder."

"There's no law prohibiting me from talking to the girl's parents, is there?"

"Reporters do it all the time." He grinned sourly. "They got easier access to a victim's relatives than I do. They're not officers of the court." But he wasn't entirely easy about a civilian nosing into police business. "What are you going to ask them?"

"Who her closest friends were. And how close."

"Finch has talked to them already and interviewed the friends. I can find out when he files his report."

"He was interested in their alibis. I want to know if she was as much a loner as her apartment implies."

Shaughnessy studied the wall somewhere over my head. "Let me know what you find out."

"Of course."

"I'll do what I can about Vengley. Call you at the same number?"

The clutch of real estate sales people waiting at the show home's entry looked hopefully at me as I pulled to a raw and unscuffed curb. Sprinklers threw a mist over the new sod where brown lines showed seams. Spindly saplings anchored by wires bent under a steady, hot wind from the canyon. I asked an eager face for Steven Glover; the face lost its welcoming grin. "Inside."

"Hi, there—good to see you again! Be right with you." Glover looked up to smile and nod toward a coffee urn. "Help yourself."

I did. Maybe it came out of Glover's commission. I waited until the man had totted up figures on a calculator and then entered them on the long and detailed sheets. He shut the file and stood to shake hands.

"Closing another sale this afternoon—one more satisfied customer, and they're really moving fast. But we're already planning additional units in an area that hasn't been developed yet. You've got a chance to buy early and get a really choice location."

"I'm here to talk about Shelley Aguirre."

The wide smile hesitated and he peered at me with sudden recognition. "Let's step outside where we won't bother these other folks, okay?"

I followed the tall, slender man around the side of the house. As we walked slowly, Glover pointed at different corners of the development that spread cloned condos across the mesa toward the rim of steep canyon walls. I was told about the clubhouse, the swimming pool, the recreation park and tennis courts still to be installed. Maybe he was covering with his boss who might overhear us, maybe he was talking to give himself time to think. I didn't believe he was trying to sell me. "Californians live for the outdoors, you know? I mean with a climate like this, you want to take advantage of it, right?"

"You know Shelley's dead?"

We stopped well out of earshot from the show home. A string of fluttering plastic pennants rose from a stake in the yard's corner to the roof of the condo. "I heard about it. On TV. It's terrible."

"I understand you and she were dating."

"Well, we went out a few times. But just friends, you know?"

"And that you two were in the same Kabbal."

The pennants crackled. Glover's tongue wiped across his lower lip. "What's that mean?"

"It means you were in the same Satanist cult. I talked to Shelley before she died. She told me."

One of Glover's shoulders bobbed. "Hey, everybody's got a right to their religion, you know?"

"Do these people know you're a Satanist?"

"I don't brag about it, if that's what you mean. But then none of them come up and tell me they're Catholics or Mormons or whatever. Religion's not something we talk about."

"What rank are you in the Kabbal?"

"That's none of your business."

"I found Dorcas Wilcox."

"Yeah? Good—that's fine. Makes her folks happy, right?"

I shook my head. "Not so fine. She's in a commune in Denver and doesn't want to come home."

"Yeah? Good ol' Dori. Sounds like something she'd do."

"Dwayne belongs to it, too. The Temple of the Shining Spirit."

The tongue wiped again and then Glover shrugged. "Don't know anything about it."

"Have you seen him lately?"

"No."

"Dori said he came back to San Diego."

"I wouldn't know."

"Is Dwayne planning on becoming a High Priest soon?"

"You'll have to ask him."

"I'm trying to find him."

"Good luck. I don't know where he is."

"When's the last time you saw Shelley?"

"Three days ago," he said promptly. "We took in a movie."

"Have the police talked to you yet about her death?"

He nodded. "A cop asked me some questions. When was the last time I saw her, what I was doing when she was killed." He added, "I've got an alibi and if you're interested in what it is, ask the cop."

"Did he know what good friends you were? And that you belonged to the same Kabbal?"

"It didn't come up."

"Do you think the cop would be interested in finding out?"

Glover's blue eyes narrowed. "I don't care. I didn't have anything to do with Shelley's death and I got a good alibi."

"You say your employer doesn't care about your religion. Do you think he'll care about your being linked to a homicide?" I gave him a sample news item: " 'Steven Glover, employee of . . .' "—I read one of the "For Sale" signs—" 'Bracken Realty, was questioned in the murder of a young woman. Both Glover and the woman were members of a satanic cult . . .' Think that might sell a few houses?"

"Just what the hell are you after?"

"Dwayne Vengley."

"I told you, goddamn it, I don't know where he is!"

"But you can get in touch with him through the Kabbal." I handed him another slip of paper with my telephone number and reminded myself to invest in business cards. "Tell him to call me. It's important—for me, for him, for you." I left the man standing in the sun; the hot wind tugged at his regimental tie and slapped it against his white shirt.

CHAPTER

What would I say to Vengley when I found him? Any attempt to separate Dorcas from the Temple would require some kind of leverage. And an appeal to the man's kinder nature didn't seem too promising. Perhaps some sort of quid pro quo. But the only quid I had was Vengley's involvement in David Gates's death. That would take someone willing to testify that it wasn't an accident. So far the only one who had hinted at that was Dorcas, and to use her against Vengley would place her in even greater danger. Perhaps I might offer to stop looking into that death if Vengley told Dorcas to return home. I didn't like that idea. As an actual success, it had the same probability as divine intervention. But maybe if Vengley was worried enough . . . and if I could attribute testimony to someone other than Dorcas. And if Vengley believed me at all.

And now there was Shelley's murder. No evidence, but I had suspicions. Certainly, Glover had bent a little under the pressure of being linked to Aguirre. Which was all I could tell Shaughnessy when the policeman called later that afternoon.

"Here's Vengley's address." He gave me the apartment number on Island Street.

"He's not there. I checked. The woman he shared the apartment with said he moved out a couple months ago—owing rent."

"That's all the DMV has. And no recent arrests, so no update of his records." Shaughnessy paused. "How about his work address. Have you tried that?"

"No. What is it?"

"Alef Distributing Company. It's down in National City." He gave me the street and number. "That's the best I can do so far. I'll keep working on it."

It took me a while to find the street and then the address. Decades ago the area had been metal shops, steel fabricators, chemical plants. They supplied goods and materials to the once active navy yard where the mothballed fleet now rode at anchor. I vaguely remembered some of the old companies. I had sought work among them during the summers of high school. One job had been the gritty aching labor of lifting steel blanks from one die onto a dolly to be carried to another cutter. It was a job soon to be replaced by another machine. Its greatest profit had been to convince me of the benefits of college. I could still see the gleam of amusement in my stepfather's eye as, worn with eight hours of heavy lifting, I dragged home to check another day off the summer months.

Now much of the heavy industry had gone to Japan and Korea, and other factories across the border to Mexico. Electronics and biotech had replaced it, along with wholesalers, trucking depots, warehouses, shops for repairing or salvaging auto parts. The occasional welding shop could still be found, and a few of the steel fabricators had shifted to construction beams or ornamental ironwork.

It was between two large metalware storage yards fenced off with sheets of rusty galvanized roofing that I found Alef Distributing. A sand-colored Quonset hut; the arched end-wall held two doors, one large that said "Do Not Block," and a smaller one that said "Office" and held the only window. Tires crackling on the gravel, I pulled into the parking apron where a new and gleaming sport truck was the only other car. The office area was boxed in by plywood walls and a waist-high counter, all painted institutional green. Two desks, empty but used, were behind the counter. A small bell sat beside a hand-lettered sign that said "Push for Service." I thumped the plunger and leaned on the shelf to wait. The ring echoed against the silence of the rest of the building. A few seconds later, a door leading to the back opened and a young man in a flowered sport shirt and cutoff jeans leaned through. "Man! I thought I heard that bell—just a minute."

It was a bit longer than that. But he came back smiling politely and scratching his chest. "What can we do for you?"

"Are you Dwayne?"

"No. I can take a message for him, though."

"I'd like to talk with him. Do you know where he is?"

The man shook his head. A narrow plume of hair hung down his nape and wagged. "He's in and out a lot."

"Can you tell me what his job is here?"

The smile went and caution took its place. "You—ah—you looking for Dwayne for something special?"

"What's that mean?"

"I mean like are you a cop or something, man?"

"No. I'm trying to get a message to him. About a mutual friend."

"Oh." He studied me as if he intended to remember my face.

"What's his job here?"

"Marketing director. That's why he's gone all the time—on the road, like."

"Who's the owner?"

He hesitated. "Mr. Lyles."

"He around?"

"Not now. He'll be in tomorrow morning."

"You run the place yourself?"

"Well, pretty much. I mean there's not that much to it."

"What do you distribute?"

Another pause, this one longer. "Novelties, mostly. Advertising flyers. Whatever people want distributed. Look, man, I got to get back to work. You want to come back tomorrow, you can talk to Mr. Lyles. Okay?"

Nervous, the young man didn't wait for me to say I would. He nodded good-bye and quickly shut the partition door behind him. I heard the latch click and then lock.

There wasn't much to see down either side of the corrugated steel building. The neighboring fences ran to the edge of the property line and blocked my view. A slow tour down the alley behind showed only a square of weedy lot protected by a chain-link fence topped with spirals of razor wire. The empty lot seemed unused, but the wire looked new. I pulled my car to the side of the alley and waited for a truck to lumber by. Then I walked back to the dumpster that had splashed on its side the same street number as the Alef building. The back of the Quonset had a small fire door and a large window protected on the outside by heavy mesh and on the inside by whitewash across the glass. I tried to keep the iron lid of the dumpster between me and the building as I rifled through the trash. Most of it was shipping debris: plastic peanuts, air bubbles, strapping. Wads of perforated strips showed a lot of computer printing. I did find some boxes with address labels and I tore those free. Empty bottles and cans of toner and fix, wrappings from photography paper as well as plastic shipping guards for videotape boxes. Some broken glass—bottles, lightbulbs, an incandescent tube—and some rags and empty cleaning-powder cans.

Ignoring the glances of workmen in the steel yards, I gathered the scraps with the addresses and sat in my car to thumb through them. Many were from local photography supply stores. A number of others were from Fantasy Products Ltd. on Imperial Highway in Inglewood, CA. One came from a computer supply firm—Data Documents—with a size marked "9 ½ × 11," which I took to be computer paper. A few from an outfit in Garden Grove, CA, called A & D Products, twenty-four to the carton, color white. There was no outgoing correspondence. The Age of Floppies had done away with carbon copies and discarded ribbons. I did find a couple of envelopes that looked as if they'd held bills. One was from CompuRepair in San Diego, another from Southland Photographic Supply Warehouse, also local.

I finally found a public telephone with its directory intact and flipped through the business section for the number. Compu-Repair's secretary was both friendly and helpful.

"I don't know how it happened," I said. "I must have torn part of the bill when I opened the envelope. If you could read it to me, I'll get the payment in the mail."

"That's happened to me, too. Would you like a duplicate sent out?"

"Not necessary. I'll just jot down what you tell me."

She listed the items from her file: cleaning, adjusting, and routine maintenance. The big charge was to replace the head on the printer. Then she cited the total with tax. "That help?"

"Yes, it does. Thanks."

But it didn't. The computer repairs were generic and could apply to any business. The luck was a bit better with Southland Photographic Supplies. That order was primarily for videotape cartridges, color paper, and chemicals for developing and printing.

"It's pretty much the same monthly order you always give us," said the woman.

"I know. I just want to be sure it's entered right."

I thanked her and stood a few minutes in the telephone hood to let some ideas begin to congeal from what few facts I'd turned up. Then I headed toward downtown and the harbor area.

The restaurant was almost empty at this time of the afternoon. Only the bar held people, and one or two occupied tables filled up the gap between lunch and dinner. Tommy was in his small office tucked into a corner near the kitchen. "Jack! I was just talking about you. I been calling around to some of the guys and they want to get together. So I'm setting up something in a couple weeks. A little chow, a few drinks, a lot of lies and laughs. How about it?"

"A couple weeks—sounds good." I settled into the wooden

arm chair placed in front of Tom's desk. "It'll be good to see them."

"Aw, yeah. I told them you were back and everyone wanted a get-together."

"Right—we always had a hard time getting a party going."

"How about a luau? A little sand shark and rum?"

"Followed by a trip to TJ. It does sound familiar."

"Man, those were the times." Tom shoved back from the desk and grinned at the ceiling. "Remember when Cookie got caught at the border with that bottle of Bacardi under his front seat? Told the customs guy it was something his mother left there?"

"Didn't do us much good."

"Yeah. But you'd think the customs guy would give us credit for the day's worst lie. Still funny! Every now and then I find something hidden away somewhere, I think of that: 'Must have been something my mother left there.' " He shook his head. "Over twenty years ago. How the hell did we get so old so fast? And why in hell didn't we get our asses slung more'n we did?"

"Luck."

"Yeah. A lot of that. But Jack, I think times were different, too. A kid could do things, nobody would get too bent out of shape about it. Nowadays, I don't know. Kids now, it seems the stakes are a lot higher, you know?"

There was some truth in that, though I was less convinced it was the changing times than our changing ages. Granted a lot of our survival had been luck, but not all. Try as I might, I couldn't think of anything we'd done that was vicious. Wild at times, certainly careless, thoughtless, and often with the universal selfishness of youth. But nothing intentionally mean or predatory. Driven by the need to discover life and explore the rapidly widening boundaries of adolescence, we still knew there were things you did for others, not to them. There were rules you didn't have to put into words. In fact, it seemed corny when somebody—usually an adult—did. Instead, they existed in the puzzled expressions, the wondering question when a violation did occur: "Now why would he go and do some dumb-ass thing like that?" And the usual answer: "Guy's fucked up."

One generation older than Dori. A mere couple of decades. And what might have happened to us if one of our gang had been Vengley?

"Hey, Jack—you've been chewing your knuckles for five minutes. What's bothering you?"

"It's this job for Admiral Combs, Tommy. The missing girl is only part of it now. And I don't like what I'm digging into."

"Hey, you can't shovel shit without raising a stink."

"For a philosopher, it's a good thing you run fast. Ever hear of Alef Distributing Company?"

Tom frowned, head wagging no. "You want information on them?"

"Any way I can get it?"

"If they're local, I can help. I subscribe to this new business data bank. It's mostly for restaurant owners—you know, restaurant supply companies, food wholesalers, cleaning equipment and supplies, that kind of thing. Gives you the specialty, a record of service, comments from people they deal with. The kind of stuff you want to know before you sign a contract." He turned to the small p.c. on a stand beside his desk. "Let me punch it up, see if it's in the bank."

I watched him type a series of commands on the screen and enter answers to the queries that came back. Then I spelled the name for Tom. A few seconds later, the machine beeped irritably and flashed "No Information Available," followed by a menu of suggested alternatives.

"Let's try the general directory."

A happier beep heralded the brief entry.

"Yeah, what I thought. But the stuff here's from public records, is all. Corporation officers, BBB rating, that kind of thing." He shrugged. "What the hell, it'll save you a trip over to the county building."

I noted the entry under Alef Distributing as Tom explained that the data people, to fill out their files and make them look impressive, dumped all sorts of crap into the memory bank, even stuff anybody could get from the various public records offices. "That's where they get it themselves."

Alef was licensed to undertake any legal business. Its stock was privately held and the major stockholder was a holding company, Mesa and Mountain Investments. The president of Alef was Ralph Lyles, business address supplied, and the corporation treasurer and secretary weren't listed, which wasn't that unusual, Tommy told me. The address was the familiar National City street. Under the heading for type of business was noted "General distribution services." About as enlightening as the purpose for incorporation.

"Can you look up Mesa and Mountain Investments?"

"Sure."

Again the rattle of the keyboard and the tweedle of machines talking to each other through the modem. Then the entry. The president of the holding company was Arthur Iacino. Their address was a post office box in downtown San Diego. The type of business was general investments.

"Do you any good?"

"Maybe. Do you subscribe to a credit information service?"

"Hell, yes, a couple services. Got to—plastic money, checks, that's all people use anymore. I'm on the A plan. Costs a little more, but it's worth it in the long run."

" 'A' plan?"

"Complete credit display. 'B' plan just lists the names or card numbers that have been flagged. Most retailers use an issuer-approval system. You know, you hand them your card, they run it through a reader. A few seconds later they stamp your purchase. It's okay for most retail stuff. But I got to tell you, Jack, customers come in here, some of them run up bills that make even my bunghole pucker. I need more than somebody saying the card's good—I need to know how much the card or check's good for, and where to call if it bounces."

"Try Ralph Lyles and Arthur Iacino."

Tom started rattling keys. "They might not be here. Some-

body deals in cash, they don't have an entry. Like the mob."
The screen flickered, the lights blinked from green to red and
back, a beep said the Lyles request was answered. "Bingo."

Ralph Lyles had a good credit rating. His established bank
references were a checking account in First National of San
Diego and a savings account in Great Western S & L. He'd
recently bought a Datsun 280Z from All-American Auto Sales
and completed the payments early. His mortgage payments to
Nichols and Nichols were regular. His employer was Alef Distributing, and his home address was 403 Chestnut Court, Chula
Vista.

"See what I mean, Jack? Anybody that borrows money or
gets a loan fills out a form—employment history, residence,
income, closest relatives, bank account numbers, debts, credit
history, references. The whole bit. Information from the form
ends up in the data bank. Guy like this bounces a check on me,
I know where to find him, where to go to garnish his wages."
Tom added, "Of course, with Lyles's record, he's not likely to
do that. I'd take his paper." The keys rattled again. "Let's see
what's on Iacino."

Three Arthur Iacinos were listed and the computer wanted
additional information to sort them out. Tom typed in Iacino's
employer. The screen flickered and brought back a brief entry.
The date of record was several years old; the man had taken
out a house loan but no other transactions. His home address
was on Hilton Head Road in San Diego County. "Probably a
pretty big house," said Tom. "That's prime real estate up
there."

"Try Dwayne Vengley."

The only response was the disgusted beep.

I thanked Tom and promised again that I'd be ready to party
in two weeks. It was a good thing to look forward to, and if I
hadn't other things on my mind at the moment, I might have
enjoyed the prospect even more.

The San Diego regional map led me to Lyles's home. It was

on a short street, the last of a series of wandering lanes carved into the hills overlooking Telegraph Canyon. Beyond the street's dead end, brown manzanita and rocks covered hills that might have been city open space. More likely, it was private land waiting for the developers. The view was to the southwest. Over a series of lower, smoggy ridges crenellated with roofs, the Pacific made a coppery glint through the city's haze. I swung around in the empty street. The stucco house was new and sprawled under a bright red tile roof whose gables tilted up in a vaguely Oriental manner. A key-shaped portal of long bricks framed doors carved with Spanish motifs: California's own style of Hong Kong hacienda. The doorbell was a soft brassy chime.

A faint scratch behind the bullseye mounted in the door told me someone was peering out. I must have looked almost harmless; a moment later one of the twin doors opened to the end of a short chain. "Yes?"

"Afternoon, ma'am. I'm looking for Mr. Lyles."

A pause. "Does he know you're coming?"

"No ma'am. His assistant at the shop told me I might find him at home, though."

"Oh. Just a minute. I'll call him."

The woman left the door open on its chain. I heard her voice call "Ralph." A few seconds later the slap of loose sandals came to the doorway. Lyles closed the door briefly. The chain rattled and then he reopened it. "You want to see me?"

"Jack Steele." I shook hands with the man whose paunch pressed against the bathrobe. A towel hung around his neck. Water marks traced from his thongs across the tile entry to the living room rug and out sliding glass doors to a pool beyond. "I'm looking for Dwayne Vengley. I understand he's your sales representative."

"Dwayne? Yeah—sales, marketing. Why?"

"He's acquainted with a girl who was missing. I'd like to talk to him about her."

"A girl? Who?"

"Dorcas Wilcox."

"Never heard of her." The man scratched at his chest. "When—ah—where's she missing from?"

"Her parents live in La Jolla. She has a place up in Julian."

"Oh. You mean a grown girl. An adult."

"Yes."

The balding head with its tufts of gray hair sprouting over the ears wagged. "Don't know anything about it."

"What kind of products does Alef distribute?"

"What kind? Novelties, advertising circulars. General distribution. Why?"

"You don't do photography?"

The man's eyelids dropped a fraction and he tugged at a fold of whiskery skin under his jaw. "Sure. We do a lot of photograph work. Advertising sheets, illustrations for the circulars, photoduplication. Why?"

"I'm having trouble finding Dwayne." I smiled. "Maybe if I know more about what he does, it'll help me."

"Yeah? Well, you tried his home? You know where he works, you got to know where he lives."

"Lived. He apparently moved a couple months ago."

"Oh, yeah? News to me. He spends a lot of time on the road. Tell you what. Give me your name and number. Next time he phones in, I'll tell him to get in touch with you."

I wrote the information on another slip of paper. "Do you know Steven Glover or Shelley Aguirre?"

The balding head shook again. "Who're they?"

"Friends of Dwayne."

"Never heard of them."

"Thank you."

I wasn't certain where the questions had taken me or if they had taken me anywhere at all. I had learned in counterintelligence that you kept trying, first one avenue then another, even if the direction of inquiry seemed to lead away from what you expected. "You can think of some of the things all of the time, and all of the things some of the time . . ." A parody of Lincoln's phrase that had been popular folklore during those situations when none of the leads seemed to go anywhere and all of the painstakingly gathered details seemed to be just that: details without meaning or pattern.

CHAPTER

I guided the car down through the sandy hillsides and then northwest on 94 for El Cajon where Shelley Aguirre's parents lived. Theirs was an older stucco home that looked dated and out of place surrounded by the waves of condos and apartments. A small black bow and a white cross were tied to the screen door. In the welcome shade of the deep front porch, I smelled the odor of cooking oil and spices. An Hispanic man with cropped black hair and baggy eyes answered my knock.

"Are you a relative of Shelley Aguirre?"

"Her father. Are you with the police?"

"No." I explained a bit about Dori, stretching a point here and there.

"I remember her. Shelley brought her here a couple times when they were in college. A real pretty girl."

"I'm very sorry about Shelley, Mr. Aguirre. And I know this is a painful time for you. But perhaps Shelley mentioned something—a name, an address—that might lead me to Mr. Wilcox's missing daughter."

The light brown eyes, a shade similar to Shelley's, blinked and Aguirre swallowed quickly. "That poor man. Sure—come on in. I'll help if I can."

The living room, too, had an old-fashioned quality to it. A

large wood-framed arch linked it to a formal dining room with its heavy table. Set off behind stubby wooden pillars that rose from a waist-high divider was a parlor where doilies spotted a large couch and a matching pair of overstuffed chairs. The room felt little used. The television set was in the dining room. Above a mantel over the clean fireplace, Christ looked toward a glow in the sky and pulled his robe open to show a bleeding heart radiating love. On the mantel, votive candles flickered in front of a framed photograph of Shelley. A small silver crucifix was draped with a rosary.

"Shelley was a practicing Catholic?"

The brown eyes glanced at the candles. "She was when she lived at home. When she moved away . . ." Aguirre flapped a hand. "Have a seat. My wife's in the kitchen. I'll see if she feels like talking."

Maureen Aguirre was the source of Shelley's blond hair. Heavyset, she had lank, red-blond hair, recently permed.

"I told her what you wanted," said the man. "She says she'll try to help, too."

"Thank you, ma'am." I had been looking at the family portrait gallery arranged on the paneled wall. Shelley was the youngest of four—three boys and her—who had close family resemblances. "Shelley's brothers?"

The woman nodded. "Paul's in the navy, now. He's the oldest. Then Bradley, then Jerry. Shelley was the youngest."

"She was the only one went to college," said the man. He jerked a thumb over his shoulder toward the window. "We sold off a lot of the ranch to give the kids their start in the world, you know? Ranching, you can't make a living from that no more, and this isn't good land for orchards. Not with the price of water these days. So we finally gave in to the developers."

Mrs. Aguirre stared at the picture on the wall. "Shelley really wanted to attend college. She was that way—always wanted to know about things. We wanted her to attend a Catholic college." A sigh. "Still, she liked Occidental. We went up there a lot. You know, on parents' day and all. It was such a nice graduation—outside in a kind of bowl at night and everybody wearing these robes and cheering." The voice faded.

"Did she like her work at the design office, Mrs. Aguirre?"

"Oh, yes. But it was just her first job. Something to get experience with, you know?"

"She was good at it," said the father. "We got a lot of her drawings." He leaned as if to get them.

"How about her friends?" I asked quickly. "Did she get along with her coworkers all right?"

"Oh, sure! They closed the office so everybody could come to her funeral. A lot of people came."

"Was there anyone she was particularly friendly with? Anyone she might have confided in?"

They looked at each other, waiting for the other to say a name. Finally the woman answered. "Us, I guess. She'd tell us when something funny happened at work, like that. But she didn't talk a lot about it. We just didn't know the people that well."

"How about friends outside work? Anyone she was seeing?"

"Steve," said Aguirre.

"Steve Glover. They went to college together. She dated him a lot. I think they were thinking of getting married maybe."

"He never talked to me about it."

"Well, he's just getting started, too, you know." She turned back to me. "He's in real estate. A real nice young man."

"Did Shelley have any photographs of him in her apartment?"

"Sure! There was that one, the two of them standing in front of the waterfall. Remember, Aurie? The big one on the wall."

The father nodded. "Took it last spring. They went up to Yosemite."

"Did she keep a photo album, too?"

The mother slowly shook her head. "I don't think so. A few pictures maybe, but never a whole album full."

"Letters? An address book?"

"I . . . I guess. That officer, he didn't ask us these things."

Aguirre nodded. "Is it something we need to know about?"

I smiled. "I'm just looking for names that might lead to Dori Wilcox. That's the way these things are done: you start with one person and talk to his friends. Then to their friends and so on."

"Well, she talked about Dwayne. He was another friend from college."

"Dwayne Vengley?"

"You know him? Shelley talked a lot about him. He was nice to Maureen at the funeral. You could see he . . . cared."

"Anyone else?"

"Tim Gifford. But he moved away a few months ago."

I made a show of writing the name. "Any others?"

They waited for each other to come up with more. Finally Aguirre said, "That's all we can remember. Maybe later . . ."

"I appreciate what you've told me." I jotted down my name and telephone number. "If you do remember any others, please call."

Montgomery Freeway to State 75 and across to the south end of Silver Strand Boulevard. This late in the afternoon, even the side streets were clogged with homeward-bound traffic. Between ads for men's clothing, home furnishings, automotive painting, and grocery chains, the radio gave updates on road conditions. The vague temptation I felt about heading out to Iacino's home had been easily overcome. All the freeways were jammed, the San Diego north was gridlocked, and 94 was stop-and-go as far east as Lemon Grove. A telephone call could probably do the job, and I wasn't sure right now if I even needed to talk to the president of Mountain and Mesa Investments.

But there were more questions I had wanted to ask Lyles. The man wouldn't have answered, though. As I followed the Strand up through the fenced, grassy fields of the Naval Communications Station, I tried to figure ways to get the information.

Turning out of traffic, I wound through the short streets to my driveway. Mrs. Gruening across the street had set up a plastic water slide for her two kids and, it seemed, the rest of the neighborhood as well. The screams of excitement and joy rattled dimly against my front windows. Children had more room to play in the front yards than in the back where docks and boat slips took the place of grass. I poured myself a beer and checked the day's mail, then the telephone answerer. Buried among buzzing blank spaces and electronic voices selling this and that to electronic ears, a voice whose tension made it almost unrecognizable said, "Dad, it's Karen. Call me as soon as you can."

She knew Jerry had loved her. That knowledge brought both an excitement and a sense of power because he was someone from whom that kind of emotion hadn't been expected. It had even made her feel a kind of love for him. Well, if she was terribly honest, a refreshing love for herself through him. Growing aware of his eyes on her, she began to see herself through the lens of his estimation, and gradually she regained some of the self-value that had once been hers so long ago. It wasn't that other men hadn't wanted her—Dwayne, in his own tortured way, also loved her. Had loved her since high school and, she guessed, in the core of her heart she loved him. How else to explain the magnetism that drew them together again and again? And there were other men who stared at her hungrily, too, even when she tried her best to efface herself. Dwayne had told her a long time ago about what he called the burden of a woman's beauty. It had puzzled her why some boys wanted to force their longing on her as if they looked at someone who really wasn't her. "They do," Dwayne had said. "You're a dream made flesh for them—a living symbol of what they want. They think if they're lucky enough or persistent enough or sexy enough, they can own that dream."

"I'm not a symbol. I don't want to be owned."

But he had shown her a collective yearning that far outweighed her isolated and lonely struggle for self. He had also shown her the power that was in that yearning—a spiritual embrace that healed without embarrassment because she could admit what she really was and what she had done; she could join those who either did or wanted to do things as bad. And Dwayne had shown her the widening dimensions of sexual power, as well as the mindless, totally submerged enjoyment of it.

Jerry, however, had a certain distance. His was a love less of her as embodied symbol than of the act of love itself—at first, anyway. He, like Dwayne, sought. But unlike Dwayne, he had not found certitude, and there was something temporary in his joining the Kabbal. He was testing, trying, and—still dissatisfied—moving on. He had some kind of vision that differed from Dwayne's. It was more . . . not self-confident; that wasn't the term. Nobody she'd ever met was more self-confident than Dwayne. More . . . sincere. Perhaps even spiritually innocent. As if, in contrast to Dwayne, Jerry would be open to any truths his search brought him rather than measuring them against a certitude he already had. It was something she'd tried to explain to Dwayne but at the time he had only smiled and said Jerry just refused to admit truths that were self-evident.

"But he's sincere. He really wants to know."

"Up to a point. If he was all that sincere, he'd admit the truth of what I've shown him."

"He doesn't?"

"I think he's just another dabbler. We'll see in time."

But she knew that the same earnestness that attracted her drew Dwayne as well. Jerry was for Dwayne a challenge, a prize. In some ways, he was to Dwayne what she was to those men who saw whatever it was they longed for in her. And, ironically, perhaps it was Dwayne's fascination with Jerry that stirred her own. And then, of course, he had begun to show interest. And had begun to ask questions.

"You're trying to make me feel ashamed. Well, I don't! Not one bit—"

"No, I'm not trying to make you feel ashamed. Why the hell should I? You're acting out of belief, Dori, and I respect that. In a world where there's so little belief, where so few commit their souls to something other than money, I'm not going to scoff at any act of real belief." He handed her the toke and, with a long drag, she soothed the hazy anger that had been stirred by his questions. "What I'm asking about isn't your act of belief, but its object: Dwayne's whole value system. Despite what he says, he's still in the material world—for him the world of the spirit is just a device, a means to get more things. Look what we ask: 'O Dark Lord Satan, we demand your help in winning gold and gaining power over our enemies.' "

"And tell me people don't pray to God for a good price on their stocks or for a winning lottery ticket!"

"Sure they do. It's no different. And there are the hypocrites who say they have money because they're blessed by God, therefore their money's blessed, too. What I'm saying is Dwayne's approach ignores a whole spectrum of possibilities. There's strength and knowledge in denial, too."

"He doesn't believe in denial."

"That's my point, Dori! He won't even accept the possibility of a value system outside the Judeo-Christian tradition." He waved an arm at the books stacked in the board-and-concrete-block bookcases on each side of his desk. "Read some of these—they're by people who've searched for the same things and thought as deeply—deeper—about them than Dwayne. He's closed off possibility; these keep it open."

From down the hall, a door slammed loudly, its echo twanging against the muffled jumble of stereo sets in neighboring dorm rooms. Outside, a squeal of rubber on the asphalt parking lot followed by the loud, drunken laughter of students coming back from town. Saturday night.

"Are you going to leave the Kabbal?"

"It's given me all the answers it can. But I still have more questions. I don't know if anyone or anything can give me an-

*swers to all the questions, but I know I have to keep looking."
He squinted into the smoke of the final end of the roach. "I'd
like you to look with me, Dori."*

*It was the way she had felt, too, when she first came to Oxy.
That same kind of excitement at being on the borders of knowing,
the daring involved in pushing out from the familiar. Even a
sense of exhilaration at the chance to leave behind and forget.
But that had been before she was with Dwayne again. Before
she once more accepted his catechism as the limits of search.
Now she felt a tingle of envy: Jerry still had the yearning. He
was still willing to voyage outward. She, in trying to master those
nagging fears, had become static. "Maybe we won't know it all
until we cross over."*

*"Maybe we won't know it all even then. But that's not the
issue—it's how much can we know here and now. And now the
Kabbal is more restrictive than liberating. The road goes on,
Dori; it doesn't stop with Dwayne. Not for me, not for you."*

*But it had stopped with Dwayne. She wasn't sure how he did
it, but Dwayne had some role in Jerry's suicide. And, God help
her, so did she. She would not join him in leaving the Kabbal;
she who, despite what they said in each other's arms, would not
let her feelings for Jerry become the kind of love that gave without
asking in return. His had been, and she had not known its value
until it was gone. Jerry's suicide was as much out of jealousy
over her role in the Kabbal, Dwayne said, as despair for his
search in this world. He said that Jerry talked about the power
of denial and the trap of materialism, but when it came to Dori's
role in the Kabbal, he couldn't get beyond jealousy. Dwayne
had been with him for two days and on the third, Jerry finally
saw no other way.*

*But even Dwayne had finally felt remorse. He wrote to her in
Tahoe where she had fled the ghosts of voices and arguments
and memories, trying to find peace in the mountains with their
timeless, vast power that dwarfed the self and, wordless, argued
against the vanities of human struggle.*

"We've Broken the Circle, Dori. I guess it's Jerry—I can't quit

thinking about him and the talks we had when he was planning on leaving the Kabbal. Maybe there was some truth in it, I don't know. Anyway, I'm moving away from The Practice. I know there's something for me somewhere and I intend to find it. Keep in touch, I'll let you know what I find. And you let me know, too, if you find what you want . . ."

CHAPTER

24

Karen answered the telephone. "Dad—are you all right?"

"Yes, fine. Is something wrong there? You sound pretty tense."

She didn't answer his question. Instead, she asked, "Do you know anybody named Aleister LaVey?"

The skin at the back of my neck prickled with lifting hairs. "The name sounds familiar." Aleister Crowley and Anton LaVey—well-known in Satanism, and the combination of the names was a thinly disguised code. "Why?"

"I found a strange note slipped under our front door. It's signed by this man."

"Read it to me."

" 'Karen—Tell your father to leave things alone. We know about you and Rebecca. Aleister LaVey.' "

"That's it? Nothing else?"

"That's it." The line was silent a moment. "I don't like what I hear in your voice, Dad. Maybe you'd better tell me what's going on. Are you really retired?"

"Yes, Karen. This is something else. A little job to help some friends."

"What kind of job? And who is this Aleister LaVey?"

They must have found some reference to Karen and Rebecca

when they searched my house. My address book—they'd have read through that. But how would they know by Karen's married name that she was my daughter?

"Dad? Are you there?"

"Yes. Listen, I want you to call the Sacramento police as soon as you hang up. Tell them you've been threatened and give them my name and number. Tell them to call me and I'll fill them in with as much detail as I know."

"How about filling me in, too, Dad? It involves Chuck and Rebecca and me, and we have a right to know what we're faced with."

They had a stronger right not to be involved at all. I told her about Dorcas Wilcox and Dwayne Vengley, and added that I wished I knew what we were faced with, too.

"Satanism? This Aleister LaVey's a Satanist?"

"It's a phony name, but, yes, that's what it means."

"What can we do, Dad? What about Rebecca? I don't like her being in danger."

I didn't like endangering any of them. "I'll telephone her as soon as I can. Listen, Karen, I don't know how long it will take me to straighten things out. That's why I want you to notify the police. Does your firm make use of private detectives?"

"Yes. I don't know any of them personally, but we do have several names."

"I'll send a check. Hire a man to see if he can find out who left the note. But you and Chuck go on about your lives. Just use some caution and common sense, okay? Lock your home and car, stay away from isolated areas, be suspicious of any strangers hanging around or any packages, okay?"

"Yes . . . of course. But how long will we have to do that?"

"I don't know, Karen. Not long."

"I feel like we're suddenly in a state of siege. I feel as if all the things around us have suddenly become enemies." She added, "I'm frightened, Dad."

"That's what this person wants, Karen—to scare me off through you."

"Well, he's succeeded in part!" A sigh. "But I know he won't ever scare you off. And, Daddy, when I think about it, I don't want him to." Her voice gained a fierceness. "It makes me angry. No, it makes me goddamned mad! Nail him, Daddy. Nail his ass to the barn wall! And Chuck and I'll do everything we can to help. So don't worry about us!"

It crossed my mind that my elder daughter was going to make a pretty good lawyer.

Shaughnessy wasn't all that excited to hear from me, especially so close to quitting time. But when he heard about the threat, the man's voice quickened. " 'Aleister LaVey'? I guess they couldn't have said it any clearer."

"It's a serious threat, Sergeant."

"Yeah. The crummy shits." Then, "How'd they find out about your daughters?"

I'd been thinking about that. And about the teakettle I'd found on the stove. "I had a letter from Karen in my mailbox when they went through the house. I think they steamed it open, read it, and resealed it."

"When was that?"

"While I was in Colorado. Two, three days ago."

"I see."

It gave them time to fly up to Sacramento, to check out Karen's return address, to leave the threat. It was a not-too-subtle hint how easy it would be to harm or kidnap her, and I made an effort to modulate my icy anger. It had gradually replaced the spasm of fear that came when Karen first told me about the threat. Old Beltline wisdom: don't get mad, just get even. Granted there were times when it was best to fight mad, but this wasn't one of them. "Is there any way I can make sure the Sacramento PD takes this seriously?"

"I got a contact up there. I'll call and talk to him." Shaughnessy added, "Not that they wouldn't do their job anyway."

"Just so they know Karen's not a crank complainer."

"I'll tell him."

"I haven't been able to find Vengley."

"The work address didn't pan out?"

I told Shaughnessy about that and my visit to Ralph Lyles and the Aguirres.

"A large photograph of Glover and the girl?"

"At Yosemite. Hung on the wall."

"Well, no shit . . ."

When the line remained silent, I added, "Alef Distributing should be looked at, too."

"We can't get a warrant on guesses."

"Can you look at their paper trail?"

"Yeah. But I don't know if I'll come up with any more than you've already got. I'll do what I can, though."

"Want to look at Mesa and Mountain Investments while you're at it?"

"Hey, call it happy hour—two-fers."

"Anything new on the Aguirre killing?"

"Nothing Finch wants to tell me. And I haven't found anybody yet who corroborates that she was a Satanist."

"That's not surprising, is it?"

"Naw, I guess not. The people who'd know are in it with her, and the people not in it wouldn't know. I'll get back when I hear something."

Later, a Detective Lewis of the Sacramento police called to find out what I had to say. "You don't have any idea who wrote the note?"

"It could have been Vengley. No one I've talked to knows where he is."

"Uh-huh. Well, Mr. Steele, we'll pay attention to the threat, of course. But there's not much we can do unless the lab turns up something on that note."

"What about protection for my daughter and her husband?"

"I've arranged for drive-bys. And I've given your daughter a quick-response phone number to call in case anything suspicious happens. Beyond that . . ."

"I understand."

Which left me pretty much where I was earlier—on my own. And worrying about Rebecca, who could pose an even more difficult security problem. Counting the difference in hours between California and western France, the school's offices should be open now. The overseas operator took all the information and in a few minutes, I heard a woman's voice, delayed a few beats by distance, answer in French.

"This is Mr. Steele in the United States. I'm trying to reach my daughter, Rebecca Steele. Is she there?"

"Is it an emergency, *m'sieur?*"

"Please don't alarm her, but it is very important. Is she there, please?"

"I think all of our students are back now. If it is not an emergency, I will have the concierge give her a message to call you as soon as possible. Will that be satisfactory?"

"Please. Here's my new telephone number—she might not have it yet. Tell her it's not an emergency—no one's hurt. But it is very, very important that she call collect as soon as possible."

"I will tell her, *M'sieur* Steele."

There would be no telephone in the dormitory rooms, of course. Probably the person I talked to was the residence manager, and Rebecca would find a note in her mailbox when she came back from classes. If she looked. Then she would have to use the pay phone, a basement location probably, and maybe stand in line to get to it. But there was nothing I could do now except wait.

The call came about two hours later as I absently chopped up an avocado and whatever for a supper salad. I watched but did not really see the daily "sunset regatta" as the neighbors took their boats out for after-work cruises. When the telephone finally rang, I almost knocked it off the shelf in my haste. When I heard Rebecca's voice—with that familiar, slightly breathless quality that sounded so much like Eleanor—my suddenly relaxing muscles made me realize how tense I had been.

"Dad! I got your letter—I just mailed an answer yesterday. I just can't imagine you retired!"

I told her a little more about it, leaving out the mandatory part. "Listen, Becky, I hope you're not too upset about my moving to California. It seemed like the best thing to do at the time, and I've got a job lined up out here."

"That sounds great, Dad. Can you talk about it?"

The question an intelligence operative's daughter would ask. "I'll tell you more about it when I write. Before I left Fairfax, I talked to the Richardsons—they say you're welcome to stay with them and Sue this summer if you want to."

"I haven't really thought that far ahead yet. I mean it's nice of the Richardsons and all, but I was thinking of staying over here a little longer after school's out. I can get a job—secretary or au pair or something." She added quickly, "If it's okay with you. There's a real shortage of secretarial help and with the EEC and Eastern Europe and all, it's really exciting to be here now."

"Of course it is!" I hoped the heartiness didn't sound as false as it felt. "I put all your gear in one of the upstairs bedrooms—your bedroom, when you want it. I unpacked the clothes, but the rest is still boxed up."

"Leave it that way for now, Dad. Until I find out what I'm doing."

"Will do. Hey, I'm sitting here watching my neighbor hoist the jib on his sloop. He takes it out every evening."

"Neat! Is it a big one?"

"Looks around twenty-five feet. We'll go boat shopping when you get here. One of my old high school buddies says he has a few contacts in the boat business."

A pause. "You really won't be too disappointed if I don't come out there before school starts in the fall?"

"Not too, no. I'd be a lot more disappointed if I thought you were coming back when you didn't want to and didn't have to."

"You're sure? You won't be lonesome?"

"Hey, I've got plenty to do here, believe me. In fact, the last couple weeks have been a lot busier than I planned on."

"Good—I'm really glad to hear it, Dad. I wasn't worried you'd turn into a couch potato. But . . . I don't know. Sometimes when people retire, they sort of don't know what to do with all their time."

"Believe me, Becky, retirement has not meant inactivity."

"Well, you're what they call over here 'le bel âge.' "

"What do you know about *le bel âge?*"

She laughed. "We women talk! Have you met some California blonde yet?"

"Maybe you ladies talk too much. No, I haven't—not the kind you're hinting at, anyway." Megan crossed my mind, but for no clear reason I preferred not to mention her. My love life was a topic where joking masked a serious concern on Rebecca's part. I believed her sincerity when she said I ought to remarry, that I had too much life left to stay single out of fear of what she or Karen might think. But I also suspected that my daughter wasn't entirely convinced she'd like it and that she spoke from some noble sense of sacrifice for what should be right for me. "Besides, anyone I happen to get serious about will have to pass muster with you and Karen. So don't worry about that."

"I'm not worried. How are Karen and Chuck?"

I told her they were doing well, wondering how to caution her without either alarming her or generating some silly notion of dropping out of school to fly home and protect me. Rebecca had been the one to take Eleanor's place as my helpmate. Karen, away at college, was spared the daily emptiness of the house and the routines of shopping, cleaning, and laundry. "Is everything okay with you, Becky? Any problems or . . . or anything you need help with?"

"I'm fine. Everything's going swimmingly, as Barbara says. Oh, she wants me to go over to England with her in a couple weeks. I think I might—we have another vacation coming up."

"Another one?"

"A long weekend—one of those national holidays."

"That sounds fine, and have a good time." I added, "Listen, Becky, if you need help at any time, remember just call me. When I'm not at home, I have the phone answerer on. I'll get right back to you."

"Is something worrying you, Dad?"

"No. It's just you're a long way from home. The usual fatherly concerns."

"Well, don't be concerned—I can take care of myself."

"I know that. But if something happens that you can't handle, or aren't sure about, call. Don't hesitate at all. Ever. Hear me?"

"All right. I hear you."

"I'll be talking with you again soon."

We would be, she assured me. And we gave each other our love and said good-bye.

I stared at the telephone with that slightly empty sense of talking a lot but saying little that seemed memorable. If I'd told her about the threat, she'd have worried more about me than herself. Enough, perhaps, to insist that she could contribute something. Right now, her contribution was to be out of harm's way. Moreover, I didn't want to spoil the obvious enjoyment she was finding in her year abroad.

Oh, to be in England in the spring. I might even fly over for a couple of days just to say hello. By then, I hoped, there'd be no reason not to. Hoped, hell. I was certain. Because I wasn't going to let this Satanist garbage drag on that long.

CHAPTER

Annette Vengley was apologetic. "No, Mr. Steele, I haven't heard a thing from Dwayne since we spoke. Have you found out anything about Dori yet?"

"I finally traced her to Colorado. She said Dwayne had been there, too."

"That's news to me—I didn't know he'd moved there."

"I'm not sure he moved. I was told he was there for a while and then came back here. Is there any possible place you can think of, no matter how tenuous, that he might be? It's extremely vital that I get in touch with him." Across the calm waters of the bay, the mountains behind the city rose yellow and brown as they faced the flat glare of a setting sun. On one of those ridges, somewhere to the right of that bright cluster of downtown high-rises with sun-sparked windows, was Mrs. Vengley's apartment.

"As I said before, he doesn't talk to me very often."

"Did you read about Shelley Aguirre's death?"

"Yes. That poor girl." The telephone was silent. "You're not . . . implying anything about Dwayne, are you?"

"Why do you ask that, Mrs. Vengley?"

"Well, you say you know where Dori is. But you're still looking for Dwayne. It seems to imply a connection . . ."

I wondered if her question was because she sensed something to distrust in her own son. But all I said was, "Shelley's death came after I talked to her."

"I don't see your point. The paper said she was probably killed by a burglar."

"She belonged to a Satanist cult, Mrs. Vengley. She said Dwayne was a member, too."

"A what?"

I repeated it to the shocked silence. "Did he collect books on devil worship or sorcery? Do you remember any radical personality changes—moodiness or withdrawing or losing his sense of humor?"

"I . . . I really can't remember his reading anything like that. It was several years ago. He's been on his own since he left for Occidental. And as for being moody, I thought that was the definition of a teenager."

"How about suddenly changing his friends?"

She thought about that. "No. When he went to college, he stopped seeing most of his high school friends. Except for Dori, of course. But that's only to be expected—new school, new friends."

"And you've never suspected any kind of cult activity on his part?"

"Of course not. No. Why did Shelley say such a thing?"

"Because I asked her about it."

"Mr. Steele, I can't remember anything like that. I can't imagine Dwayne surrendering himself to any sort of group like that. He's always been so—" She groped for a word. "Self-contained."

"Did he ever mention a Gaylord Pettes?"

"No. And I'd certainly remember such a name."

"Or the Temple of the Shining Spirit?"

"No."

"Did he ever talk about his work at Alef Distributing?"

"I didn't know he was working anywhere. In fact, with all your questions, I'm beginning to wonder what we do talk about." She added, "And they're beginning to frighten me a little, too. It sounds as if you really are implying that Dwayne has something to do with Shelley's death."

"Mrs. Vengley, I don't have evidence of anything at all. But I do know of David Gates and Jerry Hawley. And now Shelley Aguirre. Your son's friends seem to have bad luck and that does raise questions. But please don't think I'm making accusations. I'm not."

"It's difficult to think otherwise, Mr. Steele, given the tenor of the questions you've been asking. You came to me asking if Dwayne knew Dori Wilcox. Now you're making all these . . . these innuendos about my son!"

"Dori's involved in another cult, one which Dwayne seems to have some tie to." I could have added that I was also trying to find out if Dwayne knew about the threat to my daughters, but the woman was too near the edge already. "Please, Mrs. Vengley, I'm just trying to discover the facts. And to do it, I need to speak with Dwayne. It may be in his best interests to talk with me, too. Do you have any inkling where he might be? Can you think of any names or addresses—new or old—that might be a lead to him?"

"His father, of course. Have you talked to him?"

"Only one time. Like you, he said he rarely sees Dwayne."

"He sees more of him than I do, I know that. But I don't know how often that is." Hesitantly, she added, "You might try Willy Davis. He lives over in Coronado somewhere—Ninth Street, I think. He and Dwayne used to be very close friends. But Dwayne hasn't mentioned him in a long time."

I noted the name. "Anyone else he used to see a lot of?"

"Those girls in high school. Dori, Stacey, the other two."

"Kimberly and Margot?"

"Yes. They were good friends their senior year. But as I say, that was quite a while ago."

"Before David Gates's death?"

Her voice faltered. "Yes."

"Anyone else?"

She thought. "He mentioned a Michael somebody. But that's all I can think of."

"Thank you, Mrs. Vengley. You've been helpful."

There were several Davises in the Coronado directory, but only one W. listed for Ninth Street. I thought about dialing the number and decided not to. It's harder to close a door than hang up a telephone. Besides, I wanted to see the man's eyes. I made the short drive up the Strand and turned north from Orange Avenue.

Like most of the streets in Coronado, this was a quiet one. The homes were smaller than the mansions closer to the beach. There, old money mixed with retired admirals and generals. Here were the more modest homes of retired captains and colonels. An American flag fluttered from a standard in front of a corner split-level. The glimpses over patio walls showed tiny gardens lush with flowers and citrus trees and care. The Davis house was a ranch-style duplex running down the depth of the narrow lot. A matching white stucco wall blocked off a small patch of front yard. Then it continued around the property line to enclose a larger rear patio. Apparently the garage was in back, approached from the alley.

I let myself through two green wooden gates and pressed the bell of the rear unit. A wrought-iron grille sheltered the door. It opened to show a man with his hands wrapped in a dish towel. "Yes?"

"Are you Mr. Davis?"

"Yes."

I introduced myself and told Davis what I wanted.

"Dwayne?" A hand came out of the dish towel to tug absently at the collar of his Hawaiian shirt. Davis was somewhere in his late thirties, about five-seven, gaunt, with a fleshy nose and deep lines running from it down to the corners of his mouth. His complexion had a kind of grayness that matched the narrow face and showed little effect of sun. "I haven't seen him for a while. Can you tell me why you're looking for him?"

"He might be able to help me with a case I'm working on."

"You—ah—you're a policeman?"

"No. I was looking for a missing girl. But it's gotten a bit more complicated. Dwayne might have some information that will help." The doorway gave a glimpse of the living room. Hung on the wall was a large charcoal sketch of a male Negro, nude and lounging against an ottoman. An end table bore a lamp whose base was an elongated female figure in smoky glass. "Can you suggest any place Dwayne might be?"

"What do you mean, 'complicated'?"

I smiled. "Well, it involves reasons why the girl was missing. Reasons why she might not want to return home."

"I see, I think."

"Did Dwayne ever mention the Temple of the Shining Spirit?"

Davis's almost black eyes stared up at me and after a moment he shook his head. "No. Not that I recall."

"It's in Denver. Did he ever talk about Colorado?"

"No. Look, I haven't seen Dwayne in a long time. I just don't know what he's up to now."

"Up to?"

Davis's lower teeth glimmered as they nipped at his upper lip. "I didn't mean anything by the phrase. But perhaps it was a dicey choice of words. Freudian slip, perhaps. 'Doing.' I don't know what Dwayne is doing now. I don't know where he is and I haven't talked to him in at least two years."

"I understand from his mother that you were very good friends for several years."

"We were, yes."

"How'd you meet him?"

Davis seemed surprised at the question. His eyebrows lifted to wrinkle a narrow forehead. "We, um, shared some interests. I met him at a bookstore."

"Interest in the occult?"

The man's eyes narrowed slightly. "Well, yes. Spiritual explorations."

"Satanism?"

"There's nothing illegal about it."

"I didn't say there was. Do you belong to the same Kabbal as Dwayne?"

"Kabbal? No—coven. I practice the Craft now. I gave up Satanism."

"Is that why you and Dwayne stopped being friends so suddenly?"

Davis hesitated and then nodded. "In part, yes. He's more into Satanism. I explored it for a while, but Wicca is more positive. It's a positive energy; Satanism's a negative energy." For the first time the man smiled, a quick lift and fall at the corners of his mouth. "We used to have some good talks."

"So you had shifted to witchcraft before you stopped being friends?"

"Yes."

"Was there any other reason you stopped being friends?"

Davis debated something. I waited. At last he bobbed his shoulders. "We had an argument. Quite an argument."

"About what?"

"Well, I happen to be homosexual. I'm not ashamed of it. But I don't flaunt it, either." He looked to see if I believed him. "Just like heterosexuals, there are responsible and irresponsible homosexuals. I happen to be a responsible one."

"Dwayne is homosexual?"

"Bisexual. Or so he claims. I suppose it's possible, though I have my doubts."

I asked, "How was he irresponsible?"

"He brought a little friend to my house once. Someone he picked up over on the beach. He expected me to join in the fun and games. I kicked them both out."

"A little friend?"

"A boy. Eleven, twelve. I am not a chicken hawk. I don't believe children have the maturity to make decisions about whether or not to join an adult in sexual activity—they can be too easily manipulated. By money or gifts, by emotional pressures. A great part of their innocence is their ignorance, Mr. Steele, and they don't really know what they are getting into." He took a deep breath. "I was a sexually abused child; I know what I'm talking about." He added, "That's not why I'm homosexual. Besides, Wicca teaches us to respect the wishes of others: 'As you harm none, do what thou wilt.' "

"Was this the first time you saw Dwayne with a child?"

"And the last."

"Do you know if he made a practice of pederasty?"

Davis shook his head. "We were friends for two or three years before this incident. He never even talked about it. I suppose that's why, when the two of them showed up right here where you're standing, I was shocked. Totally shocked." Another of those quick smiles. "And perhaps even verged on the irrational in my disappointment with Dwayne. At any rate, we've had no contact since then."

"Can you think of any place at all where he might be? Places he likes to hang out—bars, restaurants? Friends he might be staying with? Anyone he talked about a lot?"

"Well, as I said, the store where we met—Demeter Books. I went with him once to a bar over on the north side, Pony's, a gay place. As for people, he didn't really speak too much about other friends. Dwayne could be quite reticent about his personal life. Mostly we discussed the relative merits—or lack thereof—of Wicca and Satanism."

I got directions to the bookstore and bar and, thanking Davis, drove through the lingering twilight. The lights of downtown made a glare that dimmed the glitter of the bay bridge and brought the sky close to the streets. Demeter Books, like many shops but perhaps with more reason, was open until nine. It was a deep store with a narrow front and bookshelves running down the long axis. A handful of people, mostly men, browsed here and there. The clerk wore a full beard and a large chain and pentagram medallion around a pudgy neck. He nodded hello as I walked in.

I browsed down the aisles. Sections were labeled The Occult,

Wicca, Satanism, Spells and Incantations, Ceremonies. There was even a glass case offering a sale on bells, books, and candles. Mounted over the rear door, a ram's head with massive horns glared down with wide, glassy eyes. I wandered back to the proprietor. He smiled and placed his hand over his heart in a gesture I'd seen recently.

"Is that a greeting?"

Teeth shone white against red lips. "If you were a club member, you wouldn't have to ask. It's no secret; it's just like shaking hands among us."

"Satanist?"

"Of course. Thumb and little finger are the horns, bent middle fingers the head. Horns are sacred to Satan." He bobbed his head toward a shelf. "Read Hobbleston. He explains it all. In fact we have a special on it this week: *The Graffiti of the Dark Lord: Signs and Symbols of Satanism.*"

The youth at Alef Distributing . . . he'd placed his hand on his chest that way. "Accurate?"

"Mostly. But the graffiti section's dated. Hard to keep up with that—it changes too fast."

"I've been told by a friend that Dwayne Vengley comes in a lot. Have you seen him lately?"

"Dwayne?" The man's full lips pulled down. "He was in, what, a week or so ago just to say hello. I haven't seen him since then."

"Did he come alone or with someone?"

"By himself." He shifted on the stool that lifted him level with the counter. Down an aisle, one of the browsers coughed loudly and blew his nose, an absent honk of discomfort. "Why?"

"I'm not a cop, but I'm trying to find him. Nobody seems to know where he moved to."

"He moved? From that place on Island Avenue?"

I nodded. "Did you visit him there?"

"No. It's just where I send the mailing lists."

"What mailing lists?"

"He buys my outdated mailing lists. Helps me cover the overhead."

"He hasn't sent you a new address?"

"He probably will. I'm due to revise it next month. Twice a year it gets revised. With the cost of postage, I should do it more often than that. But even with the computer it's a bitch of a job."

"What's he do with your list?"

The lips pulled down again. "Says he mails out advertisements."

"What kind?"

"Don't know. It's not," he said pointedly, "my business." The man looked past me and smiled at a waiting customer.

I stepped aside as he cheerily rang up the sale. It was an hors d'oeuvres book and bar guide for Perfectly Satanic Hospitality. After the satisfied customer left, I asked, "Did he ever mention the Temple of the Shining Spirit?"

"Shining Spirit. I can't recall. But we sell their publications." He pointed to a shelf marked by a poster bearing a lotus figure surrounded by an aspen shape of radiating wisdom.

"Are they a satanic cult?"

He shrugged. "I don't know. I haven't heard that they are, so I put them in our occult section." Teeth glimmered again. "Prices are marked on the covers. And club members get a twenty-percent markdown."

The Pony Club was a place for homosexuals to see and be seen. The clients were mostly men, many young Hispanics. In the dimly lit room with its rough wood siding and barnlike decor, a few tables collected small groups of women. They held hands and rubbed each other's backs while they talked aggressively against the clatter of male voices. Some of the men eyed me suspiciously. Others rogueishly. I put my foot on the rail and waited for the bartender to work his way down the crowd. The sign indicating restrooms had an additional sign underneath: "One at a Time." Near the cash register, glittering in the faintly blue fluorescence of bar light, the trophy of a cowboy riding a bucking horse bore a hand-inked card: "World's Best Bare Back Rider Award." Along the bar, collection glasses with various wads of bills solicited for the AIDS Assistance Fund.

"Help you, sir?"

The youthful bartender, like most of the other males, wore a mustache and tight jeans.

"Has Dwayne Vengley been in lately?"

He hesitated, then asked a trifle too loud, "Are you a policeman?"

The men sidling up on each side quickly moved away. "No. He's a friend of mine."

"Oh." Suspicion narrowed the bartender's eyes. If I wasn't a cop, I was an older fag looking for his young lover who had probably gone on to someone else. Either way, I was trouble. "I really haven't seen him in a long time. At least a month. You might ask a bartender on another shift . . ." He raised shaped eyebrows. "Want to order a drink?"

"Maybe next time."

I stepped out into the quiet street with a feeling of relief. Willy Davis might have been comfortable with his homosexuality. But the restless hunger I saw in the eyes and gestures of those in the Pony Club depressed me. Like any singles bar, homo or hetero, the smiles were too wide, the laughter too strident, the saucy hints too desperate.

CHAPTER

The depression stayed with me back across the bridge and down the Strand. Deepened, perhaps, by my worry about Karen. When I reached home, I dialed her number, counting the rings until Chuck answered.

"No, we haven't heard a thing, Jack. A detective called and gave us his private number in case we needed it. He thought your idea of hiring a private detective was a good one. In fact, he gave us a couple names and I'll call first thing in the morning. Do you have anything new?"

"Nothing. I talked to a detective up there—Lewis. He said the police would provide drive-bys, but that's about all they could do."

"Yeah. He told us." Chuck's voice pulled away from the telephone and then came back. "Karen's more angry than upset now. But of course we're both worried."

"You'd be foolish not to worry."

"Yes. Karen wants to know if you reached Rebecca."

"I did. She's well and happy. I think if they went after anyone, it would be you first—you're closer."

"All right; I'll keep that in mind. Karen's here—she wants to say hello."

She and I spent a few moments trying to talk each other into feeling better. Her message was clear: she wanted me to know they were holding up. It was the kind of quiet courage I'd seen in a lot of service families. They were the ones who faced directly the nation's eruptions of war, terrorism, or other "military options"; and they also bore the accidents and deaths claimed by the dangerous practice of rehearsing for war. I suppose a lot of nonmilitary families have the same courage, but I can only speak for what I know. And I knew, too, that Karen was her mother's daughter.

The call came about an hour later. I'd finished a shower and was listening to the ten o'clock news while puttering around, checking the commissary for the groceries and household items I'd have to restock soon.

"Mr. Jack Steele?"

The voice was unfamiliar. But as soon as I heard it, I knew. "Yes."

"This is Dwayne Vengley. I understand you're looking for me."

"Where can we meet?"

"I haven't said that we could, yet. What is it you want to talk about?"

"Dori Wilcox, to start with. Why it would be good if you convinced her to come home."

"Me? Dori's a big girl, Mr. Steele. She can do what she wants to."

"She says she's staying in the Temple because you're going to join her and the baby there. That you've left Satanism."

"Well, there you are. What more to talk about?"

"About why you will tell her that you haven't left the Kabbal. About why you will tell her to come home."

"Care to amplify on that?"

"When we meet."

The line was silent. Then, "All right—neutral ground. You know the Coronado Ferry?"

"Yes."

"Catch the eleven-thirty. I'll meet you at the landing on the San Diego side."

The new San Diego–Coronado ferry was a mere ghost of the large boats that used to link the island with lower downtown. It was now against the law for an operator to run car ferries— the bridge had to be paid for. But plenty of foot passengers used the new one. Most were tourists or workers who could walk to their offices or grab easy public transportation from quayside. It left San Diego on the hour, Coronado on the half hour. A new parklike shopping mall of small shops and restaurants had replaced the light industry and junk waterfront that had been. Somewhere around the gift shop where I bought my ticket, I had labored all one summer rebuilding a '39 Ford into a version of a sports car. The finished product had been pretty bad. I learned a lot—mostly that I shouldn't have tried. But the car ran well enough to get me up to Stanford, through the school year, and into an oak tree one slightly fuzzy afternoon on a fast run back from Rizzotti's Beer Garden. But the landmarks that would give me the exact location of that summer's labor were gone, for better or worse, like a lot of other things.

I joined a crowd of tired tourists queuing up on the pier. They wore an assortment of T-shirts with neon messages and they lugged drooping, fussy children onto the ferry, which looked like a modified tug. With a shudder of engines and a thrash of foam, it started back across the black water.

I found a breezy seat at the bow. In high school one summer, I'd spent a lot of time this way on the old ferry. At four-thirty every morning, I'd cross to pick up the *San Diego Union* and run it around the island to the route carriers. Even the cold, late-night air and low-tide smell were familiar. Musty, rank. Almost stagnant salt water mixing with drying algae and seaweed. The smell also brought back nights spent drinking beer and telling jokes with Tom and the rest. And staring across the harbor at those lights to see an occasional boat glide past or the silhouette of a porpoise fin cruising just offshore.

Tommy. And Roger—now dead of cancer, rest his soul. He

had been a fine young man and I was sure he'd turned into a fine grown man as well. I regretted not having kept in touch with him. Those were the memories that, after the frittering away of all the other things that seemed to fill the days, made up an individual's history and past and home. The kind of past that no one would ever know except those I shared it with. No others could share it. My children had their own memories, and to them mine were just words. I remembered my mother telling me about her trips to Point Loma with her mother, before World War II. They drove out on Fridays in a new '36 Chevy to search the horizon for the black smudge of coal smoke that told them the fleet was coming back to port. In telling me, she had tried to include the detail that her young girl's eyes had seen: the pale yellow cactus flowers that sprinkled the dry gullies running down the ridge's spine. The tears stung from her eyes as they faced the icy sea wind. The excitement of knowing Daddy—my grandfather—would be home soon. And the warmth of standing next to Momma in her heavy coat as they stared. But even her detailed re-creation of it couldn't bring it alive for me. My reliving of my own memories for my girls would never bring them alive for them. The real life—the only life those events had—was in the actual living of them. And that living was trapped forever in each single, atomistic memory. And goddamn anyone who, out of their own selfishness and arrogance, corrupted the lives of other human beings and embedded their memories not with joy but with horror. Especially children.

The ferry gave a honk and reversed engines as it drew under the high wharf of Harbor Street. At the navy pier, a missile ship was moored. A sludge barge pumped its bowels clean, and its open hatches showed the white clutter of shipboard life. The only people were the shadows of the watch at the quarterdeck; most of the crew would be on liberty while the ship was serviced. Across the way, the berth for the cruise boat was empty. The brightly lit dining and dancing vessel was somewhere down the harbor on its nightly tour. Searching the almost empty wharf,

I held back to let the eager passengers step from the bobbing rail to the float and clatter up the gangplank to the wharf above. Then I joined the final stragglers.

This late on a weeknight, Harbor Drive was almost empty. A few cars sat with lights on in front of the neon of Anthony's Fish Grotto waiting to pick up diners. Across the divided street, empty parking meters formed rows of iron pickets. A few cars swung from Harbor up Broadway toward the center of town. The crowd from the ferry dispersed, hurrying for cars or the last trolley that waited a few more moments and then pulled away. With their disappearance, the darkness seemed heavier. The restless water around the pilings made a faint sucking sound as the tide ran in. My ears and eyes strained to catch any movement as I stood by the empty gangplank and waited. It was a good place for an ambush.

Finally, a tall figure stepped from behind an ill-lit cluster of oleander and palm trees. It walked slowly toward me.

"Mr. Steele?"

"Dwayne Vengley?"

Neither of us offered to shake hands. Instead, we studied each other for a long moment. Vengley was an inch or so taller than I. His pale-blond hair curled down his nape and in front of his ears. His rounded chin thrust aggressively beneath a straight nose and he stared at me with eyes set deep under a prominent ledge of eyebrows.

"This way."

He jerked his head in command. I followed him back toward the darkness that pooled around the foot of the navy pier. Vengley found a concrete bench and sat. Beyond him, toward the end of the pier, the lights of the missile ship lifted above the sharp crease of its bow. Except for the shrubbery, the area was empty of places for people to hide. It was a broad stretch of wooden dock that ran between the cutter and the towering flanks of a dark troop ship moored at the next pier. I could make out her name glimmering in the dark: the *Daniel I. Sultan.* One of my uncles had sailed on her to Europe in

World War II; I had spent forty-five glorious days on her, crossing to Okinawa from this very port. God only knew what generation of cockroaches sailed aboard her now.

"Well?" Vengley's voice was a soft drawl.

"All I wanted was to find Dorcas."

"And you found her, right?"

"Among other things."

The young man's body leaned forward. "What's that mean?"

"Why did you kill Shelley?"

"That's a stupid question, Mr. Steele. Are you a stupid man?"

"And why threaten my daughter?"

After a long moment, a smile tightened Vengley's lips. "I don't know about any threats. Still, if it was my daughter, I'd be very, very worried. In fact, I'd feel grateful that someone cared enough to warn me."

"Funny me. I'm not. I'm just curious to know what you're hiding. And ornery enough to get pissed when somebody threatens me or mine."

"What do you mean, 'what we're hiding'?"

"You overreacted, Vengley. When I was looking for Dorcas. The question is why. The answer is you're hiding something."

He was silent a moment. "Look, Steele, I don't know what in the hell you're talking about. You said you had something to tell me that would convince me to send Dori home. So tell me."

"That's the price for me to quit digging. And for me not to go to the police with what I know now. That, and no more threats against my daughters."

"Let me get this straight: I tell Dori to go home, you back off. That it?"

"That and no more threats."

Vengley stood and dusted off the seat of his pants. "You think I've got something to be afraid of if you don't back off?"

"Somebody killed Shelley Aguirre. Somebody killed David Gates. Somebody talked Jerry Hawley into killing himself."

The shape stared my way through the dimness. "That's what you believe."

"Yeah."

"Well, I'll think this over, Mr. Steele." He glanced down the dock. "Now you better hurry or you'll miss the last ferry back."

The ferry was almost empty. Only a few stragglers like myself rode back to Coronado at this hour. I watched the city lights pull away and wondered if that little charade had accomplished anything.

Vengley was a handsome youth, and those deep-set eyes under a tall forehead gave his gaze a charismatic intensity. I could understand Dorcas's fascination with him, if she only looked at the surface. Or if she believed she was saving his soul. And he seemed used to giving commands, expecting obedience. He would be the kind of personality that could sway weaker ones, the kind they might even be attracted to in order to share his strength. But beneath all the arrogant self-consciousness had been a faint tremor of concern.

He had come to find out something—there was no reason for him to get in touch with me otherwise. The young man seemed intelligent. Bright enough, anyway, to know that if I had any real evidence concerning the dead, I wouldn't offer to step away. Something I was doing was worrying him enough to make him threaten, and then meet with me.

By the time the boat docked, the cluster of harborside shops had closed for the night. Their display windows glowed white in the increasingly misty air. A giggling man and woman sprinted past me down the dock for the last ferry to San Diego. I turned toward the small, unlit parking lot and my car. My shoes scuffed in the gravel and echoed against the closed walls. In the distance, a car raced its engine and squealed a stretch of rubber on the pavement. Then the island was quiet. As I bent to unlock the door, a darting movement reflected in the window.

Turning, I bent low to guard against whatever it was.

Two men, masked by stockings pulled down to twist their

features, lunged for me. One swung a short pipe before him. The other, a step or two back, circled to get behind me. The pipe chopped toward my head and I caught the metal bar on my crossed forearms. Its thudding blow numbed my hands but I twisted hard against the grip of the man's thumb. Behind me, the other man rushed in to wrap an arm around my neck and pull back. He tried to pull me down and I wrenched the pipe out of the clutching hands and jabbed backwards with it. It jammed solidly against something that mashed and jerked and grunted a curse. The arm dropped from my throat and, spinning, I snapped a side kick at the first man's knee. It hit and drove him far enough away so I could get my car at my back. The two hesitated, then they dove forward. One came high, the other low. I parried one set of snagging fingers with the pipe. The other tangled in my legs and twisted, pulling me over despite my elbow thudding repeatedly at the back of the man's head. A stunning, glare-splintering blow caught me somewhere on the side of my skull and I felt myself going down. Another fist dug into my ribs. Elbows flailing, I tried to hit what I could, but the sting of gravel and dirt mashed against my face and a heavy shoe caught my stomach, emptying my lungs and doubling me as much in pain as self-defense.

I tried to get to my feet but another fist clubbed the back of my neck and jarred my spine with numb tingles.

"You fucker!" Another kick. "You want to poke around? You want to stick your goddamned nose where it don't belong?" The questions were punctuated with kicks. "You keep the hell away—you want your goddamned kids to live, you keep the hell out of our fucking business!" A final kick aimed at my head. It bounced off my hunched shoulder, and the sound of feet ran into silence. I heard the slam of doors and a moment later the yelp of tires as a car made a sharp turn for the bridge.

I lay still to let my body tell me if anything were broken. Nothing seemed to be. But I'd have to move to know for sure. Gingerly, I crawled from under the side of the car. Using the fender, I levered myself to my feet. The twinge of bruised flesh snagged in my back and I felt the burning throb of scrapes on my arm and cheek. But it was my ribs that worried me. Every breath brought a stitch of pain that could be a bad bruise or, worse, a break.

Clumsily, I lowered myself behind the wheel and slowly drove toward the main gate at the North Island air base.

The corpsman joked about drunken sailors getting rolled. Holding up a wet sheet of X-ray film, he pinned it against the glow of the viewing light for the doctor to study in the morning. Watching from the examining table, I asked what he saw.

"I'm not a radiologist, but I don't see any obvious breaks, sir. I'll tape you up. Either way, you ought to be taped up. A doctor'll look at the X-rays tomorrow morning. You can call the main desk and they'll tell you if anything's broken."

The pain of breathing had lessened considerably. I didn't think there was a break either. The corpsman washed out the scrapes and bandaged what needed bandaging, then he started rummaging for pills.

"What'd the other guy look like?"

"Not as bad. There were two."

"Well, Colonel, you're lucky. At least they didn't use knives. Or razors. We see our share of that every Saturday night."

He handed me a small bottle of white pills that I recognized as the navy's cure-all: APCs. "If you have persistent headaches or blurry vision, or if you notice infection, see a doctor as soon as possible."

"Right."

The long drive home was through empty streets. When I finally collapsed on my bed the tetanus shot and pills swirled me into a sweaty, dream-racked sleep. The telephone was the first thing to wake me, and my twanging muscles the second. I grunted hello and Admiral Combs's voice gave a crisp good morning and said he was just checking to see if I'd come up with anything to get Dorcas home.

"Good question, Admiral. I don't think I've been too successful."

"What's the matter, Jack? Is something wrong?"

I told him, the words muffled through swollen lips.

"Beat up? How bad are you hurt, Jack?"

"I've been to sick call already. I'll live."

"You'll stay right there, too. Jenny and I are coming over."

Rolling to my side, I eased out of bed and stumbled into the shower to soak in water as hot and hard as my scraped flesh could stand. Gradually, bending and twisting, my body loosened up and the aches began to ebb. By the time the admiral and his wife rang the doorbell, I even had some appetite back, which was good. It was a sign I didn't have a concussion.

"Oh, my God, Jack!" Jenny started to reach up to my face but then paused. "Does it hurt much?"

"Of course it hurts, damn it!" The admiral closed the door and stared at me. "It was Vengley, wasn't it?"

"His people." I limped into the kitchen. "Coffee?"

"Let me, Jack." Jenny insisted I sit down while she heated the water and even cleaned out a cantaloupe for me.

"They wouldn't have done this if they weren't worried, Jack."

"I'm glad I didn't worry them anymore." One thing was certain: if I was going to be a professional snoop, I'd have to work out in a gym as well as run the beach. The reflexes forgot a lot when all they did was hold down a desk.

"Can't I fix you some eggs or something?"

"This is fine, Jenny. Thanks."

"I'm sorry we got you into this."

I couldn't tell the admiral I was overjoyed, but I didn't want him feeling guilty about it, either. "I could have pulled out anytime. Now I've got a personal stake." I told them about the threats to my daughters.

"My God . . ." The admiral frowned at his coffee cup. "They could do something to them, couldn't they? Beating you up says that."

"It tells me we don't want to take a chance."

"Dorcas can't know about any of this—she can't!"

"No, Jenny, I don't think she does. She really believes Vengley's left the Kabbal."

"Do you think he might do something to her now?" The admiral's eyes were hard as two blue marbles.

"The police—they have to help us now!"

I tried to make Jenny and the admiral believe that Dorcas was all right. But I couldn't convince myself, either: during the restless night, I'd remembered another place I saw the satanic hand sign—at the Temple's lodge in the mountains. When they left, I promised to call Shaughnessy and see if he could suggest any way to persuade the Denver police to help get the girl out of the Temple.

CHAPTER

27

Shaughnessy himself answered the telephone. I told him about meeting with Vengley and about the assault.

"You think Vengley set you up?"

"He knew I'd be on the ferry and when. All he had to do was drop a dime and tell them I'd be coming."

"Uh-huh. Sounds possible." The telephone was silent. "You all right?"

"A few sore spots. I don't think anything's broken."

"That's good. Can you identify your assailants?"

"No. They wore stocking masks. I didn't even see their car."

"So no real link to Vengley."

"Just my suspicions. And their warning to keep my nose out of their business or look out for my kids."

"So what makes you think they were amateurs?"

"A lot of wild swinging and kicking. I went down. They could have done some real damage if they knew what they were doing."

"I don't know that I'd complain about that, Mr. Steele." He asked, "Are you going to keep out of their business?"

"It's my business now."

"Uh-huh. Thought you might feel that way. I did some snooping for you."

"What'd you get?"

"Not much, but something. Among the major stockholders of Mountain and Mesa Investments is one Arthur Vengley."

"How in hell did you find that out?"

"A phone call—it's a public corporation. Does it make any sense to you?"

"Not yet. But it's interesting."

"Does it lead anywhere on the Aguirre homicide?"

"If it does, I'll call."

"You be damned sure you do."

I promised again that I would, and then I asked about any possible help from Denver in getting Dorcas away from the Temple.

"No way, Mr. Steele. The most they could do for us would be go by and ask her if she's all right. If she wants to stay, there's no way they can take her without some criminal charge."

That was what I'd figured. I hung up and started working my stiff body into a coat and tie. As I was finishing, the telephone rang. It was Megan.

"Jenny told me what happened, Jack. Are you all right?"

"Hey, marines—ex-marines—call that rest and recreation."

"Right. I've read the propaganda. You and John Wayne."

"He's dead."

"That's what worries me."

There were a couple ways to take that. And what the hell, John Wayne, even dead, wouldn't play it too cautious. "If that's what it takes to worry you, I'll do it again."

It was her turn to pause. "Suppose I just worry without it."

"And suppose I set your mind at ease over dinner."

"You are all right, aren't you?"

"I am now."

We set a date for Friday. Megan had one request. "I'd just as soon we didn't tell Jenny about this, Jack. She might jump to an . . . unreasonable conclusion."

I didn't want to listen to her gloat either. "It's a deal."

———

Mountain and Mesa Investments had their headquarters in a new high-rise office that had sprouted a few miles north of downtown. The suite was on the twentieth floor behind a band of tinted windows overlooking the lines of traffic on Interstate 805 below. Arthur Iacino had placed his desk so the glare from the windows highlighted his profile for visitors; the rest of the office breathed comfort and financial security. I ignored the stare of the receptionist. Iacino politely ignored my battle scars. He offered me a deeply upholstered leather chair snuggled under the leaves of a large ficus.

"We do a variety of investments, Mr. Steele. We started in real estate over fifteen years ago, and since then we've diversified into a number of areas." He nodded at a chart on the wall whose pie slices indicated the percentages of corporate funds going to different types of investments. "Real estate is still the bulk of our holdings—the profit's still there. But we've cushioned ourselves against fluctuation in that market by wise and selective money management. That, and our streamlined administration, is why we can offer a return that's several points higher than you'll find in any bank."

"And the risk?"

"Of course there's risk." Iacino's dark eyes smiled merrily behind the yellow-tinted lenses of his aviator's glasses. "You don't get this kind of return without some risk. But the diversification keeps it within sound limits. If—and it's not very likely—the bottom dropped out of real estate tomorrow, we'd be cushioned by our other sectors. It's the same principle used by the most successful mutual funds. We just apply it to local and regional markets. An investment area, I'm pleased to say, that we pioneered."

I made a few notes on a small yellow pad. Iacino had given me a glossy brochure that showed a well-dressed, gray-haired couple smiling widely at an equally smiling dark-suited figure handing them a check. The caption urged readers to make their retirement money work harder by purchasing shares in Mountain and Mesa Investments. "And the initial share is ten thousand?"

"Yes, sir. After the initial buy-in we offer the opportunity for incremental purchases in five-thousand-dollar amounts." He added, "Many of our clients find that the income from a one-hundred-thousand-dollar investment is quite suitable for their retirement needs." He shrugged. "It all depends on your tax situation and age. Many of our investors combine their social security with their dividends." He smiled again. "I assume you'll be starting a second career and would prefer to let the dividends accrue until you reach sixty-five?"

I nodded. As one more recently retired government employee seeking better return on my accumulated retirement fund, Mountain and Mesa had caught my eye. "Well, I like the idea of using the money to develop local businesses. It seems to be responsible capitalism."

"Oh, yes—well put. The local economy profits . . . and so do we."

"I understand Alef Distributing is in your portfolio. Can you give me an idea of how well it performs?"

"If it's there, it must be doing well!" He turned to a computer terminal and punched up a menu. Then he rattled keys. A few moments later a printer clattered into life. Iacino tore off a page and scanned it before handing it to me. "You can see it has a very impressive earnings record."

It did—on paper at least. Over the last three years, the company's investment had returned an average of twenty-three percent.

"They must do a tremendous business."

"Well. I don't have access to their detailed statement, just to our returns from them. But, yes, it must be good. I think it's typical of our portfolio, Mr. Steele. That's the kind of business we locate and develop. That's why we can almost guarantee our high yield every year."

"I didn't know distribution was so profitable."

"They're certainly doing something right, aren't they? But

as I say, our expertise is the local economy, and we constantly monitor the earnings of each and every investment. We know which companies will pay off."

"Exactly what does Alef distribute?"

"Well . . . I'm not sure. But I can check with our market analyst on that, Mr. Steele. All I have here is the bottom line. Are there other holdings you'd like to know about?"

I had the man select two or three at random and, though they didn't come near the profitability of Alef, they contributed handsomely to the company's returns. Finally, I shook hands and gathered up my brochures and graphs and told a slightly disappointed Iacino I would think carefully about the investment.

A lot of money. Low costs and high profits added up to a lot of money being made by Alef. Those profits could come from volume trade or an outrageous margin on each item. Or a combination. On a product that no one seemed able to identify . . .

The blinking light on my answering machine told me I had a message and I ran the tape to Play. A cautious voice whispered, "Mr. Steele, this is Dori Wilcox. I'm at the Temple in Denver. I've found out something horrible—it's horrible— please help me. I'll try to call again. Please help!"

Now she understood what the phrase "born again" meant—well, not meant, exactly, but felt like. It felt like you were suddenly light and free and clean. All the dark and heavy thoughts and nagging worries, all the restlessness that made nights sweaty and broken, all that was gone. Gone, too, was the weary feeling that for so long had robbed each day of its freshness so that she had even forgotten what it was like to welcome a morning. She felt like a little girl, childlike in touching with eye and finger the brilliant colors of a flower, in losing herself in the slow, awesome shifting and magic of towering clouds, in discovering a sweet sense of kinship with all other living things. Now she woke to each day eagerly and happily, now she slept at night with a sigh of contentment and a prayer of gratitude for the blessing of God's generous forgiveness and the kindness of the Pastor's guidance.

When she first arrived, she had been suspicious of the happiness she saw in the others. She had distrusted the comfort they found in the passages from the Vedas that they read and meditated on twice a day. They were putting on a charade of wide-eyed smiling faces and mild answers, trying to convince themselves as well as her that they knew the secret of living with joy. But, as the Pastor gently reminded her, she had come to the ashram of her own free will to see—so why not truly see? Why not set aside her suspicions and preconceptions, her worldly cynicism, and just use her eyes and ears and soul and let them tell her mind what they discovered, instead of her telling her senses what to see?

She still could not point to the exact moment of revelation. Some could—Sister Jolene said it was when she was meditating late one night and suddenly she saw herself through her third eye, and from that new angle of vision and distance wondered why that anxious person below was struggling so hard against something that was so simple and good for her. Something that was there waiting for her to take it up. From that moment on, Sister Jolene said, she accepted, and in accepting, had found the Peace of Spirit that others in the Temple shared.

But for her, the acceptance had come more slowly, and in small stages. Perhaps because she had so much more to slough off than Sister Jolene or some of the others. Perhaps because she had a deeper reservoir of cynicism and distrust of herself as well as of others. Still, come it had, and she remembered that morning when she woke early, long before the others and while the sun was only a pink streak low under the cool gray of dawn. Alone, she had climbed the stairs to the roof and settled to watch the world stir into life, and then she realized she felt peace. Deep, pervasive, thorough peace. And acceptance.

It was what Dwayne had tried to tell her. It was what he said Shirley had discovered, too. But she hadn't believed him. At first she would not believe either in the peace she seemed to have found or in Dwayne's claim that Pastor Pettes and the Temple of the Shining Spirit had cleansed him of his submission to Satan. And Shirley, who had gone up to the lodge before Dori arrived at the Temple, wasn't around to tell her if what Dwayne said about her was true. But he didn't insist. Not even in the subtle way he used to have of insisting even while he talked about letting people do what they wanted to. Instead, he stepped back and left her to talk to Pastor Pettes and the others as she would, left

*her to the quiet and benevolent—that was the only word—guid-
ance of the Pastor. And, gradually, she had discovered what that
peace was and that she could share in it.*

She and Dwayne and the baby.

*As if, at the end of a long and weary journey that seemed to
have no direction, suddenly she glimpsed a place of rest and
welcome.*

CHAPTER

Dori had not called back and my calls to the Temple were answered by a taped message that gave the office hours, urged a turning away from earthly concerns, and told where to send donations. I tried to reach Shaughnessy but he was out of the office and the clerk wouldn't give me the man's home number. Standard procedure, but it made things damned awkward. I left a message for him citing Dori's words and asked that he request the Denver police to interview the girl as soon as possible. Calling the airlines, I reserved a standby ticket on the last red-eye to Denver. Then I telephoned the admiral and Henry to tell them about it. They both urged me to go and wanted to know what they could do to help. Finally, I telephoned Karen and told her I'd be out of town for a little while.

"Colorado? Why do you have to go there?

"It might have something to do with this mess, Karen. I'll let you know as soon as I'm back."

Megan wasn't home. Since she refused to get an answering machine, I couldn't tell her I might not be back by Friday. Maybe the admiral would tell her where I was. Maybe I'd better wrap this up and get my butt back by then.

This late at night the palm-lined roads looping around the airport lay empty under the metallic glare of streetlights. I checked in at the ticket counter and was told the gate number. Then I settled into one of the molded plastic seats to wait. Loading started with the usual call for people traveling with children, those needing assistance, and those flying first-class. When the final section of reserved seats had been summoned, I and a few others stood at the counter while the crew checked the passenger manifest. Finally my name was called and I hurried down the loading ramp.

Most of the flight was spent in restless drowsing and uneasy thoughts. The seat backs, curved to fit everyone, fit no one. A pillow finally gave me support for the small of my back and an aisle seat let me stretch my legs. Half-awake, I glimpsed the icy white of a full moon gleaming on the tops of cumulus clouds and felt the lurch of air pockets. When finally we glided down the Rockies and over the sprawling grid of lights that was Denver, it was 3:00 A.M. Mountain Time, and the long day's weariness had settled into a headache that pressed against the tops of my eyeballs. A sleepy clerk filled out the paperwork for the rental car. A shuttle finally took me through the chilly night air to the vehicle compound.

I tried the Temple again at seven-thirty from my motel. This time a breathy female voice answered, "Temple of the Shining Spirit."

"May I speak to Sister Dori, please. It's a family emergency."

". . . Just a moment. I'll see if she's here."

It was more than a moment before a male voice came on. "Sister Dori's in meditation right now. Who's calling, please?"

"Jack Steele. I've just arrived from San Diego, and I have a very important message from her father."

"I can deliver it to her."

"No. He asked me to tell her myself. It's personal."

"Well, we can't interrupt meditation. If you want to call back after nine, you can speak with Pastor Pettes."

"No. I'll come by and speak with Sister Dori."

"Well, I'm afraid—"

I hung up on the voice and plunged under the heat of a

scalding shower. A quick breakfast and then I threaded my way across east Denver in the morning rush hour. This time when I parked in the guest slot behind the red-brick building, the children in the day-care center were gathered in a circle on the far side of the sandy playground. Sister Rhona, even more pregnant, looked up from the desk on the converted back porch.

"Welcome to the Temple. Can I help you with something?"

"I called earlier. I'm here to see Sister Dori."

"Oh."

"I was told she's in meditation. I have an emergency message from her father."

The woman's light brown eyes blinked. "I'll have to talk to the Pastor." She pushed herself up from the desk with both arms and walked heavily into the hallway. Her sandals slapped loudly on the polished wooden floor.

When she came back, she smiled apologetically. "I'm sorry. The Pastor isn't in yet. And I'm not allowed to interrupt meditation. If you want to leave your telephone number, I'll ask Sister Dori to call you after Morning Rites."

"I need to see Sister Dori now. It's very important. I'm not here to make trouble for her or for you, but I do need to talk to her."

The woman smiled and shrugged. "But what can I do? Only the Pastor can interrupt Morning Meditation, and he's not here."

I stood. "She meditates upstairs?"

"Wait—you can't—"

But I moved faster than she did. I passed the closed door to Pettes's reception room and headed for the stairs. Before I reached them I heard the muffled jangle of an electric bell and the quick thump of bare heels above. I was a few steps up when two young men, robed and alarmed, appeared at the landing and glared down at me. A third man, a few years older, leaned over the railing. "You're trespassing. Outsiders are forbidden in this area. Go back down."

The two young men, ready to fight, came slowly toward me.

"I have to talk to Sister Dori. It's vital."

"Then you have to ask the Pastor when he gets here. He'll give you permission to talk to anybody in the Temple. Now, I ask you to go in peace. We don't want to violate the Temple with anger."

The two came down another step, followed by the third man. I backed down to the first floor. Behind me, I heard Sister Rhona's heavy breath.

"I tried to stop him. He wouldn't—"

"That's all right, Sister Rhona. He's leaving now."

At the bottom of the stairs, the two stepped away from each other, ready to close on me from both sides. The third man spoke gently. "We don't like violence. But we've learned to defend ourselves."

"Fine—I'll take your word for it. But will you please tell Sister Dori she has a visitor?"

"I will if the Pastor tells me to."

The two eased within kicking range, herding me toward the doorway. Sister Rhona stood rigid and frowning as I backed down the outside steps.

"Please don't come back, Mr. Steele," she said. "You're not welcome anymore."

"I hope I don't have to come back with a warrant, Sister Rhona."

"You don't frighten us. We've had people harass us before. The Spirit protects us."

"Be sure and tell Pastor Pettes and the Spirit that I'll be back to see Dori."

The screen door slammed. I searched the windows of the second floor for any faces, any movement of a curtain. But they remained blank and empty. Feeling Sister Rhona's angry eyes on my back, I walked down the redstone walk to my car. A robed woman was busily raking the parking area and picking up trash in a black plastic bag. As I unlocked the door, I heard a voice whisper "Sir?"

"Yes?"

"Don't look around—they're watching."

I opened the door and sat, not yet starting the car.

"Sister Dori's not here." The murmur barely carried over the scrape of the straw rake. "She's at the Retreat. They took her up there two days ago."

Unfolding a road map, I held it in front of my face. "Up in the mountains? Near Ward?"

The screen door slapped and one of the two young men came out on the back stairs.

"The mountains—yes!" The mutter hurried. "Help us. Help the children." The woman picked up a final shred of paper and walked slowly back toward the building.

I closed the car door and backed into the alley. The youth on the porch watched me out of sight.

I left the car parked by one of the silent cabins near the gate to the lodge. Cutting through the fringe of brush beside the road, I found a relatively open avenue among tall pines and began to work my way toward the log-and-stone building. Staying in the shadows, I paused frequently to search ahead through the binoculars I'd bought in Denver. The light day-pack with its smell of new canvas began to heat my back, and I tied a bandanna around my forehead to keep the sweat from burning my eyes. The pack held what little I needed, and though the new canvas shoes wouldn't do for an extended hike, they were light and quiet and gripped the tilted surface of boulders.

When I came within view of the ranch, I pulled farther back into the woods and studied the buildings. Half a dozen cars and vans were parked in the open area in front of the main lodge, but only a few people could be seen. A woman wearing a tube top and cutoff jeans sat near the slide leafing through a magazine. Beside her, three children—two boys and a girl somewhere between seven and nine years old—played desultorily in the sandbox. At least, two of them seemed to be playing. The third, the younger boy, just sat and gazed away from the house toward the woods.

Through the binoculars, the windows of the lodge trembled in magnified heat waves from the stone-and-log walls. A pale wisp of smoke rose from the main chimney, the only sign of life inside the lodge. Except for the woman and three children, no one moved. I walked a long, roundabout way to a ridge overlooking the lush green meadow and the buildings. A film of caked dust dried on my face and neck; occasional deer flies zoomed in to sample my flavor.

The binoculars picked up a stone-lined path that arced across the small creek behind the barn and disappeared into a thick stand of lodgepole pines. The parallel lines of evenly spaced and whitewashed stones gave the trail a formal look. I made my way through the trees to follow it. In a corral beyond the screen of brush, a horse snorted as it caught my scent on the light breeze. The trail wound through the thick woods to a circular clearing carved out of an aspen grove. A thick carpet of mown and trampled grass formed a level bed. Across the circle sat an ornate wooden chair. Made of the smooth trunks of aspen saplings, it had a high back and wide arm rests and sat on an elevated platform of split logs as if it had grown almost naturally from the earth. Smaller twigs made the design of an upside-down star on the seat back. Along its base a frieze of sticks spelled out runic letters that I could not read. Directly in front of the chair, a low stone served as a base for open fires, and a mound of ashes covered its face. Around the central fire and including the throne, a line of small quartz rocks made a circle. I paced off its diameter—three paces: the nine feet I expected. Another line of stones made a triangular shape beyond the circle, one of its points aimed at the throne. There the grass was longer and undisturbed. According to what I'd read, that was where the spirits that might be harmful would be summoned while the worshipers remained safe in the circle. Aleister Crowley's design, which, true or false, he claimed to get from runic texts and which by now had the authority of unholy writ among those who wanted to believe in Satanism.

The circle was a primary symbol in a number of faiths, Christianity among them. Witches and Satanists used it to focus their psychic energy when practicing magic. If a coven grew too big for all members to fit in the nine-foot circle, a new group had to be formed with its own circle. Some of the texts I'd read said the range of effectiveness of the magic was three miles around, so new covens had to be far enough away not to overlap and confuse each other's spells. That meant a six-mile diameter— not a bad impact zone for low-budget weaponry.

Looking, I found the five stakes that would hold string forming a pentagram when certain rites were performed. It wasn't as ornate as some sites I'd read about, but the basics were here: magic nine-foot circle, signs and symbols, throne for priest or priestess or even Satan's spirit in some ceremonies. The grass, carefully picked of rocks and thorns and brush, provided bedding for the sexual revelry that followed most rituals. And the miles of empty forest around gave the necessary isolation. I didn't see an altar, though. Perhaps they elected one of the women to be a living altar, bracing her with a portable rest stored nearby. I could imagine a group of people, robed or nude—skyclad, as they called it—lit by the fire on the central stone and intoning whatever chant was called for. What I had trouble imagining was Dori—with her forswearing of Satanism—joining the circle willingly. Certainly the groping, half-terrified voice of last night's telephone call wasn't that of a willing participant. I touched the ash-covered stone sitting in front of the throne. It was still warm.

The smell of fresh ashes was heavy in the hot air. Smears of greasy candle fat glinted on the arms of the throne. In the highest rituals, the candles were supposed to be made of the fat of babies, and the odor from the smears did nothing to dispel that idea. More greasy wax formed melted lumps at the points of the pentagram. The only sound was an occasional insect and a distant squawk from a mountain jay somewhere up the steep ridge that began a hundred yards or so beyond the glade.

At the far side of the glade, an unmarked path of newly trampled grass led into a dark gap in the treeline. It twisted between the thick trunks of old and large ponderosa and across roots that lifted like wooden veins from the packed earth. Branches closed around heavily, and the shadows breathed a moist chill that the sun, reaching this far only as pale spots, could not dispel. A charred smell and shriveled pine needles told me that those who took this path in the dark used flaming torches to light their way. An occasional broken branch said that people stumbled and grabbed out for balance.

The trail twisted steeply uphill as the ridge began to close in on the sides. Then it snaked between two massive boulders that choked the narrow gulch. Beyond the boulders, a steep cliff formed a ragged wall.

This was the place of sacrifice. They had come and gone, leaving behind signs and stains and a tangle of odors that even the tingling smell of pine and dust hadn't erased. A soot-stained cliff sheltered the small gully on three sides. Under the overhang of the back wall, which was mottled by patches of lichen and dark streaks of old water courses, a large boulder rested like an altar. Around it in a semicircle, smaller flat stones looked like the pedestals of missing columns or seats of honor for an inner circle. Farther back, toward the open end where I stood, the ground was scuffed by traces of feet, and the sparse grass was flattened and dying.

The odor of piss-wet charcoal came from the large pile of ashes and charred wood. It mingled with the unnatural sweetness of heavily perfumed candles. Under it was an almost sour smell that reminded me of a butcher shop after a busy day. That came from a soggy patch of ground at the foot of the altar rock. A reddish-brown stain had run from a now-dried pool in one of the rock's hollows to the gritty and sticky earth below. Above the gentle sigh of pine needles, I heard an erratic, nervous whine, and an occasional glint of steely green leaped and swirled and settled again on the stains. But it wasn't the odor or the feeding flies that made me feel sick. It was the knowledge that I was too late.

By the time I made my way back to the trees overlooking the lodge, the sun was almost straight overhead. Another car had joined the row of parked vehicles, and the woman and three children had disappeared to leave the grounds empty of life. I searched each window, but saw little. The large ground windows gave a shadowy view into the lodge's main hall. It held a scattering of chairs and sofas, worn and sagging as befit a summer house. A towering mossrock chimney formed the wall at one end, and over the black fireplace was a gigantic ram's head mounted like a hunting trophy. Through the binoculars I could see two pinball machines in an alcove, along with a pair of video games and a child's plastic pony. A pair of open doors led to a dining room that held wooden trestle tables and benches. Unless you knew about the clearing in the woods, the lodge looked like any other dude ranch. An occasional figure strolled through the room, but none of them was Dori.

From this distance, I wasn't going to find out if she was in there and alive. Slipping around through the trees, I put the barn between me and the house and worked closer.

The horses snorted and tossed their heads as I paused by a corner of weathered boards and scouted the outbuildings. Sliding between the rails, I crossed the powdered dust of the corral and entered the barn's side door. The shade lifted the heat of sun and was filled with the quiet smell of hay. Listening for footsteps or a voice, I edged toward the large doors that opened to the parking area and lodge beyond. From a dark corner, I again searched the lodge's windows with the binoculars. A rattle of crockery and a murmur of voices floated from the kitchen. But from this angle I couldn't see into it. Then a screen door slapped. Dwayne Vengley and a young boy came out on the front porch.

The blond man said something to the boy, who stared down at his feet and swung a toe in short arcs against the porch boards. It was one of the children from the sandbox, the one who had simply sat in silence. Vengley patted him on a shoulder and guided him toward the barn.

I pulled back into a horse stall as they came up to the front of the barn and leaned on the rail to feed something to one of the horses.

"Don't you like being up here, Brian? We sure like having you." Vengley's voice was a pleasant murmur. "The Pastor was telling me just yesterday that you're one of the nicest boys we've ever had to visit the ranch."

The boy said nothing. He held out a handful of oats and gingerly let the horse mouth them from his palm.

"Rusty and Sandy like you, too. Don't you like them?"

"Yes. I guess so."

"Well, why don't you tell me what's wrong, Brian? I can't help if I don't know what's bothering you."

The boy mumbled something to the horse.

"What?"

"I'm scared!"

"Well, there's nothing to be scared of! Has anyone hurt you? Tell me, has anyone hurt you at all?"

". . . No."

"Then what makes you frightened?"

"What they'll do. What the Pastor said they'll do."

"Oh, that's only if you tell somebody. You're not going to tell anybody, are you?"

"No!"

"Then you don't have anything to be afraid of, do you? Are Rusty and Sandy afraid?"

"I guess not." He added, "But they've been here before, too."

"And they wanted to come back, didn't they?"

"I guess so."

"Oh, you know they did. They invited you along, didn't they? Do you think they would have done that if they were afraid?"

"I don't know. I guess not."

"Of course not." Vengley patted the boy's shoulder again.

"Look, I'll tell you what—anytime you feel afraid, you come see me, okay? You're a very special person to me, Brian. I'll take care of anything that makes you afraid."

"I won't have to make any more movies?"

"Not if you really don't want to."

"Pastor won't get mad if I don't?"

"No. Not mad. He'll be disappointed. You made a promise, remember? You promised to do what we told you and we promised to let you ride horses and camp out and go fishing, remember?"

"Yeah. But . . ."

"And Rusty and Sandy will be disappointed, too. They like having you make movies with them. And isn't it really a little bit fun sometimes?"

"Sometimes, I guess."

"Sure it is. And how many young men and women your age get to be in real movies? That's something special. It's not like there's anything wrong with it, Brian. My goodness, do you think the Pastor or me or any of the family would want you to do something that was wrong?"

"I . . . I guess not."

"But we have to keep some things secret from other people. That's why Pastor said those things about what would happen if anybody told."

"He scared me."

Vengley stroked the back of the boy's head and they started slowly back toward the lodge. "Well, you're not going to tell, so there's not a thing to be afraid of. Come on—I'll bet the camera's all set up now and I'll bet Rusty and Sandy are wondering where you are."

Understanding fully now, I rose from my hiding place to watch the two stroll across the sandy patch toward the lodge. Behind me I heard a hissing grunt and jerked around to see the twisted, bristly face of the caretaker just before the end of an axe handle smashed my vision into ringing black.

CHAPTER

It might have been the thick and sour taste of dried blood in my mouth. Maybe it was the rip of pain across my forehead. Something stirred me into consciousness and then, when I turned my head, made me wish I hadn't. The pain rolled into a throb of heavy aching pulse that I could almost bite with my jaw teeth. The sound of my own groaning voice came muffled to my ears, and as my eyes focused, I made out the glossy varnish of a peeled log wall shoved against the edge of a bare mattress.

I was tied. My wrists were lifted to the upper end of an iron bed frame. My ankles were hooked to the lower. My mouth had opened to let a dribble of blood and saliva dry down my chin and neck and on the striped ticking of the stained and lumpy mattress. I was in a small room and it was empty. A curtainless window showed a square of pale blue sky where a fly buzzed persistently against the screen. Carefully, I tilted my head up to squint through its ache. A closed door. Then I let my head sag gently back against the thin mattress and shut my eyes again.

The second time I woke it was to a patch of late-afternoon sun glinting on the varnished log wall. I felt an insistent shake of my leg and looked down. The frowning, whiskery face of the caretaker bent over the end of the bed and the man grunted when my eyes opened.

"Didn't think you was dead."

"Water."

The man thought that over while he stared at me. Then he went out of the room and a few minutes later came back with a heavy glass tumbler full of water. I tried to raise up to drink but my arms were too tautly stretched. The caretaker put a wide, callused hand under my head and tilted the glass to my dry lips.

"Guess you was thirsty."

"Your name's Sam?"

A faint flicker of surprise. "You know me?"

"Sister Dori mentioned your name. Is she here?"

Sam didn't answer. Instead, he gave a quick look at the nylon straps holding my ankles and wrists and left, leaving the glass on the old bureau.

The headache ebbed a bit, but it came back if I lifted my head or turned it quickly. The dusty, scarred bureau was shoved against one wall. Beside it, another closed door looked like it led to a closet. The ceiling was made of perforated squares set in a gridwork of metal hangers. One corner had old water stains in a brown pattern that looked something like a bobtailed kangaroo. I wondered how much time I would spend studying that stain and counting the rows of perforations.

The patch of sunlight climbed another log. I tried to avoid the stiffening of my bound muscles by shifting my body as much as I could from side to side on the cot. Steadily, I worked against my bonds. The nylon didn't stretch, but it gave my muscles relief. The headache lessened and I was glad I didn't feel drowsy or nauseated, both welcome signs that I didn't have a concussion. I'd been hit on the head before, but I couldn't remember a blow that hard. Or maybe being over forty had something to do with it. The twinges and tingles of my flesh told me that old injuries and new bruises were beginning to add up to a slower recovery time. Something I'd have to think about one of these days. Right now I could still see Sam's arms swing across his body and the axe handle whip with the man's wrists. If I hadn't heard something—if I hadn't had that half second to roll away from the swing of the club—Sam might have been right to worry about my being dead.

Then again, he hadn't seemed all that worried. Maybe he was planning to try again. It would depend on how much they thought I knew. On whether they thought I'd come up here alone. On how much they thought they could get away with.

I tried the straps again. But the nylon webbing had been designed for just this purpose. A loop slipped over each hand and foot, and a ring of some sort clamped it firmly. I figured that the wrist straps, like those I could see on my ankles, were buckled securely to the bed frame. But the leg straps were too short to let me do more than tickle at the metal rail. Still, I grunted to wrench my torso around and try to gain an extra inch, two inches, that might let me feel the wrist buckles and the strap running through them.

The sound of boots outside the door sagged me back against the gritty striped cloth. Dwayne Vengley stood in the doorway and gazed at me for a long moment.

"Sam said you were feeling better."

"I'd feel even better if I could take a piss."

The young man shrugged. "Go ahead. It won't embarrass me."

"Thanks. I'll wait."

He shrugged again and leaned against the bureau. His weight made it creak slightly. "Sam also said you were asking about Dori."

"She wasn't at the Temple. I figured she might be up here."

"I see."

"Is she? And is she all right?"

He didn't bother to answer. "You're not in a position to worry about anybody but yourself, Mr. Steele. I'd think you'd have realized by now you're not really welcome around here. And that Dori doesn't want to talk to you."

"I have a message from her father. All I want to do is give it to her. Then I'll go."

"Give me the message. I'll tell her."

When I didn't answer, Vengley asked quietly, "What did you see from the barn?"

"I saw you and that boy come out. Then you went back."

"And what did you hear?"

"Nothing. You were too far away."

The man shook his blond head. "Sam heard us. He was farther away than you."

"Wish I'd have heard him."

For the first time, Vengley smiled. But it stayed on his full lips and didn't make it to his green eyes. They looked at me with cold objectivity from beneath the ledge of his brow. "Good for us you didn't. Now, Mr. Steele, your health and welfare depend on your being scrupulously honest with us. Why did you come up here?"

"To find Dori."

"What have you found out since you've been here?"

"That you're involved in child pornography."

Vengley nodded. "That's better. I figured you heard Brian and me. Well, I know a number of things about you, too, Mr. Steele. Such as your daughters."

"They don't know anything about you. I'm the only one who does."

"Um-hmm. You went out to Alef Distributing, didn't you?"

"Yes."

"And you can guess what goes on there."

I tried to read the young man's green eyes. They gave away nothing. "Film processing. Storage. Shipping."

Vengley nodded again. "It's a very lucrative business, kiddie porn. Tremendously profitable." There was even a little pride in his statement. "We ship all over the world."

I didn't trust myself to say anything. I watched the face of the young man who gazed back as if not quite seeing me. Finally Vengley wagged his head once. "You just had to keep asking questions, didn't you? Nosing around. Until you've become a problem."

"Where's Dorcas?"

"I suspect you'll see her soon." He pushed away from the bureau. "You've caused us quite a bit of trouble. Quite a bit."

"People are waiting for me to report back."

A chilly smile. "Then we'll just have to hurry up and make our decision, won't we?" He paused at the doorway. "The High Priest will be here soon. You should feel honored: he's flying in just for you." The door closed.

I listened to the boot heels fade down the hallway. From somewhere beyond the window came the *chirr* of a humming-bird claiming his territory and the slam of a car door followed by an engine starting. Then silence.

It was pretty clear that Pastor Pettes recruited the children from the Temple's day-care program, and that meant some of the Temple members were involved. But not all. The woman sweeping the parking lot had pleaded with me to help the chil-dren. And I guessed that Dori, too, had found out something about the porn racket and that's why she called me. From what Brian had said, the satanic rituals were used to keep the kids quiet about what happened to them. And the filming took place here, too—deep in the woods on private property so they wouldn't be seen or heard. Too, the isolation allowed Vengley and the others better control of the children: no place to run, no other adults to appeal to, no one outside the group to say what they did was wrong. It was a separate world the children could be brought into, exploited, and then brought back from. Their memories of what had happened would be set off by distance from their other, ordinary world, and they would be reluctant to tell their parents about it.

A lot of money, Vengley had said. Alef Distributing's profit sheet backed him up, and probably that was only what the company reported for tax purposes. No wonder they had tried to scare me off. As well as to kill Shelley Aguirre, who had been weak—who, perhaps, had said too much to me. And now Dorcas was a threat. Certainly I was. The meeting would not be to decide whether to kill me, but when and how.

My steady working on the straps loosened them only a bit more, but I didn't have much else to do. I tried to keep my mind off the increasing pressure of my bladder and the thirst that had returned to be tantalized by the empty glass sitting on a corner of the scarred bureau. Finally, after the patch of sunlight had moved halfway up the wall and faded in the shadow of afternoon rain clouds, the door opened again.

Sam brought in a plastic tray with a bottle of mineral water, a tumbler full of ice, and a sandwich and orange. He set it on the bureau and went out again, returning with the axe handle. "Dwayne says you ought to be getting hungry about now."

"Dwayne's right. I need to use the bathroom first, though."

The weather-beaten man grunted and loosened the buckles on my ankle straps with one hand while clutching the axe handle with the other. Then he undid the wrists.

I rubbed the sore flesh and looked at the nylon webbing with its system of guides and clamps and buckles. "Pretty effective."

Sam's smile was proprietary. "They'll do." The axe handle beckoned. "This way."

The narrow hall led between a row of closed doors to a bathroom at the end. Two fiberglass shower stalls, four mirrors and sinks with a long shelf running above them and a litter of soap ends, used toothpaste tubes, scraps of paper, two toilet stalls. Sam held one of the doors open and stood behind me while I relieved myself. When I was through, I headed for a sink.

"What you doing?"

"Washing my hands."

"Hurry the hell up. I ain't got all damned day."

Lathering, I glanced at a rusty razor blade on the shelf. In the mirror, Sam caught the look and his lips tightened. "You try it." The axe handle smacked against his thick palm. "Just you try it."

"I wouldn't even think of it, Sam."

A grunt.

While I ate, the man stood by the door, swinging the axe handle. Then he made me lie down and buckled first my wrists, then my ankles. He pulled the straps tight against my tensed muscles.

"Acting like a goddamned horse fighting the cinch, ain't you? Won't do you a goddamned bit of good."

It didn't. If anything, I was drawn tighter than before. But at least my hunger was gone and the headache had faded into a sullen throb that came only when I lifted my head.

The light from the window dimmed and I heard the long, rumbling crash of mountain thunder echo along the valley. A sudden darkening was followed by the sound of heavy raindrops crackling on the shingles and the ripple of runoff in a nearby downspout. A light spray glinted on the screen and the shower passed over. The room slowly grew light again with a weaker and lower sunlight and the cool smell of damp wood and leaves. After a while it became hard to make out the details of the room in the dusk, and when it was almost black, the hall light flicked on to show a wide streak of glow under the door. Vengley flipped on the unshaded bulb and nodded at me.

"The High Priest is here. He wants to talk to you."

Hands strapped behind my back, I was led along the hall by Vengley while Sam and his axe handle followed. Our feet clumped loudly on the plank stairs down to the lounge with its scatter of worn and sagging couches, easy chairs, end tables, and lamps. Indian rugs brightened the log walls, and in the dimness of the high ceiling at the large room's far end, the ram's head loomed. Its glass eyes reflected the lamps with a cold gleam.

On the other side of the empty lounge a side door opened to a smaller room crowded with folding metal chairs that faced a plain wooden table. A many-branched candelabrum at one side of the table held a cluster of snuffed candles. At the other a single, thick candle like a column of gray suet stood cold and unlit in its holder. Overhead, the varnished boards of the ceiling made the room feel cavelike. Behind the table, wearing a plaid woolen shirt and a black silk cravat, sat Arthur Vengley.

"You're the High Priest?"

The man's thin lips smiled affirmatively. "I can't say I'm pleased to see you again, Mr. Steele."

"You and your son—a family of Satanists?"

"Actually, Dwayne is the third generation. Haven't you ever heard of a third-generation Episcopalian or Baptist?"

I had, but generational Satanism still seemed bizarre. "Does your wife know about it?"

"Ex-wife. No. I didn't marry her for her beliefs but for her father's money." It was an admission he seemed proud of. "If, over the years, she has had suspicions, she's been too weak to face them."

"For good reason."

"We do nothing we're ashamed of, Mr. Steele. But we also find no profit in drawing attention to ourselves, or flaunting our beliefs in front of those who would fail to understand. We prefer to go in our own faith, and let the rest of the world go in theirs."

With, perhaps, the exception of a few children here and there. "Where's Dorcas?"

The elder Vengley made a little tent of his fingers and rested his narrow lips on it as he studied me. "My son tells me you are interested solely in Dori."

"Is she all right?"

"Of course." He added, "She's also free to do as she wishes. To stay with us or to go home. Whatever."

"When can I see her?"

"That's up to you."

"Meaning?"

Vengley senior didn't answer right away. Instead, the lawyer rubbed the tips of his fingers together as he stared over them.

Behind me, I heard Sam sigh a breath through his nose and shift his weight like a patient horse. From somewhere in the building came the sound of running feet and the high-pitched, nervous laugh of an overexcited child.

"I mean, Mr. Steele, that I would be willing to let you talk to Dori—even to take her home, if that's her desire—in return for your solemn promise of silence."

"About your kiddie porn?"

"It's not my kiddie porn. That's Dwayne's enterprise. His and some others'. But, yes, that would have to be included in the ban."

"You don't mind your son exploiting children?"

"Our basic tenet is freedom. Dwayne is free to do whatever he wants to do. Or can do."

Including sacrifice and murder, as well. "What if I don't promise?"

"Well, in the first place, you have absolutely no evidence of any wrongdoing. You only have your suspicions, based on a misunderstood and overheard conversation that is inadmissible as evidence. Without evidence, Mr. Steele, no case."

"And in the second place?"

"Even if there's no case, the possible notoriety would make things very awkward for us and the Temple. It would also make things awkward for you. And for your daughter in Sacramento."

"You're saying I have no choice."

"I'm saying I think you're to be a man we'll be able to trust. What I offer is a quid pro quo—Dori for your silence."

"Did you give Shelley Aguirre the same option?"

"You're asking if we killed Shelley? The answer's no." He gazed at me levelly, searching for a sign that I didn't believe him. "We don't like violence. It's counterproductive. For a group as nonconformist as ours to draw the attention of the police would be suicidal. We just want to be left alone. That's all I'm asking: you leave us alone and we'll leave you alone."

"That sounds fair enough."

"And I'm sure we can rely on your word for that."

"Why not? You have insurance."

"I'm glad you understand that. And you understand further that our group has members everywhere."

"Including Sacramento."

One of the man's shoulders lifted. "And Bordeaux."

CHAPTER

I wasn't strapped down this time, but Sam and his axe handle kept me company while we waited in my room. Dori, Dwayne said, was resting. He'd let her know I was waiting to talk to her. When the knock came, Dwayne and Sam flanked me once more and we crossed the balcony above the main lounge. Below, the woman who'd been with the children at the swing sat near the fireplace warming her back. She looked up to watch us come down the stairs. Straight, dark hair framed an expressionless face as she sipped something from a coffee mug.

A couple of other figures in denims and sweatshirts lounged on the overstuffed and sagging furniture. I didn't recognize the first of the two men. But the second, who stared back impassively, was one of the young men who had chased me from the Temple so long ago this morning. From the kitchen area came the sounds of children eating and talking. But the varnished plywood shutters closed off the serving windows and only the voices, oddly domestic and piping cheer, could be heard.

We went down another short hallway. Dwayne knocked gently and opened a door. The axe handle nudged me in.

Dori sat in a straight-backed wooden chair between a bed and a small writing desk. In a pale and drawn face, her eyes were wide over dark circles. When I came in she seemed to lean back away from me.

"Dori, are you all right?"

The blond head nodded. But the cords of her neck stood out tautly.

"Would you like me to take you home?"

"Home?" She looked at Dwayne and then back to me. "Go?"

"You can stay or go with me. That's what Mr. Vengley said."

Mutely, she looked at Dwayne again.

He nodded. "The High Priest gave his word. It's your choice, Dori. You know what I want you to do—I guess we've talked about it enough. But it's your choice."

"Really?"

"It's always been your choice. That's our basic tenet. You know that."

She started to stand, leaning heavily on the table. "Go."

Vengley stepped forward quickly to support the unsteady woman. "She had a miscarriage," he told me. "She still feels a little weak."

"Go."

"All right," shrugged Vengley. "I'm sorry that's your choice. But we're going right now."

Walking painfully and slowly, Dori didn't reply. She leaned against Dwayne, who led her out a door at the end of the hallway and gently down three board steps at the side of the lodge. A small Toyota pickup truck with a low camper shell was parked close to the building.

"Dori," said Vengley, "you sit up front with Sam. It'll be easier on you there."

"Where are you taking us?" I asked.

Dwayne closed the rider's door. "To your car. You left it somewhere down the road, right?"

"Yes."

"Well, it's obvious Dori can't walk to it."

Sam's voice came over my shoulder. "Put your hands behind your back, Mr. Steele."

"Why?"

"I feel better driving with you tied up. I'll untie you when we get to your car."

His fingers were busy a moment and I felt the familiar yank of nylon loops and a quick, efficient tug to tighten them.

"Now you crawl in back there." Sam lowered the tailgate and held up the camper shell's door. I crouched to clamber awkwardly on my knees into the low space.

Dwayne leaned over the tailgate. "Not all of us trust you, Mr. Steele. But the High Priest says we have to. Just remember, we made a deal. I hope for your sake you keep your part of it." He thought a moment, then added, "You remember, you don't have any evidence of anything. And we know a lot more about you than you do about us."

"I understand."

"Good. Have a safe trip home."

He lowered the camper shell's door and the truck rocked as Sam got in. Then the engine started and the vehicle bounced slowly over the rough earth and past the parking area toward the long road out.

I rolled on the cold, ridged metal of the pickup's bed. Bracing my shoulder against the lurching side, I worked my knees under me enough to peer through the front window into the cab. The dim glow of dash lights showed Sam's frowning face staring ahead where the lights picked rocks out of the gullied road. Dori leaned weakly against the seat, her head tilted down. Behind us, I saw the lodge's windows and outside lamps glimmer through tree limbs. Twisting, I tried to stretch the nylon cuffs but they bit into my wrists. A quick look around the metal bed showed a wadded burlap sack and a hoe handle without the hoe. That and a scattering of gravelly dirt were the only other things in the truck. Feeling with my hands behind me, I groped down the metal flange that anchored the lower rim of the camper shell. A long bolt poked through, giving a rough dowel of a few inches. Rattled by the jounce of the rough road, I struggled to jam the bolt end into the cuffs and twist. The straps seemed to give a little—either that or the searing bite into my flesh numbed my wrists and made me think they loosened. I twisted again, surer this time. Then I writhed sidewards and on my back to shake my pants pockets and use two fingers to fish out the sliver of soap I'd stolen from the bathroom shelf. Awkward and straining against joints and tendons, I managed to smear stinging soap on my raw wrist. Again, I hooked the strap on the bolt and twisted. The loop that gripped my arm widened and slid a little further down my slippery hand.

Through the tinted plastic of the shell's back window, a faint glow moved behind us in the blackness of forest. I paused to study the glimmer, not surprised when it congealed into a pair of distant headlights. A car followed from the lodge. I had a good idea what its purpose was. An automobile accident in my own car—a steep cliff, a missed turn and a rock wall. A fire, perhaps. Something that would make my and Dori's accidental deaths take place well off the Kabbal's property. I twisted savagely against the straps and felt the soap burn anew into freshly torn skin. But with the wrench the webbing slid as far as my knuckles. I began rocking my hand back and forth. The little knuckle—if I could just slip the strap over that knot of bone . . .

The truck swung down and up and halted, engine still running. Sam opened the driver's door and I watched him unlock the gate and prop it wide. Then the man clumped down beside the truck and I quickly flopped on my back. The upper door lifted. "Where'd you park your car at?"

"Second cabin up on the left. It's in their driveway. You can't see it too well from the road."

A grunt and the door closed. The truck jolted forward again, Sam not pausing to close the gate.

I lay on my back as the vehicle's low gears ground and it rocked back and forth with the ruts of the road. Then it turned left sharply and tilted up and braked. The glow of headlights reflected on the ceiling went out and the motor stopped. A door opened and shut and boots mashed into gravel beside the truck.

The back door lifted and the tailgate fell open with a metallic clunk.

"All right, Mr. Steele. Come on out."

Sam was a shadow outlined by the gleam of stars in the ribbon of sky over the road. I pulled myself toward the tailgate with my heels, arms bound behind. A thicker blackness in the trees indicated the silent cabin. Tiny reflections from the truck's shining parking lights showed my rental car.

"Come on out so I can get those cuffs off you."

I scooted under the lip of the camper shell and swung my feet over the tailgate. Sam's teeth glinted in a smile or a grimace. He stepped back. The axe handle came at my head in a heavy, level swing.

I thrust the hoe handle up. Lunging my full weight behind it, I bayoneted the center of the man's shadow. It struck bone as the axe handle whistled through the dark and I tumbled away, pivoting myself off the tailgate. Sam's breath burst in a "hunh" of pain and surprise. The axe handle clubbed against the camper shell, sending splinters of Plexiglas whirling into the night. I tucked and rolled to come up on my feet with the long stave at guard position. I thrust again, using the end of the handle to gouge at Sam's face. The wood struck and Sam cursed and swung wildly as I parried high and right to glance the axe handle away. Then I closed. I drove a knee hard into the panting man's groin. He sagged and stumbled back into the night, axe handle dragging in the grit.

"Goddamn . . . goddamn you I'll kill you . . ."

Sam came at me again. The club lifted high overhead in both hands and caught the glow of headlights bobbing across the rough road behind us. I waited until, with a savage grunt, Sam started the axe handle down. Then I stepped forward under the blow and used both hands to drive the slender shaft of wood into Sam's throat. The man's plunging arms caught me on the shoulder and the axe handle whipped down to thwack hard across my hip. But its force was broken and Sam dropped to clutch noiselessly at his neck. His eyes bulged wide and sightless in the brighter glow of the approaching headlights as he staggered to his knees, hands tugging at his crushed throat. As the second car stopped at the end of the short drive, I gave him a hard kick in the face.

"Dori—Dori . . . come on!"

"What's happening? Why are you fighting?" The girl stood rigid by the truck's open door and stared wide-eyed at me, at Sam, at the headlights that began to turn up the short drive.

"They want to kill us. Let's get out of here."

"But Dwayne said—"

"He lied! His father lied! They can't afford to let us go." I grabbed the girl's arm and pulled her into the wedge of blackness cast by the truck. We stumbled past the cabin and into the thick, snagging limbs of the pines as, behind us, we heard the slam of car doors and a startled mutter of voices.

Wordless, I dodged between the thicker blackness of tree trunks, a hand up to protect my eyes against limbs and twigs. The other hand pulled a tottering Dori. Her steps were noisy and unsure on the rough and black earth. I took quick bearings on the headlights splintered by the trees and angled back toward the road. At least I knew where that led. And if I could get to it, I might drag the girl fast enough to keep us from being caught.

A looming shadow of large boulders forced us around but also shut off the last of the glare. I paused to listen for hurrying boots but heard only Dorcas's gasping breath as she leaned heavily against the cold rock.

"Can you keep going, Dori? We've got to keep moving."

"I . . . I don't know. I'm bleeding again."

I groped to feel the girl's pulse and forehead. She was clammy and her heart beat rapidly. Maybe she was moving into shock, but there was no time to treat that. The cure now would be to keep her alert. And to keep moving.

"When was the miscarriage? How long ago?"

"Yesterday."

"After you called me?"

"Yes . . . I found out . . ."

"We can go slower now. Slow and quiet. Can you do that much?"

"I'll try."

I led her through ponderosa trunks and around heavy thickets of aspen. How long we struggled, I couldn't say. But Dori's weight grew heavier and she began to lean on my shoulder.

"You want to rest?"

"Yes."

We stopped. The girl sank to the dark earth. I stood and listened and searched the blackness for any movement.

"Mr. Steele?"

"Yes?"

"I . . . I don't think it was a miscarriage. I think it was an abortion."

"What?"

She took a deep, shuddering breath. "We came up to the lodge. They said we were going on retreat and it was my turn. But they gave me something . . . I don't know . . . the contractions started. Sister Gwen said I was going into premature labor . . . they said they'd get a doctor but it would take a while. They gave me something that made me sleep. I had terrible nightmares—things . . . I hurt . . . and when I woke up, my baby was gone. They said I miscarried. But they took my baby, Mr. Steele. I know they took it! There was this hole in my arm . . ." She rubbed at the inside of her elbow. "And I felt so sick."

"How many months, Dori?"

"Seven. Almost seven."

"You said Dwayne was the father?"

She nodded. "He came up to Julian a few times. To talk about us, he said. We didn't plan on it—it just happened. But when I told him I was pregnant, he was happy. It . . . he said he left the Kabbal after Jerry died and we didn't see each other for a long time. And one day he came into the store . . . he was different—changed—he told me about the Temple and said we could find a way to start over there. A new spiritual path. And he was so happy when I got pregnant . . ."

"I see."

"He never said anything about an abortion. Nothing—nothing!"

"That's all right, Dori. It's okay."

But it wasn't okay. She took a breath that shook her shoulders in a convulsive shudder. "Mr. Steele—I think they took it. You know, the fetus. I think they used my baby for the Beltane ritual."

I remembered the flies buzzing around the stained altar. "A sacrifice, Dori?"

"Yes." She whispered, "A long time ago, Dwayne told me he wanted to be a High Priest. Like his father. A High Sacrifice is one of the steps to the priesthood. It would have been Dwayne's firstborn." She was crying again. "I didn't know, Mr. Steele. I swear—I didn't know!"

"I understand, Dori. I know you didn't."

After a few long, shaky breaths, she added, "I think something happened to Shirley. Shirley Graham."

The girl who preceded Dori. The one who, Dwayne had written, found peace in the Temple.

"You think they killed her?"

"I wrote her. At her home. The Pastor said she'd gone home for a while. But the letter came back forwarded to the Temple." She shifted her weight uncomfortably, the pine needles rustling. "I think she learned what I found out. I think she's dead."

"Is that why you called me?"

"No. I didn't even think of it until now. I didn't know about this . . ." Catching herself with another sigh, she said, "It's the Temple. What they do at the Temple. The children."

"The pornography?"

"Yes. And they sell them."

"What?"

Her voice teetered on the edge of hysteria. The words began to tumble out. "Sister Gwen told me. She's been there four years. She's had four babies. They sell them to people who want to adopt babies, she said. She said Pastor Pettes tells them he runs a home for unwed mothers who can't keep their babies. It's God's work, she says. She says she's bringing souls out of purgatory into life so they can find God. She says by getting pregnant we're obeying God's command to be fruitful and multiply. But that's only part of it—the children—they make pictures of them . . .''

"The pornography?"

"The Temple gets money that way, too. That and selling babies. They're born there in the Temple so no one knows they're even alive. They don't have any records, Mr. Steele— they can do whatever they want to with the babies because no one knows they're alive. So no one knows when they're sold or when they die . . .''

"And you didn't want to do that?"

"I didn't know about it! At the lodge, I saw some pictures of the children doing those things . . . Jennifer . . . Allan. Children I know!"

"That's when you called me?"

"Later—when I woke up once and everyone was gone. To . . . to Beltane. I didn't know who else to call . . . I'm sorry . . .''

"Shhhh." A faint light moved through the trunks. In the sudden silence I heard the grind of a car engine.

"They're looking for us, aren't they?"

"They sure are. Can you walk again, Dori?"

She grunted painfully to her feet. "I think so."

CHAPTER

31

I wasn't sure how long we had been moving. Dori's clammy sweat had changed to a warm one. I tried to keep her quiet but she kept whispering, feverishly, telling me about the full moon, about Beltane, about high sacrifice and Dwayne. At least it kept her awake, kept her moving. After a while she said the feeling of blood had stopped. As long as we moved slowly and rested often, she said, it was all right. She was a brave girl, and when this nightmare was over she would testify against Dwayne and his father and Pastor Pettes. She had promised me that in a whisper as fierce as a witch's curse. Maybe that's what gave her the strength she needed for the hours we struggled.

I tried to stay parallel to the road, to keep some sense of direction in the twisting blackness that was our path. But we had to stay in the rough dark of trees. Dwayne and his people had spread out. We had seen the lights of vehicles prowl the two-rut road leading from the ranch and past the dark cabins. It was a good bet the cars had dropped someone off along the road to wait for us to stumble across them in the dark.

The county road, too, would be under surveillance. But our chances would be better there. We could move faster once we reached the level glimmer of that wide, graveled track. And then how many miles to the well-traveled highway? And would she be able to make it? Dori leaned more heavily against me, her breath a rhythmic gasp. She no longer said anything. She only concentrated on putting one foot in front of the other. I was hot and tired and so thirsty I didn't even want to think about water. And Dori—with her loss of blood—must be suffering even more.

"Can you keep going?"

"Yes . . . keep going . . ."

But it was clear she couldn't. And something else was clear: the shadows of the tree trunks were more distinct and I could now see the paleness of my tennis shoes against the black of earth. Dawn was coming; with it our concealment and our safety faded.

"I need to stop, Mr. Steele . . . I'm sorry . . ."

"Sure. Sit against this tree. I have to go ahead a bit and see where we are."

I pushed through a stand of old aspen. Their smooth boles made pale streaks against the pines. A sinuous smear of sky among the trees showed me where the access road was. It also showed me that the stars had dimmed in a paler sky. As I watched, I heard the restless grind of an automobile and Sam's pickup truck swung around a bend, lights out, to patrol the road and pass me with a squeak of springs and the smell of hot oil.

Dori had heard it, too. "They're still after us?"

I nodded. "But we're near the county road. It'll be easier going, then."

"I don't know if I can make it, Mr. Steele."

"Yes, you can. Sure you can. You've come too far now to think you can't."

"I don't know."

I got her on her feet. We stumbled forward a bit more easily as the sky began to show us the stones and logs in our path.

"Dori, when we get to the road, I'll find a place where you can rest safely. Okay? Then I'll go for help. It's just a little farther. It can't be much farther now."

". . . Yes . . ."

"Hang on. It can't be much farther."

We lurched on through the tangle of limbs and brush. As I half-carried Dori and looked ahead for dim figures waiting for us, I almost didn't recognize the county road when we reached its wide cut. A screen of thick brush and a high bank masked it and I pushed through to stand suddenly exposed on the crumbly lip of earth before I jerked back and crouched. An automobile was parked almost out of sight near the access road.

Dori's voice whispered over my shoulder, "They're here."

"Yeah. I figured. Sit still—they didn't see anything or they'd be all over us."

"It'll be light soon. They'll see us when we move."

"No, they won't. Not if we keep low and move quietly. Come on."

I led her back into the trees and we picked our way behind the brush that screened the graveled road.

"Are you all right?"

"No. I'm—I don't feel very well." She panted lightly and I could see the dark flesh under her staring eyes. The front of her long and now torn dress was spotted with blood. "I don't think I—" That was her last sentence before she fell against me. Her knees gave as she plunged and I grabbed her boneless flesh to lower it gently to the pine needles.

She was alive, but her pulse was light and rapid and, as far as I could tell, uneven. Her shallow breath tensed her upper body and a sheen of sweat felt cold on her forehead. Loss of blood . . . shock . . . exhaustion. She would need help soon.

I tugged her farther back into the brush and wrapped my wool shirt around her as warmly as I could. Propping her feet high, I made certain she could breathe easily. Then I gathered fallen branches and built a screen around her. I hoped, too, it would be a sign when she woke to know I had hidden her, that she was supposed to stay until I came with help.

Creeping to the edge of the road, I tied a strip of my T-shirt to a shrub. Then I started jogging toward the paved highway somewhere ahead.

How far I'd gone I didn't know. At first I counted my strides, trying to keep track of hundreds until I reached the seventeen hundred I figured was a mile. But my mind wouldn't stay on the steady rhythm of my feet. It drifted back to Dori, ahead to what cars might be waiting at the juncture of the dirt and paved roads, over the revelations the girl had made. The ground rose in long hills, fell away in much shorter declines. Rose again with a drain on my strength that was almost inimical. And I felt that strength ebb. My legs sank past the sense of burning and into numbness. My ankles no longer adjusted to the uneven and rocky earth but turned occasionally with quick jabs of pain. I couldn't afford a sprained ankle now. Shoving through the growth at the side of the road, I slipped and skidded down an embankment to the hard but even graveled surface. Running faster, I let my body look after itself as my consciousness drifted away in the steady thud of my canvas boots against packed clay. It was that familiar state I reached on the longest runs when my flesh had been pushed to its limit and my gasping, numb body was defining an even higher degree of effort. Fixing first on one tree or telephone pole, I ran until I reached the landmark. Then I chose another and focused on that.

A metal strut, bracing a telephone pole, caught the low morning sun with an orange glow. I was aiming for that when the growl of an approaching car finally registered. I saw it over my shoulder, the high silhouette of a large pickup that, when it spotted me, began to accelerate.

Stumbling and numb, I plunged across the roadside ditch for the trees as the vehicle scratched to a halt in the loose dirt. Glancing back, I saw the youth from the Temple fling himself out of the truck and shout something into a radio handset. Then he sprinted through the weeds and loose gravel of the ditch. I sucked in air and goaded my legs into a sprint.

I pictured my route in my mind, trying not to make angles and turns that my pursuer could use to cut across and gain on me. But the legs chasing me were well-rested, and as I panted through a flicker of lodgepole pines I saw the pickup truck move down the road to keep pace with the man who ran after me. Still, the road was my only guide, my only chance to find help for Dori. Somewhere up ahead was the highway and surely by now I had come the three miles from the access road.

Behind me I could hear running boots. Through a dry and burning throat my breath rasped. If I couldn't outrun the man . . . maybe I should turn and fight while I had some strength left . . . Stirring beneath blind weariness and the numb thud of my legs, I felt the spread of rage. An old, almost forgotten rage that I thought I'd left in the sticky, stinking mud of Viet Nam: it was the red rage of killing.

Lurching around an outcropping of boulders, I pulled back against the cool rock and waited. The running boots rounded the mossy shoulder: a blur of open-mouthed face and an arm cocked with a radio near the gasping lips. From my knees, I swung both fists into the man's unguarded stomach and felt the deep, sweet joy of crippling my enemy. The youth said, "Oooop" and doubled over my arms, grappling to catch me and protect himself at the same time. I brought the blade of my hand down hard against the man's nape and stamped my heel on the fallen radio. As the youth struggled to his knees and reached for anything he could grab, I stumbled away into the woods again.

My legs moved much slower now. Not only the fight but the halt had broken the mindless lift and thrust of muscles. If the man behind me was on his feet again, it wouldn't be long before he would catch up. But the truck didn't follow along the dirt road. It stayed waiting for guidance from the radio. I stumbled over the road's berm and ran tottering on the easier hardpack of gravel and clay, trying to reclaim my rhythm and that blessed distance between thought and flesh. Then an engine sound grew in front of me and turned into the loom of another vehicle. A blur of shape and chrome and a windshield glinted harshly in the full morning sun. I knew that my running was over. I couldn't run another step. But I could still fight. What little was left I could use to fight with and if I was lucky I would take one of the bastards with me. But the running was ended. There was nothing left to run with.

I aimed myself at the stopped vehicle, eyes fighting the reflected glare to see the man I wanted to kill. My voice grunted with a last effort to make this lunge a fatal one.

The car door opened and a figure stepped out. A glint of silver flashed on his pale blue shirt. "Whoa, now—hold it, now! You wouldn't be Mr. Jack Steele, would you? You need help?"

"I'm going to fly her home as soon as she's able to travel." Henry stood by the cold cheeriness of an illuminated soft-drink machine. Its muffled vibration was a faint hum in the late night silence of the hospital corridor. "The doctor says she wouldn't have lasted much longer. He said they had to give her three units of blood."

Freshly shaved and showered, I tried not to step too heavily on blistered feet as I sipped my fourth ginger ale. After a while, water had felt too heavy on my stomach, but I was still suffering dehydration—a combination of long hours sweating, no liquids, and Colorado's low humidity. But that and the blisters were the only damage. The doctor had checked me for a concussion as well as exhaustion and mentioned something about my being a remarkably fit man.

"Dori wants to testify," I said. "She'll have a lot to go through." More, I thought, than either she or her father realized yet. For with testimony came confession and the acceptance of her responsibility. But the long run through the forest had proved she was a strong girl and a determined one. I felt she would do what she had to. And the admiral, when I called to tell him the outcome, felt that way, too. Dori had seen—and shared—evil. But it was an evil of human creation, not of Satan or any other devil or god. Dori knew now that to blame something other than man for the evil of the Vengleys was to excuse them and to deny the rest of us the privilege and duty of combating that evil.

Henry rubbed at the puffy flesh under his eyes and stifled a yawn. His flight had arrived in the late afternoon and now it was long after sundown. Dori was still in intensive care, but the nurse said they would soon be moving her to a room. "Jenny and the admiral send their gratitude, Steele. I forgot to tell you earlier. I—ah—I want to thank you, too."

"How's Margaret doing?"

"Well, she needs help. We all know that. But she told me she wants to try AA." Henry lifted his can of soda pop in a mock toast. "We'll both be going. It's a start, at least."

It was a good start. The Vengleys and their crew were in custody. The Denver district attorney had raided the Temple earlier that afternoon and found enough still undestroyed evidence to bring charges against Pettes. Detective Shaughnessy said that the San Diego police were drawing up charges and extradition papers, as well. He also thought Vengley senior was working on a deal to turn state's evidence on his son's involvement in the Aguirre murder.

"Thanks for looking after me," I told Shaughnessy.

"I just asked the Denver PD and the Boulder sheriff to keep an eye out for you. I told them you might be in trouble. They're the ones that did all the work."

"Still, I owe you a beer."

"I'll collect when you get home."

Home. The word sounded good, and I caught myself no longer thinking about the costs of the past but of the promise of the future. The red-eye would leave in less than two hours—that gave just enough time to make the drive to Stapleton Airport and turn in the rental. To call Karen and Chuck. To tell Megan that I would, indeed, make our dinner date Friday. Then I could sleep on the flight home.